Saving You

Love Wanted in Texas
Book Two

Kelly Elliott

piatkus

PIATKUS

First published in 2014 by K. Elliott Enterprises
First published in Great Britain in 2016 by Piatkus
This paperback edition published in 2016 by Piatkus

1 3 5 7 9 10 8 6 4 2

A CIP catalogue record for this book
is available from the British Library.

ISBN 978-0-349-41344-0

Printed and bound in Great Britain by
Clays Ltd, St Ives plc

Papers used by Piatkus are from well-managed forests
and other responsible sources.

MIX
Paper from
responsible sources
FSC
www.fsc.org   FSC® C104740

Piatkus
An imprint of
Little, Brown Book Group
Carmelite House
50 Victoria Embankment
London EC4Y 0DZ

An Hachette UK Company
www.hachette.co.uk

www.piatkus.co.uk

WANTED
family tree

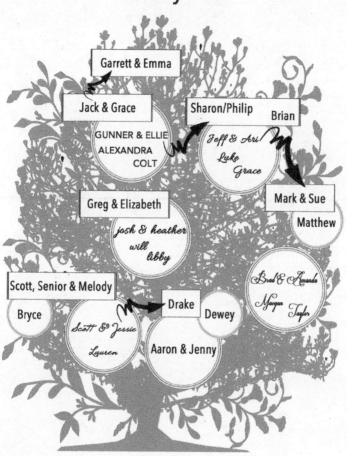

Garrett & Emma

Jack & Grace

Sharon/Philip   Brian

GUNNER & ELLIE
ALEXANDRA
COLT

Jeff & Ari
Luke
Grace

Greg & Elizabeth

Mark & Sue

Matthew

josh & heather
will
libby

Brad & Amanda
Maegan   Taylor

Scott, Senior & Melody

Bryce

Scott & Jessie
Lauren

Drake   Dewey

Aaron & Jenny

tossed in my bag. I went to get in and when he took my hand to help me up, I let out a small gasp. I was pretty sure he hadn't heard it. Glancing back at him I smiled weakly as I whispered, "Thank you."

Luke smiled, winked, and shut the door. He headed around the front of his truck but was stopped by a guy who had been running. The guy was dressed in a Texas A&M T-shirt and jogging pants. His blond hair was longer than Luke's and his body not anywhere near as nice as Luke's. My eyes moved to Luke as I watched him stand there and talk to the guy. Luke was dressed in jeans that fit his body better than they should have. His tight, light-blue T-shirt clung to his toned muscular body and made his green eyes seem almost gray blue.

I bit down on my lower lip when he ran his hand through his brown hair. Luke never was one to worry about his hair. He didn't really wear it in any type of style. It always looked like he woke up and ran his hands through it and that was it. It worked for him, though.

Luke reached out and shook the other guy's hand as they said their good-byes. Then he slapped the other guy on the back as he threw his head back and laughed. The runner was a bit taller than Luke, probably six feet tall. Luke stood at five-feet-eleven inches. He thought he was short, but I thought he was the perfect height. When we used to dance together, I fit perfectly up against him, and he would rest his chin on the top of my head. Smiling, I thought about all the times we danced together growing up.

Looking away quickly, I attempted to take charge of the emotions trying to build up. I missed him. I missed my best friend.

The door to the truck opened and Luke jumped in. "Sorry about that, Lib. That was a guy from one of my classes. He had a question about something."

I continued to look out the passenger window as I said, "No worries." I looked back at him and smiled. He gave me that damn sexy grin of his and then put the truck in drive and took off.

He reached over and turned on his radio. Mantz Brothers' "One Kiss At a Time" started playing. I closed my eyes and leaned my head back against the headrest.

This is going to be a long drive.

"ARE YOU HUNGRY, Lib?"

I looked up from my chemistry book and saw we were in Austin already. Glancing over to Luke, I couldn't help but smile back at his stupid sexy grin. I shrugged my shoulders. "I'm kind of hungry. Are you?"

He smiled bigger. "I'm starved. Franklin's?"

I laughed and shook my head. Luke and his barbeque. The bastard knew Franklin's was my favorite, except if you didn't get there first thing in the morning you were out of luck. They sold out every day by noon. "Luke, there is no way they are going to have food left." I glanced at my watch. "It's almost eleven thirty. The line is going to be around the block."

Luke turned right and started heading toward Eleventh Street. "You still like brisket, right?"

I nodded my head even though he wasn't looking at me and clearly ignoring what I had to say. "Yeah, I do."

He chuckled and said, "There ya go. Let's go get some of your favorite brisket."

Shaking my head, I sighed. We were wasting our time.

Luke pulled into the parking lot and parked. The place was practically empty. I looked around and only saw a few cars.

"Where is everyone?" I asked as Luke turned off his truck and got out. He made his way around the front of the truck and opened my door. When he held his hand out for mine, I wanted to push him. *Why is he being so sweet to me? I hate it when he does this. It confuses me.*

We started walking toward the restaurant. There was a closed sign up. "They're closed already, Luke," I said as I reached for his arm. He shot me a sneaky grin and grabbed my hand, pulling me toward the door. The butterflies deep in my core caused me to place my hand on my stomach.

Luke pushed the door open and I was overtaken by the smell of heaven. I glanced around the restaurant. There was no one sitting at any of the old fashioned tables. All the red chairs were pushed in and the place was spotless.

The yellow walls always made me smile. I wasn't sure why. Looking down, Luke still had a hold of my hand in his and I wasn't about to pull my hand away. Any touch from him, I'd take.

I heard someone say Luke's name as I raised my head and saw a guy walking toward us. He looked to be about our age and had dark-brown hair, almost black. He held out his hand to shake Luke's. Reaching out, Luke shook his hand while he kept his grip on mine. I swallowed hard as he let go of it as he talked to the guy.

Luke smiled warmly and said, "Manny, thanks so much for doing this for us."

Manny looked over at me, smiled and then turned back to Luke. "I always said I owed you one, I just never thought you'd be asking for something like this."

Luke chuckled and nodded his head. "Manny, this is Libby. Libby, this is Manny. We met last year at A&M. Manny's dad is the best friend of the owner of Franklin's. He's also the general manager here."

Reaching out my hand, I shook Manny's. "It's a pleasure to meet you."

Manny slapped his hands together. "I hear the brisket here is your favorite." I laughed as I nodded my head. "Well you're in luck." He motioned with his hands for us to sit. Turning, I followed Luke to a table as he pulled out the seat and pushed it in for me as I sat.

As Luke sat, he and Manny talked about football and how well A&M was doing. I smiled at a young girl who walked over to our table and sat down two plates and silverware. She peeked over at Luke and smiled. She couldn't have been more than six-

5

teen. Her dark-brown hair and deep-brown eyes led me to believe she was related to Manny. They looked almost alike.

"Libby? Lib, are you listening?"

I looked over to Luke. "I'm sorry, I was … um … thinking of something," I said as I felt my face heat up.

Luke looked at me and tilted his head as if he wanted to say something but didn't. He was about to talk when the same young girl brought out all the food. My stomach growled as I inhaled a deep breath.

"Okay, well let me leave y'all be so you can eat and talk," Manny said as he began to take a few steps back. I smiled and gave him a thumbs up since my mouth was full with brisket.

Luke made a sandwich and took a huge bite and then let out a moan. I giggled as I swallowed and said, "I know, right? It's heaven. How did you do all of this? *Why* did you do all of this?"

Luke's eyes filled with what appeared to be sadness before he masked it over with that damn smile of his. "I can't do something for one of my best friends? I knew how much you loved this place and Manny owed me a favor. They were closed today, but he talked his dad into opening up for us." Luke winked at me and laughed. "Plus they are catering a huge party at the capitol, so …"

I laughed and shook my head. "In other words, you lucked out on timing."

He took another bite and nodded his head. "I did." Smiling, Luke asked, "How are you liking A&M, Lib?"

I let out a small breath. "I'm enjoying it. It's different that's for sure. It's harder, but not as hard as I thought it would be. I mainly miss the girls. Colt, too, of course. I wish Alex and Grace were going to A&M." Luke's eyes caught mine and we stared at each other as if trying to read one another's mind. Luke looked away and cleared his throat. He stood and looked at me. "Peach cobbler? I bet I can rustle some up."

Smiling weakly, I wanted to ask him why he was pushing me away. Looking down, I thought about that day last summer when Luke had told me he loved me. My stomach dropped like it does every time I think of that day.

I WALKED INTO the clubhouse and began looking around for Alex's change of clothes. Luke stumbled in behind me talking about some stupid song that was on the radio he liked.

I had to tune everything out. My body was craving Luke's touch more than ever. His smell, his laugh, even his slurred speech was driving me crazy with lust.

I closed my eyes and thought about the kiss that changed everything between Luke and me. The summer before he left for college he decided to kiss me. Then he just left me without so much as a good-bye. Confused and hurt.

"Lib were is ... some pants. I'm soaking wet for some reason."

Rolling my eyes, I walked over to the duffle bag that Will had left here. I reached in, grabbed a T-shirt and pants. I turned and walked to Luke.

"Here."

I shoved the clothes into his stomach, causing him to stumble back.

"Shit! Luke! Why are you drinking so much lately? You can't even stand up straight."

Luke grabbed me and attempted to stand up. He laughed and mumbled something about me being the reason.

"What?"

He looked at me and smiled. "Nothing, baby."

My stomach clenched at him calling me baby.

He began trying to take his shirt off and was failing miserably.

Reaching up, I helped him take it off. I attempted to not look at his perfect body, but my eyes were drawn to his six-pack abs. I bit down on the inside of my cheek to keep in the moan I wanted so desperately to let slip between my lips.

Swallowing hard, I began unbuttoning his pants. Luke was barely able to stand up as he placed his hands on my shoulders.

"Lib ... I'm so drunk."

I giggled and said, "Yeah, I know. I'm having to undress your ass."

He laughed and reached for the wall to hold himself up.

"Luke, can you push your pants off? I'll have to turn around while you get your pants off since you're not wearing any underwear."

The smile that moved across his face caused my body to betray me. I could almost feel my nipples get harder and the wetness between my legs was a sure sign I wanted him.

"You afraid, Lib..." He shook his head. "Lib. You afraid to see me naked?"

I chuckled nervously. At least I tried to chuckle, but it came out as more of a nervous laugh.

"No. Why would I be afraid to see you naked? We used to skinny dip in the river."

Luke smiled bigger. "Yeah, I loved doing that. I wanted to tell you how beautiful you were."

Closing my eyes, I pushed my emotions down. He's drunk.

I walked up to Luke and shoved his pants down, causing his dick to spring out. His hard dick. I let out a gasp and covered my mouth.

Oh shit. Oh shit. Oh shit. Wow. Oh ... wow.

"Um ..." I snapped my eyes up to his eyes. They were filled with what I think was lust.

"Will you ... I mean ... can you kick your pants off?"

Luke somehow managed to get his wet pants off while I stood with my back to him. My heart was beating so fast and loud, it was practically drowning out all the other sounds in the room. If only it had drowned out Luke grunting as he attempted to get dressed.

I heard a thump and turned to see him trying to put the dry pants on. Taking a deep breath, I walked back over to him. Swallowing hard, I tried to keep my hands from shaking as I took a hold of his dick. Luke let out a moan as I moved it out of the way while I zipped up his pants. My core was pulsing with desire and

Saving You

I bit the inside of my cheek until I tasted blood. Holy shit. I've got Luke's dick in my hand! *I removed my hand and zipped up his pants and took a step back when he grabbed my hands and pulled them away.*

Luke's breathing increased as he whispered, "Libby ..."

I looked into his eyes as they searched my face. He began to walk forward, causing me to step back and run right into the wall.

"Luke ... I um ... I need to get changed ..."

When I saw him look down at my lips, I licked them without even thinking. He leaned down and lightly brushed his lips across mine as we both let out a moan. He slipped his hand behind my neck and pulled me in closer to deepen the kiss.

His tongue moved against my lips making me open them to him. I placed one hand on his chest and the other up in his hair and tugged on it slightly as he moaned into my mouth.

I had been aching for his kiss ever since that day under the bleachers. Dreaming about it.

I wasn't sure how long we kissed for before Luke pulled back. His eyes were still focused on my lips before they slowly moved up and captured my eyes.

"I love you, Libby. I've always loved you."

In an instant, those eight words turned my entire world, and my heart, upside down.

FINGERS SNAPPED IN front of my face. "Lib? Earth to Libby?" I snapped my head up and looked up at him. "You were off in another world, Lib. Do you want some peach cobbler?"

"Um ... no thank you."

Luke frowned as he watched me. "Why not, Lib? You love peach cobbler." I swallowed hard and pushed my plate away. My heart was still racing at the memory of Luke telling me he loved me. "I'm really full. Maybe a piece to go and I'll eat it later?"

The smile returned to Luke's face as he nodded and called

out for Manny to pack a cobbler to go. I sat in my seat and watched him walk away as I tried to figure out the confusing feelings rushing through my head.

Chapter Two

Luke

I GLANCED OUT the window and looked at the solid line of rain coming our way. *Shit. I hate driving in the rain.* One quick peek to Libby and my heart was beating crazy again.

I couldn't stop thinking about when I held her hand as we walked up to Franklin's. Really, I couldn't stop thinking about how Libby allowed me to hold it for as long as she did. I knew I had been acting like a dick toward her. Letting out a sigh, I pushed my hand through my hair. Out of the corner of my eye I saw Libby watching me. There she goes biting on that damn lower lip of hers. I smiled slightly; she must like when I do that. Testing my theory, I ran my hand through my hair again. Libby's mouth parted slightly, causing my smile to turn into a full-blown grin.

The rain began hitting on the windshield, first coming down slow then coming in a downpour. I slowed and turned the windshield wipers on higher.

"Wow, it's really raining hard. Maybe you should pull over, Luke," Libby said as she began chewing on her fingernail. It was a nervous habit she had done since I could remember.

I rolled my eyes and said, "Nah, it's fine." Right after I said that, the car in front of us hydroplaned and veered into the other lane, causing everyone to put their brakes on. "I think I'll pull over into that HEB parking lot."

Libby folded her arms over her chest and mumbled something under her breath. I didn't respond because I didn't want to argue with her. This was the first time in months, things actually felt normal. It felt like my best friend was sitting next to me.

I pulled into the parking lot and put my truck in park as it continued to pour. Libby pulled her phone out and began texting someone. She let out a giggle and then looked out her window.

"What are you thinking about?" I asked.

She turned and looked at me and shrugged her shoulders. "Nothing. Just something Grace said to me."

My younger sister, Grace, was going to the University of Texas and I couldn't wait to see her. She was a pain in my ass sometimes, but I loved her more than life itself.

"Grace said she was surprised that you had planned the stop at Franklin's."

Turning, I looked into Libby's eyes. "Are you surprised?" She laughed and looked away. "Well? Are you, Lib?"

She slowly turned and looked at me. "Honestly? Yes."

Swallowing hard, I tried to get rid of the lump in my throat. "Why?"

She shrugged her shoulders. "I don't know. It feels like we've grown apart. You're no longer that fun guy I knew growing up."

I turned more in my seat so I could look at her. "What am I now?"

She narrowed her eyes at me. "Are we being completely honest right now?" I nodded my head. She took in a deep breath through her nose and blew it out of her mouth in a quick movement. "A jerk."

Pulling my head back, I opened my mouth slightly. "A jerk?"

She pursed her lips and nodded her head. "We used to be …" Libby looked away and out the window. "I don't really know anymore what we used to be." She slowly shook her head. "Anyway, Grace said you're not spontaneous anymore." She looked back at me and stared into my eyes. "I have to agree with her."

12

My heart ached as Libby's words echoed in my mind. *Not spontaneous?* I'll show her spontaneous. I looked out the front window at the rain. It was beginning to lighten up. I opened the door to the truck and Libby asked, "Luke? Where in the hell are you going?"

Jumping out, I looked at her and smiled. "I'm being sponta-neous." I shut the door and jogged around to the passenger side of the truck and opened the door. "Get out, Libby."

Libby's mouth dropped open as she stared at me. "You're kicking me out of the truck for being honest? Screw you, Luke Johnson."

Laughing, I reached in and picked her up. She began yelling for me to put her down. "I'm being spontaneous, Libby."

I pushed the door shut with my foot and walked away from the truck as the rain quickly began to get both of us soaking wet. I set Libby down and looked at how beautiful she was. She was staring at me like I'd lost my damn mind. "What are we do-ing standing in the rain?"

Grabbing her, I pulled her to me, pulling her body up against mine. She let out a gasp, but instantly wrapped her arms around me. "I'm dancing with you. In the rain."

The left side of her mouth slowly began to lift as she fought to hold back her smile and lost. I quickly pushed her out and spun her around and pulled her back to me as she let out a laugh.

We danced around the parking lot like we didn't have a care in the world. Libby ran over to a puddle and jumped in it, caus-ing water to go everywhere. I loved seeing how carefree she was. I ran up to her and picked her up and began spinning her around as she dropped her head back and laughed. I slowly let Libby slide down my body, holding her closer to me as we slowed our dance down. My stomach was flipping all over the damn place. I missed being with Libby like this. Missed feeling happy like this.

Reaching up, I moved a piece of hair off of Libby's face and tucked it behind her ear. She smiled and it about dropped me to my knees. Wrapping her arms around my neck, our eyes locked as our bodies moved in perfect sync.

I closed my eyes to fight the pull of her lips. I wanted to kiss her, tell her how much I loved her and wanted to make her mine. Opening my eyes again, I caught Libby licking her lips. For one brief second, I moved toward her lips before stopping myself.

She deserved so much better than me. Pulling back away from her lips, I whispered, "Was that spontaneous enough for you, Lib?"

I saw her swallow as she slowly nodded her head. "I um ... I need to change before I get back into your truck."

Letting go of her body, I watched as she turned and headed back to the truck. The rain had stopped and for one precious second, so did life. It was just Libby and me. I jumped when Libby shut the truck door. She walked toward me with a change of clothes. "I'm going to run into HEB and change." She smiled weakly as she walked past me and into the store as I stood there. I finally came to my senses and walked to the truck for a change of clothes.

I needed to get her to Mason. Then I could go out and put this whole day where it belonged—tucked somewhere deep in my heart.

THE REST OF the drive to Mason, Libby stared out the window. I tried a few times to talk to her, but no words would form. We were almost to her house when I got the nerve to talk to her.

"So this was a fun road trip, huh?"

She quickly turned and looked at me. I glanced at her as she stared at me. "What? What's wrong?"

Her mouth dropped open. "Are you serious right now?"

I pulled up to her gate and stopped. "Yeah, what's wrong?" The anger that moved across her face caused me to swallow hard. She unbuckled her seat belt and opened the door. "What are you doing?" I asked.

She got out as I put the truck in park. She opened the back door and grabbed her bag, slamming the door in the process. She started making her way to the gate when I grabbed her arm. "Lib, what is wrong? Why are you angry?"

She dropped her bag and pushed me, hard. I stumbled back a few steps before righting myself.

"You! You are what's wrong, Luke." She began shaking her head as I watched tears fill her eyes. I was always making her cry. *Always*. I ran my hand through my hair when she walked up, grabbed my arm, and pulled it down. "Stop! Stop doing that!" she screamed.

I took a step back. "Stop doing what?"

Her lower lip began to quiver as she walked away from me. Libby picked up her bag and began walking to the gate. Stopping, she turned to me.

"Why do you do this to me?"

I took a step toward her when she held up her hand to stop me. "Do what, baby?"

She shook her head and stomped her foot. "This! Luke, you can't keep confusing me like this. One minute you want to be my friend, and then you do something romantic like plan a lunch for me and dance with me in the rain. Then you go to kiss me, only you push me away." A sob escaped her mouth as she closed her eyes.

"What do you want from me, Luke?"

I knew I couldn't tell her how I felt. I knew she felt the same way about me, but something kept stopping me. I was so afraid I would hurt her again. I always seemed to hurt her.

"I ... I care about you, Libby. You're my best friend," I said as I watched a tear roll down her face. I quickly walked up to her and placed my hand on the side of her face and wiped the tear away. My heart was breaking knowing I caused that tear. She leaned her face into my hand and my heart felt like someone was squeezing it.

"I want more than that, Luke," she whispered as she closed

her eyes. "I don't want to be your best friend."

Dropping my hand, I took a step back. Libby opened her eyes and looked into mine. It was almost as if she was pleading with me to do something. Say something. I took two steps back and shook my head. "I don't mean to keep hurting you, Libby. I … I just …"

The moment I saw the hurt flash across her face, I wanted to pull her to me. She cleared her voice and smiled weakly. "I'll see you around, Luke." Turning away from me, Libby walked over to the keypad and typed in the code, causing the gate to swing open.

"Lib, let me drive you up to the house," I called out after her. She held up her hand and continued walking.

"I need some time alone. See you around, Luke."

"Fuck," I mumbled under my breath as I watched her walk down the driveway. I turned and headed back to my truck. Slamming the door shut, I dropped my head against the back of the seat. I closed my eyes and was brought back to the night my world changed.

I WAS LEANING against my truck watching Libby out of the corner of my eye. I finally got the guts to kiss her. Why I waited until the night before I left for college, I have no clue. Will was going on and on about something.

Grace and Libby started giggling when Will looked over toward them. I couldn't take my eyes off of Libby. She had been my best friend since I could remember. We did everything together. Told each other everything. I swear my lips were still tingling from the kiss we shared earlier under the bleachers.

"Our friendships are so important. I hope nothing ever gets in the way of that. We have to make sure nothing gets in the way of our friendships with each other," Will said as he turned and looked at me. "You're going off to college and all, ya know what I mean?"

My heart dropped in my stomach. What did I just do? *I was so confused by the feelings that flooded my body after Libby and I kissed.* Is Libby just as confused? Did she regret the kiss? *I turned back and looked at Libby.* I just kissed my best friend. Shit. *I swallowed hard and looked at Will.*

He was now staring at the girls. I pushed off the truck and opened it. "I'm heading off. Tell the girls I'll miss them."

"You're not going to say good-bye?" *Will asked as he looked at me with a confused look.*

I shook my head. "I did, earlier. It's best if I leave now. I've got to get up early." *I jumped in my truck and began backing up. As I started to pull out, I looked back to Libby. She was standing there with a confused look on her face. I quickly looked away and pushed down the sick feeling I had in my stomach. I couldn't risk our friendship.*

IT WAS MY *second day at school and I had already been invited to a party. I glanced down at my phone and saw Libby's text.*

Lib: *Why didn't you say good-bye? Please call me.*

Me: *Been really busy trying to get used to all this. I'll call you soon.*

Closing my eyes, I pushed my phone into my pocket and looked around. I had met Manny in fishcamp, Texas A&M's version of freshman orientation, a few weeks back. He was a sophomore, and he and his older brother lived in a house off campus. As soon as I walked through the door, Manny pushed a beer in my hand and then showed me which bedrooms were open if I was interested in hooking up with anyone.

Looking around, I checked everyone out. I was pretty sure I was the only freshman at this party. I took a drink of my beer when I caught her staring at me. I watched as she ran her tongue along her top teeth and smiled. Her wavy blonde hair fell just above her shoulders. She had on a tight, black dress that barely covered what it needed to cover. I gazed down her body to her long tan legs and bright-red fuck-me shoes and then back up till our eyes met. I nodded my head and smiled letting her know the attraction was mutual. She looked at her friend and said something before turning and making her way over to me. She couldn't hold a candle to Libby.

Libby. I needed to push Libby and the kiss far from my mind. Will's words replayed in my head about all of our friendships. Did I ruin my friendship with Libby by kissing her? I had such strong, crazy feelings for Libby. If I moved forward with my feelings for her, and if it didn't work, our friendship would be forever ruined. I'd rather have Libby in my life than risk losing her because of my feelings.

The blonde walked up and stopped right in front of me. "Hey," she said with an almost purr to her voice. "I'm Karen. And you are?"

"Luke. Luke Johnson."

Her eyebrows rose up. "Country boy. I think I just fell a little bit more for you." I laughed as I took another drink of beer. "Want to have some fun?"

Looking her body up and down, I shrugged. "Depends on what kind of fun you're talking about."

She glanced over to the stairs that led to the bedroom. "The kind of fun that has you taking off your clothes and me getting to know you better."

The entire time I followed Karen up the stairs, I rationalized that I was moving on. The kiss between Libby and me had been a mistake. I couldn't risk our friendship.

It all seemed like a blur. I was lying next to Karen staring up at the ceiling as she traced a pattern over and over on my chest. "I think you and I are going to have lots of fun together, Mr. Johnson."

I smiled as I pulled her closer to me and closed my eyes.

Libby. I'm so sorry, Libby.

OPENING MY EYES, I shook my head, trying to erase the memory of the night I betrayed Libby. I put my truck in reverse and pulled out of the driveway. Putting it into drive, I pushed the gas and sped away as I looked in the rearview mirror at Libby walking down her driveway. I'd never before had my heart physically feel like it was hurting.

Libby.

Chapter Three

Libby

"LIBBY? ARE YOU going to peel the potato or just stand there and hold it?"

I looked over at my mother and tried to smile. She looked so adorable. She had her hair in low pigtails and she was wearing black Capri pants with a light-purple shirt. "Sorry. Just thinking."

She looked at me and gave me a smile. "About?"

"School."

"How's school going?"

I smiled. "Great."

"You getting used to everything? The dorm? The food? Are you making sure you're always walking with someone at all times?"

I let out a giggle. "Slowly, yes. The dorm is okay, but really small. The food sucks, and yes I am always with someone."

"Do you get to see your brother and Luke often?" she asked as she placed an apple pie in the oven.

Hearing his name caused my heart to feel like it stopped beating. "Not too often. I'm pretty busy with school stuff and so are they."

My mother nodded her head and walked back over to the island where she began working on the stuffing. "How was the ride home with Luke?"

I snapped my head up and looked at her. "Fine. Why do you ask?"

She shrugged her shoulders. "Don't know. It just seems like the two of you used to be inseparable and now it's as if you hardly know each other."

I dropped my eyes to the ground and then looked back up. I slowly shook my head. "Why are men so damn confusing, Mom?"

She smiled softly, took the potato out of my hand, and led me to the kitchen table where we both sat. She took in a deep breath and blew it out. "Libby, I wish I could answer that for you. Your father still says and does things that have me standing there trying to sort out what in the heck he was saying or thinking."

I let out a giggle. My parents were amazing. The way my father looked at my mother was as if he couldn't get enough of her. Will and I had walked in on them more than once where they were just short of getting it on. I loved how they weren't afraid to show their love for each other. Seeing my father take my mother's hand in his made me long for that.

I turned away from my mother. "Luke told me he loved me." My mother sucked in a breath and I quickly looked back. "But he was drunk, Mom. Drunk out of his mind."

She smiled. "You know, drunks never lie."

Running my hands down my face, I let out a frustrated moan before dropping my hands onto my lap. "Mom, he pushes me away, then he pulls me right back in."

Reaching over, my mother gently took my hands in hers as she rubbed her thumbs over my skin. "What do you mean, he pulls you right back in?"

Letting out a long sigh, I closed my eyes briefly and then opened them. "He acts like he doesn't want to even talk to me sometimes. Then ... then ..." I threw my hands up in the air. "Then he goes off and pulls me out of his truck and dances with me in the rain. He almost kisses me, and the emotions start going crazy. And then bam, he pulls back! It's like I can see it in his eyes, Mom, and then his eyes go dark and I see nothing."

My mother smiled slightly and nodded her head. "You know, your father and I played a similar game. I was so in love with him, but I pushed him away. I pushed him into the arms of another woman."

My mouth dropped open some. "What?" Her eyes filled with sadness as if she was thinking back to a memory.

"I was scared. I had lost my parents not long before that and I was afraid to open my heart to anyone, Libby. I mean, so afraid. I knew the moment I let your father in, something would pull him away from me." She shook her head and looked down before looking back up at me. "Do you love him, Libby?"

Tears filled my eyes as I nodded my head. "I love him very much, Mom. So much it hurts."

"Libby, I hope to God that you've saved yourself for the one person who truly deserves that gift."

I could feel my face growing hotter, but I nodded my head and whispered, "I have." My mother smiled sweetly and squeezed my hand.

"I made a mistake one night that I will forever regret. I don't want you to make the same mistake. I wanted more than anything for my first time to be with your father, but sadly it wasn't." She looked away and took a moment before turning back to me and talking again. "Don't be pushed by anger or hurt to do something you will regret. Make sure it's something you want. I'm going to safely assume you're wanting your first time to be with Luke?"

I slowly nodded my head and whispered, "Yes."

My mother looked down and then let out a chortle before glancing back up to me. "The apple doesn't fall far from the tree. Luke's father was almost the same exact way. I can still hear Ari and him arguing with each other. Oh how the two of them pushed and pulled at each other. It was unreal."

I smiled. "Really?"

My mother let out a laugh. "There were times I was sure Ari was going to kill Jeff. A stranger looking in would have thought

22

they hated each other. Jeff did everything he could to push Ari away."

I rolled my eyes. "Like father, like son." My mother and I both started chuckling.

She let out a sigh as she said, "I guess so."

My phone started ringing as I pulled it out of my pocket and saw Luke's name. I showed it to my mother and she raised an eyebrow as she stood up. "I'd send his little ass to voicemail."

I laughed and did just that. Putting my phone on silent, I got up and walked to my mother. I picked up the potato and started back to work peeling it. We spent the rest of the afternoon laughing and cooking as we got ready for Thanksgiving.

SLAMMING MY TRUNK, I let out a sigh as I looked at my mother and father. I smiled weakly. "I'm going to miss you both so much." I felt the tears threatening to build as I bit down hard on my lip. My father walked up to me and pulled me in for one of his bear hugs. I felt so safe in my father's arms. I was sure no other man would ever make me feel safe like this. I pulled back slightly. "I love you, Daddy."

My father kissed my forehead and whispered, "I love you too, Libby. More than anything."

I dropped my arms and turned to my mother. We both smiled as she held her arms open. The moment she pulled me to her, I started crying. "Mom, I'm so confused."

She held me tighter as she whispered. "I know, baby girl. I know." Daddy walked up and wrapped his arms around my mother and me.

The sound of a truck driving down the driveway caused me to take a step back and quickly wipe my tears away. I spun around and my heart dropped.

Luke.

I watched as Luke pulled up and parked behind my car. My mother placed her hand on my shoulder and whispered in my ear, "Talk to him, Libby." I slowly nodded my head in acknowledgment.

Luke got out of his truck and I forced myself to not show what I instantly felt.

Lust. Want. Desire. Need. Him.

"Hey there, Luke. You ready to head back to school?" my father asked from behind me. Luke smiled and my knees wobbled just a bit.

"Yes, sir. The faster I get back, the faster the year ends." He walked up next to me and reached out to shake my father's hand. One quick glimpse down toward me and my heart dropped to my stomach. It was pounding so hard I was sure Luke would hear it. I turned my head and watched his every move as he spoke to my father. My eyes moved down to his Wrangler jeans that fit him just right. He had on a tight black T-shirt that clung to his body and showed off his chiseled abs. My eyes wandered down further as I smiled when I saw his cowboy boots. I moved my eyes back up to him and noticed his Texas A&M baseball cap. I moaned internally.

"We're going to head inside. Libby, don't leave without saying good-bye, sweetheart."

My mother's voice pulled me out of my trance as I quickly checked to be sure I hadn't been drooling. Luke had always had an effect on me. Since I could remember, I was captivated by his smile—his laugh—his incredible muscular body.

"Um … I won't, Mom," I said with a weak smile as I looked at her smiling at me. She took my father's hand and they began to walk up to the house.

I watched them until they disappeared behind the front door. I was wishing I could follow them. Luke cleared his throat and I looked down to the ground. "What's up, Luke?"

He took a few steps back and leaned against my car as he let out a chuckle, forcing me to look up at him. I let out a soft sigh as I waited for him to tell me what he was doing here.

"I wanted to make sure you didn't need a ride back to A&M," he said with a smirk.

I narrowed my eyes at him and stared into his beautiful green eyes. Some days you couldn't tell if his eyes were green or gray. It was one of the things I loved about him. If he was angry, I swore they turned gray. Luke had always told me I was crazy. His eyes were green and always stayed green. "I've told you three times I was taking my car back, Luke."

He lifted the corner of his mouth into a melt-my-panties-on-the-spot smile. "You did?" he asked with a slight chuckle.

I crossed my arms over my chest and nodded my head. "Yes. Yes, I did."

His eyes moved up and down my body, causing my cheeks to flush. I looked away to get my wits about me. "Maybe I just wanted to come and talk to you, Lib."

I licked my lips on impulse. "Talk to me about what?" A part of me was hoping he would finally just admit the feelings he had for me. *If only he remembered telling me that he loved me.*

Luke shrugged his shoulders. "Maybe I should follow you back. Make sure you get there okay."

I lifted my chin and stood up taller. "I'm perfectly fine getting there on my own. I'm not a child."

Luke's eyes moved down my body slowly. I was wearing black skinny jeans, my favorite pair of cowboy boots, and a teal blouse that made my eyes bluer than normal. When his eyes finally found mine, he whispered, "I know."

Swallowing hard, I looked away as I cleared my throat. "I don't need you to watch over me like I'm some little girl who can't take care of herself." I began to walk past him as he pushed off the hood of my car and followed me. Opening the driver's side door, I spun back around and looked at him. I was ready to lay into him and tell him how dare he come here and try to pretend like everything is okay. I didn't need him. I didn't even want to look at him.

When I looked into his eyes, he smiled and I was rendered speechless. I opened my mouth, but nothing came out. Luke reached up and took a piece of my hair and pushed it behind my ear. "You're eyes look beautiful with this color shirt on, Lib."

I stood there like an idiot before I finally managed to say something. "Thank you."

"Let me follow you back. Please, Lib. It will make me feel better and I'm sure your parents would feel better as well."

I was Jell-O in his hands. I always had been. I'd never forget the time he talked me into jumping out of the second-story barn window because he was convinced I could land on to the hay pile. I missed it by five feet and ended up breaking my ankle. Then there was the time he talked me into putting the frog under Grace's pillow. He said she loved the frog and would be so happy to know he was sleeping under her pillow safe and warm. Grace still brings it up to this day how she was in a dead sleep and slipped her hand under her pillow only to be woken up from touching something slimy. She flew up out of bed so fast that she tripped over her backpack and hit the corner of her eye on her desk. She walked around with a black eye for two weeks.

I pulled in a deep breath through my nostrils. Big mistake. His cologne filled my senses. I shook my head in an attempt to clear my thoughts. Luke Johnson was not going to have that kind of control over me anymore.

"Libby, honey. Are y'all ready to take off?" my mother called from the front porch. I opened my mouth and forced the words out.

"Yes. I'm ready to head out."

Luke winked and turned to my parents as he flashed them that stupid smile of his.

"I was just telling Lib I should probably follow her. Just to be safe. I'd hate to think what would happen if she got a flat tire or something." Oh. My. God. I wanted to punch him in the stomach.

"I think that's a great idea," my father said as he walked to us. I did a double-take as I looked at my father, then my mother.

"What? No. I don't need a babysitter, I'll be perfectly ..."

My father walked up and slapped Luke on the back. "Nonsense, Libby. Luke is right. You're both going the same way; I either want you to follow him, or he follows you."

I quickly came up with a plan. I'd follow Luke and go so slow he would eventually pull away and we'd lose each other. I was about to agree when Luke glanced back at me. "I'll follow Libby, Josh. I wouldn't want to lose sight of her if I pulled away."

Bastard. I pushed past him causing him to stumble. He let out a chuckle, which pissed me off even more. I walked up to my mother and hugged her. "I love you so much, Mom."

Giving me a gentle smile, my mother whispered, "I love you too, Libby."

Smiling weakly, I turned to my father. "I really don't need him to follow me, you know."

My father smiled and pulled me into his arms. "I want my baby girl to be protected always."

I pulled away from him and glanced back at Luke. "Some things you can't always protect me from, Daddy." Luke's smile faded a bit. Looking back at my father, I kissed him on the cheek. "Love you both. So very much."

Slowly I made my way to the driver's side of my door. Climbing in, I started the car and waved good-bye to my parents as I pulled out and headed down the driveway.

Operation Lose Luke was in full force.

Chapter Four

Luke

I HIT THE gas and gunned it through the yellow light. "Jesus, Mary, and Joseph. Why the hell is she driving so damn fast?"

We were halfway to A&M and Libby had been doing everything in her power to shake me. When we came to a stoplight, I pulled up next her. I put my passenger side window down and honked the horn. She ignored me of course. I honked again, this time I held it down longer. She finally turned and looked at me as she put her window down.

"What in the hell, Libby? Stop being a baby."

Her lips curled up and I was almost positive I saw a vein in her neck become engorged. "Fuck you, Luke."

My mouth dropped open as she looked back toward the road and rolled up her window. The light must have turned green because she punched it and took off. I quickly took off after her and watched as she attempted to change lanes enough times to lose me. At the next light, I put my truck in park and jumped out. I walked up to her car and banged on the window, causing her to jump. She rolled down the window and looked at me with a shocked expression.

"What in the hell are you doing? Get back in the truck, Luke!"

"Pull over at the Shell station ahead on the right," I said as I turned and walked back to my truck. I was so angry my hands were shaking as I placed them back on my steering wheel. The light changed and Libby punched it again, causing her tires to squeal as she took off. She put her right signal on and pulled into the gas station and parked in an empty spot to the side of the store. I pulled up next to her and we got out at the same time. I didn't even bother to shut my door. I walked around the back of my truck and Libby met me halfway.

"What in the fuck do you think you're doing driving like that? Are you trying to get hurt?" I asked as she balled her fists up.

"How dare you! How dare you come to my house and try to play like my knight in shining armor. You're far from it, asshole."

I inhaled a deep breath to calm myself down. "You'd rather drive like that than have me follow you? What's wrong with you?"

She took a step closer to me and pushed me with all her might, but I didn't budge. "You! You are what's wrong, like always. It's always you!"

Libby's eyes filled with tears and my world came to a complete standstill. My stomach and heart felt like I had just jumped from a skyscraper into a freefall. My eyes quickly searched hers. Grabbing Libby, I pulled her to me.

"I care about you, Libby. Why can't you see that?" I asked as she attempted to pull away.

"I don't want you to care about me, damn it!" she yelled as she continued to fight me. Reaching down, I took a hold of her hands. "Let go of me, you asshole."

I looked into her eyes and said in a calm voice, "Stop this, Libby. Calm down and understand why I'm doing this. I ..."

She closed her eyes and began shaking her head as she instantly stopped struggling with me. "Stop. *Please* stop saying you care about me, Luke."

I dropped her hands and ran my fingers through my hair. "What do you want me to say, Libby?"

She opened her eyes and I watched the tear slowly roll down her cheek. "That you love me."

29

I let out a small breath. My heart ached as I watched the tear make its way down her face. She closed her eyes and placed both hands over her face as she let out a frustrated yell, causing me to jump at the unexpected outburst. Placing my hands on her arms, I pulled them down as her eyes darted all over my face. It was as if she was afraid to look me in the eyes. "Never mind. Let's just get back to campus." She began to move away from me when I grabbed her arm and pulled her to me again. She let out a gasp as I placed my hand on the back of her neck and pulled her lips within inches of mine. Libby's breathing increased, as did mine.

"Do you have any idea what you do to me, Libby?" Pressing my lips against hers, I kissed her fast and hard. She wouldn't open her mouth to me so I began walking her backward until she was back up against my truck. In that instant her hands went into my hair and she opened up to me. We kissed like we couldn't get enough of each other. Our tongues danced in an endless motion with each other as we let ourselves get lost in the kiss. I pressed my hard dick into her stomach as she let out a moan that moved through my entire body. My hands went to her face as I started to slow the kiss down. When I pulled my lips away, I rested my forehead against Libby's.

My breathing was erratic as I tried to settle the confusing feelings running through my veins. "You. Drive. Me. Crazy," I whispered as I kept my eyes closed. I could hear her breathing heavy. I took a deep breath in. She smelled like heaven. I wasn't sure if that was just Libby or if she had perfume on. She had always smelled like a field of bluebonnets. Sweet and innocent.

Libby placed her hands on my chest as we just stood there. I was too afraid to open my eyes and look into her eyes. I knew what I had done was not fair to either of us.

Taking in a deep breath, Libby whispered, "Luke."

Swallowing hard, I opened my eyes and took a step back. I shook my head and looked away. "I'm sorry, Libby. I'm so sorry I kissed you. It was a mistake."

Shaking her head she looked into my eyes. "Why?" Her eyes

filled with tears. "Luke ..."

I took another step away. "Can't you see, Libby? All I do is hurt you."

She walked toward me. "Because you keep pushing me away. Stop pushing me away."

Libby's phone began ringing with Will's ringtone. "You better get it, Lib. You've been waiting for him to call."

I turned and headed to my truck. One quick glance over toward Libby and she was getting back into her car. As she talked to Will on the phone, she wiped a tear away.

I slammed my head back against the seat of my truck. "What the fuck is wrong with you, Johnson. Why do you keep hurting her?"

Libby began pulling out of the parking lot as I slowly pulled out and began following her. An hour later she turned and headed toward her dorm. I wanted to follow her, but I knew if I did I would end up doing something more than kiss her. I wanted to make her mine. I didn't deserve to make her mine. I didn't deserve her love.

"HEY THERE, HANDSOME."

I looked up from the book I was reading to see Abigail standing in front of me. Her brown hair was pulled up into a braided ponytail and a few pieces hung down to frame her face. She had on skinny jeans with a tight tan sweater that showed off her figure. Her green eyes were filled with lust as she looked at me. I smiled and gave her a quick nod. "Hey, Abigail. What's up?"

She sat down next to me and winked as she ran her tongue along her top teeth. "Not much. What about you? I haven't heard from you in a while."

I leaned back in my chair and smiled bigger. "Been lonely, Abigail?"

She chuckled. "Never. I have been horny though, and you haven't been calling."

My smile faded slightly. "I've been busy. This year has been tough with the class load I took on. Trying to finish up school early."

Abigail tilted her head and looked at me. "Why?"

Shrugging my shoulders, I said, "I don't know. Ready to get back home and help my father and uncle run the ranch I guess."

Abigail leaned forward, allowing her breasts to rest on the table. I got a clear shot of her cleavage, but my body didn't react like it had in the past. "I bet you look hot in those Wrangler jeans, tight white T-shirt and cowboy boots." She closed her eyes and let out a moan. "Mmm ... baby, I can practically feel you moving in and out of me. I'm so wet right now, Luke. If I slipped my hand into my panties, I'd come on the spot just daydreaming about you all sweaty and fucking me against an old truck."

Abigail had a way of getting what she wanted from me, and the only thing she ever wanted from me was sex. I leaned forward and gave her my panty-melting smile as I watched her squirm in her seat.

"You weren't kidding when you said you're horny." She smiled bigger and raised her eyebrow as she pursed her lips. "Does Abigail need some relief?"

She slowly nodded her head. "Yes. She does. And the only person who can do that is you, Mr. Johnson."

I let out a laugh as I leaned back. My smile faded instantly. It was as if I felt her before I saw her. Turning, I saw Libby standing there. I pushed my chair back and stood. "Lib, what's up?"

I watched as her eyes traveled down my body and I instantly adjusted my somewhat hard dick. She looked back up and all I saw was hurt. *Again.* Libby slowly looked to Abigail. Abigail smiled a fake-ass smile as she leaned back in her chair and began playing with her braid. I peeked over at Libby as she smiled weakly at Abigail before turning back to me.

Libby stood up a little taller and cleared her throat. "My car won't start and I can't get a hold of Will. I wouldn't normally bug you about this, but I saw you and well ..." Looking back at

Abigail, Libby's voice cracked. "If I'm interrupting something though." Abigail started to say yes, but I cut her off.

"No, Abigail and I were just catching up."

Libby turned and glared at me. "I heard."

My heart slammed in my chest and my hands starting sweating. *Fuck.* I didn't want Libby to overhear me talking to Abigail like that. Abigail cleared her throat and asked, "So you're the hot roommate's sister, huh?"

Libby's head snapped back over to look at Abigail. "Yes, Will is my brother. Do you know him?"

Abigail laughed and shook her head. "No. I don't know him that well. I've only seen him a few times."

I reached down and scooped up my books and smiled at Abigail. "I'll catch up with you later, Abigail."

Abigail placed her finger in her mouth and giggled. "Sounds good, handsome."

Smirking at Abigail, I glanced to look at Libby who rolled her eyes. Libby turned and walked to the exit. I followed her through the library and out the door. "Where are you parked, Lib?"

"Dorm."

Great. She's pissed.

"Let me drive you there, Lib."

She held up her hand and waved it. "Just meet me there. I'll text Will to let him know you're helping me."

I stopped walking and watched her quickly walk away. Turning, I headed to my truck. I pulled out my phone and hit Grace's phone number.

"Hello, big brother. What's cooking?"

"Explain women to me, Grace."

Grace busted out laughing. "Do you have a few days?"

I rolled my eyes. "Seriously. Y'all love to fuck with men, don't you?"

"No more than men love to fuck with the emotions of women. Take for instance when a guy kisses this girl in a full on passionate kiss and then tells her it was a mistake. As Uncle Matt would say, assmole move right there."

Letting out a sigh, I pulled out onto the road. "I take it you talked to Libby?"

"Possibly. What in the hell is wrong with you? Pull your head out of your ass and get your shit together. You're hurting her, Luke."

Closing my eyes, I quickly opened them again, fighting to hold back the tears that were threatening to build. "I don't mean too, Grace." My voice cracked as I talked so I cleared it.

I ran my hand through my hair. I needed to leave Libby alone. I needed to let her move on and find someone else. Someone who will guard her heart and not hurt her. Not fall into bed with the first girl who makes him forget.

I heard Grace let out a breath and sigh. "I know you don't, Luke. But you have to see how doing this to Libby is confusing her. She's not going to wait forever. Libby is beautiful and sooner or later someone is going to catch her eye and she is going to move on, Luke. Without you I'm afraid."

"Luke? Are you listening to me?"

Nodding my head, I whispered, "Yeah, I heard you." I pulled into the guest parking outside of Libby's building. I looked around and saw her car. "I've got to run, baby sister. I love you. I can't wait to see you."

"Same here. Hey, Luke?"

I put my truck in park and opened the door. Jumping out, I began making my way over to Libby's car. "Yeah?"

"Listen to your heart, not your head."

I let out a breath and shook my head. "If only it was that easy, Grace. Love you."

"Love you too, Luke. Bye."

"Bye, Grace." I pulled the phone from my ear and hit End. I stopped at Libby's car and checked to see if her car door was open. If it was, I was going to have a long talk with her about how unsafe that was. Lucky for her it was locked. I turned and leaned against it as I waited for her to show up. My mind couldn't help but drift back to holding her in my arms as we danced in

Saving You

the rain. The way she smelled. The way she smiled. Closing my
eyes I let the memory take me back.

Chapter Five

Libby

TAKING IN A deep breath, I made my way over to Luke. He was leaning against my car with his eyes closed. His brown hair looked like a hot mess. He must be working out more because I swear his muscles looked bigger. I wanted nothing more than to run my hands over his body. Memorize every inch of him.

Then her words hit me like a brick wall.

"Mmm ... baby I can practically feel you moving in and out of me. I'm so wet right now, Luke. If I slipped my hand into my panties, I'd come on the spot just daydreaming about you all sweaty and fucking me against an old truck."

My stomach flinched as I thought of Luke with Abigail. The way he was looking at her told me he was getting turned on by the way she was talking. *Why couldn't he look at me that way? Why didn't he want me like he wanted her?*

I cleared my throat as I walked up. Luke opened his eyes and gave me a weak smile. "Hey," he said as I walked by and unlocked the driver's side door.

"Hey," I whispered back. Opening the door, I pulled the latch for the hood. Luke opened it and began checking everything out.

My feet felt like lead. I couldn't move. I stood there as I waited for him to find out what was wrong with my car. He poked his head around and said, "I think it's your battery. There is a lot of corrosion on it. You wouldn't happen to have any Coke in your car, would you?"

I shook my head. "I don't drink Coke."

Luke frowned. "Since when?"

I shrugged my shoulders. "Since about two months ago."

Luke made a funny face and then chuckled. "Good for you, Lib. That shit is not good for you anyway."

I wasn't in the mood for small talk with Luke. "Can you fix it without Coke?"

I instantly felt guilty when his smile faded. He looked back at the engine and then looked at me. "I need to get the corrosion all cleaned off and then take it off and take it to get tested. The battery might be bad."

Not wanting to spend any more time with Luke, I slowly nodded my head. "Will can probably take care of this."

Luke pulled his head back and narrowed his eyes at me. "I'm not allowed to help you now, Lib? I thought we were friends."

I let out a laugh. "That's right; you haven't reminded me of our friendship in a while. We certainly aren't on the level of friends that you and the brown-haired Barbie doll at the library are. She seemed a bit pissed I walked up and interrupted your porn talk."

"What did you hear?" Luke asked as he stepped around the car and walked toward me.

Swallowing hard, I watched his muscles move under his tight T-shirt as he made his way over to me. His eyes looked up and down my body and I was cursing myself for wearing sweatpants and an A&M T-shirt. I was sure I looked frumpy. I went to talk but nothing came out. I cleared my throat. "Enough to turn my stomach."

Luke stopped walking. His eyes filled with something I wasn't sure I'd ever seen before. He turned and started toward his truck as my heart starting beating faster. "Where ... where are you going?" I called out.

He looked over his shoulder. "To my truck to get tools. I need to take your battery out and take it in to be tested."

Glancing back to my car I nodded my head.

I SAT IN Luke's truck and watched him walk out of the auto store carrying a new battery. I jumped out of the truck. "Your battery was no good."

"How much do I owe you for the new battery?"

Luke set the battery in the bed of his truck. He looked at me and said, "Nothing."

He opened the door to his truck, got in and started it. I sighed as I got back in the truck and I leaned my head back against the seat. The drive back to campus was no better than the drive to the auto store. Luke didn't utter a word to me. The radio was playing and when the first few beats of the song came on my stomach dropped. Blake Shelton's "Do You Remember" was filling the silent air in the truck cabin. It was the song Luke and I danced to the night he first kissed me. He told me it would always be our song. I turned and looked out the window. Luke probably didn't even remember. Seeing as he was able to kiss me and leave like nothing magical had happened between us.

I felt the tears trying to build in my eyes and I refused to shed any more tears over him. He didn't want me. He'd never want me.

Closing my eyes, I listened to the lyrics. I was instantly brought back to that night. The smell of his body invaded my senses. His green eyes looked into mine lovingly. He had been more than my best friend. He was my everything.

He still was. As much as I wanted to say he wasn't … he was.

"Libby, I need to tell you something."

I shook my head. "Please don't talk to me, Luke."

We drove the rest of the way listening to the song before it finally changed to a faster, louder song. The moment he parked his truck, I got out and made my way to my dorm room. As I walked by my car, Will started toward me. "Lib? Libby, what's wrong?" he asked as he forced me to stop walking.

I tried to smile. "Nothing, Will. Just trying to figure out how to move on." I looked back over my shoulder to see Luke standing there. He opened his mouth as if he wanted to talk, but he quickly shut it again.

Looking down, I turned my head back to Will. "I have a test to study for. Can you just be sure to bring me my keys?" I handed my keys to Will and walked away as I made a plan to avoid Luke Johnson as much as I possibly could.

I HAD SUCCESSFULLY avoided Luke up until Christmas break. Now that we were back home, he was everywhere.

"Let's head to the barn and see what the boys are up to," Grace said as she held her arm out. I laced my arm with hers and we headed to the barn. Taylor and Lex were talking about Taylor's last year of high school.

When we entered the barn, we could hear the guys talking. Grace put her finger up to her mouth and began tiptoeing up the stairs.

I heard Colt talking as we made our way up. "Makes me want to give up on women altogether."

"No! Don't ever talk that way, dude. A man needs a vagina to function," Luke said.

"Really? You just said that?" Will asked. We were almost to the top of the stairs.

Luke chuckled. "Hey, I could have said pussy, but I kept it clean. It's true though. A man does need pussy to survive in this world."

Colt began laughing. Grace stopped walking and turned and looked at me. I was furious hearing Luke talk like he was. I moved past Grace and stopped at the landing of the stairs. Luke was sitting in a chair, pushed back balancing on the back two legs.

Colt was shaking his head as he said, "Damn, Luke. What is wrong with you?"

Luke held up his hands and laughed. "Keeping it real. Just keeping it real."

I felt the heat move through my entire body. All I could picture was that day in the library when I overheard him and Abigail talking. The idea of Abigail having Luke and not me turned my stomach. Hearing him talk like this made me wonder if Luke was even capable of loving anyone. Maybe all he wanted was his fuck buddy.

"That's why he has his fuck buddy. No strings. Just a fun way to *survive in this world.* Isn't that right, Luke?"

Grace started giggling behind me as Will turned and looked at us. Luke looked over at me with a shocked look on his face.

"What?" he asked as he lost his balance and dropped backward onto the floor. I smiled and shook my head. *That's what the bastard gets.*

I glanced over and looked at Will. "I'm heading out for a while to meet someone. I don't have my car. Can I borrow your truck, Will?"

Grace bumped me from behind. "Libby, don't do this."

I ignored Grace as Will stared at me. "Uh …"

Jumping up, Luke looked at me with a stunned, almost frightened expression. "You're going out? On Christmas night? Who are you going out with?"

The anger kept building up. *How dare he ask me who I was going out with it!* I glared at him and he took a step back.

I had no idea where I was going to go and then I remembered Jason had texted me. "Jason's in town and he asked if I wanted to meet him for dessert."

Luke started laughing. "What kind of dessert, Lib?"

I was about to say something when Will did. "Watch it, Luke."

Walking over toward Luke, I smiled. "The kind you'll never get from me, Luke."

I walked up to Will and held my hand out for his truck keys. I needed to get away from Luke. Being around him was more than I could take anymore.

Will was staring at me. "Wait. What did you just say?"

I let out a frustrated sigh. "Can I borrow your truck or not, Will?" Will pulled out his keys and handed them to me. One quick look at Luke showed that my comment about Jason and dessert made him mad.

Good. That's what the asshole gets. Let him chew on that for a while.

Chapter Six

Luke

AFTER LIBBY HAD left, I couldn't push it out of my head what she had said. I wanted to track her down and beat the shit out of Jason. If that was who she was really with.

After everyone talked in the barn for a bit, we had all decided to head into town. We ended up at Pirates Miniature Golf where Colt and I got into an argument.

We had been bickering when I looked up and saw Libby walking by. I stopped talking and watched her walk by as she made her way over to the girls. Turning back around, I looked at Colt. "You cheat, Colt."

Colt's mouth dropped open. "I do not, you asswipe. I got that hole in three swings. Lauren, did I not get that in three shots?"

I turned and looked at Lauren who smiled at me. "Hate to say it, Luke, but he got it in three swings."

Shaking my head, I mumbled under my breath. "This night sucks." I headed over to the counter. "I need a Coke."

The few times I looked over at Libby, she seemed a million miles away. Grace would say something and cause Libby to smile. Then she would look at me and her smile would fade. I hated that I was the reason she was unhappy. I hated that I was the one who caused her to hurt. My phone went off and I pulled it out of my pocket.

Abigail: *In serious need of a good fucking. When are you expected back?*

Peeking over, I looked at Libby and decided not to text Abigail back. I looked up and Alex was looking at me. She tilted her head and mouthed, *are you okay?*

I nodded my head, but I knew by her expression she knew I was anything but okay.

Libby let out a scream and I jumped up. I quickly sat down when I saw she was smiling at Alex. "Y'all are coming to A&M next year?"

Alex nodded her head.

"What? So not fair!" Maegan shouted out.

Alex smiled bigger and said, "Yep, Grace and I are both transferring to A&M."

Sitting down, Maegan pouted and said, "Ugh."

Alex looked at her. "I thought you loved Baylor, Meg?"

Letting out a long sigh, Maegan said, "I do. It's just … I miss y'all."

As we all left Pirates Miniature Golf, I had the strangest feeling come over me. I peeked over and looked at Libby. My heart began to beat hard in my chest as the thought of losing Libby hit me like a brick wall.

IT HAD BEEN three months since Christmas break. I'd been doing nothing but working out, running, and studying in the library. Libby did her best to avoid me and I did my best to help her with that. Every time I saw her, I wanted to take her in my arms and kiss her.

Abigail was constantly on my ass about getting together. The idea of sleeping with her didn't even appeal to me anymore. I realized this morning that I couldn't keep doing this. I needed to tell Libby the truth about what had happened that first week I came to college. The night I met Karen and we slept together.

The night I tried to push all my feelings for Libby deep down inside for fear of losing her friendship. I wasn't sure how Libby would react. She might tell me to go fuck myself or she might …

I shook my head and gathered up my books and put them in my backpack. I decided I would start off slow and ask her to a movie. I headed out of the library and made my way to Libby's dorm. Glancing down at the clock, I knew she was finished with classes today and would most likely be there. I rounded the corner of Commons Halls, Libby's building where her dorm room was and stopped dead in my tracks. Libby was leaning against the building and some asshole was kissing her. He pulled away and Libby placed her hand on the side of his face and smiled. His hand was resting on her hip as they both looked at each other and talked.

All the air in my lungs was gone in an instant and I couldn't breathe. I stood there and watched the two of them. He leaned in and began kissing her neck as she dropped her head back against the building and closed her eyes. I balled my fists together. When I saw his hand move up from her hip and lightly move across her breasts, I wanted to pound his face into the ground. I was frozen where I stood. Unable to pull my eyes away from Libby in the arms of another man. I had finally decided to tell Libby the truth, but I was too late. I waited too long. As Libby laughed at something the asshole said, I slowly forced my feet to move. Turning, I walked away from the only girl I'd ever loved.

She's moved on and was now with someone else. The bile rose up into my throat as I thought about another man touching Libby. *How long had they been together? Who was this ass?* She was looking at him like she wanted more. She wanted … him. I couldn't get back to my dorm fast enough.

PUSHING OPEN THE door to my dorm, I attempted to pull air into my lungs. Images of that asshole touching Libby and kissing her flooded my mind. I slammed the door shut. I needed a drink.

"What in the hell is wrong with you?" Will asked as he looked at me with a stunned expression on his face.

Glancing at Will I asked, "What?"

Will pulled his head back and let out a gruff laugh. "The way you came storming in here just now, you look like you're about to rip someone's head off."

I looked around the room before I remembered I stashed a bottle of whiskey behind some books on the bookshelf. I walked over and moved a book out of the way and grabbed the whiskey. I took a drink from it as Will asked, "Where in the hell did you get that from?"

Shaking my head, I took another drink. I needed to forget. I *have* to forget. I tipped my head back and took another swig.

"Luke, dude, you have to talk to me. I've never seen you like this before. What in the hell is going on with you?"

I looked over at my best friend. I could never tell him I was madly in love with his sister. He was pissed at me for kissing her and then breaking her heart. I had told him about Karen almost immediately. He had bugged me for months to talk to Libby, but I couldn't. I could barely look her in the eyes the first time I came home from school.

I gave him a wink. "Nothing. I just need to release some steam. Too much fucking bullshit in my mind." I walked up to the window and looked out.

"Want to talk about it?" Will asked as my phone began ringing. I pulled it out and saw Abigail's name. I had sent her a text on my way back to my dorm.

"Hey, Abigail, are you free?"

"Hell yes, I'm free. It's about damn time, Johnson. I'm heading up to my bedroom now to get undressed. The door will be unlocked."

Closing my eyes, I inhaled a deep breath. "I'll be there in a few minutes." I hit End and shoved the phone back into my pocket. Turning, I walked back over to the shelf and put the whiskey bottle back. I headed into the bathroom to splash my face with cold water.

"Why the hell are you doing this, Luke?" Will asked.

I poked my head out and looked at him. "Doing what?"

He frowned. "Going to Abigail." I stepped back into the bathroom and shut off the water. I walked back out and just starred at Will and chuckled. "I'm going to Abigail because I want to get laid. What's wrong with that?"

Will let out a sigh. "What about Libby?"

I stopped, slowly turned and looked at him. "What about Libby?"

Will looked pissed. He shook his head and glared at me. "Do you have feelings for my sister?"

I swallowed hard as I shook my head and looked away.

"Luke?"

I turned and looked at him. "I can't. I mean, I won't do that to her. She means everything to me, and I'll fuck it up, Will. I already broke her heart with the dick move I made on her when I left for college. What if I can't ... I mean, I don't think I can ... I'm not good enough for her, Will. She deserves someone better, and she found him."

Will's eyes widened and he looked shocked. "Wait. What do you mean she found him?"

I let out a frustrated laugh. "I mean she's dating someone. I saw them, just now. I was going to ask her if she wanted to see a movie and she was leaning against the building of her dorm when some dick fucking kissed her." Sucking in a deep breath I whispered, "She looked happy." I turned away from him.

"So because you see Lib kissing a guy, you run to Abigail? Why is okay for you to be with someone, but Libby can't? Luke, did you honestly think she would wait forever?"

I knew what I was doing was wrong. The way I was acting was not fair to Libby, but if Abigail could make me forget for a bit, then so be it. I needed to forget. I reached down for my truck keys. "I haven't been with a girl in months. I need to get fucked."

I went to leave when Will grabbed my arm. "Don't do this, Luke. If you want to be with someone ..." He closed his eyes and took in a deep breath before letting it out. "If you want to be with someone, be with the person you love. Luke, Libby loves you."

My heart slammed against my chest and my eyes widened in horror. *No. No Will is wrong.* She can't love me after all the times I've pushed her away. I've never given her a reason to love me.

"No ... she doesn't love me, Will."

Will let out a frustrated moan. "Luke, for Christ sakes, will you just admit you love her? She already ..."

Will immediately stopped talking. I looked into his eyes. "She already what?"

He shook his head and glanced away before quickly looking back at me. "She was already your best friend once, Luke. Stop pushing her away. She cares about you and you ..."

I held up my hand to get him to stop talking. I had heard enough. I saw what I saw. If Libby loved me, she wouldn't be letting another guy kiss and feel her up. "I've gotta go. Abigail is waiting on me."

Will called out after me. "Don't do this, Luke. I swear to God, you'll regret it."

FIFTEEN MINUTES LATER I was making my way up the stairs of the three-bedroom house Abigail shared with two other girls. I stopped outside Abigail's bedroom and closed my eyes. The moment I saw Libby smiling at the asshole, my eyes sprung open. I reached down and opened the door. My dick jumped when I saw Abigail lying across her bed naked.

"How are we doing this, Mr. Johnson? Are we in a loving kind of mood?" she asked as she slipped her fingers into her pussy and began moving them in and out.

Shutting the door, I began unbuttoning my pants when my

phone went off again. I reached into my pocket, took it out and turned it off. I set it on the dresser along with my truck keys. "Your roommates here?"

She laughed. "Why, do you want them to join us?" I smiled and raised my eyebrows as I shook my head.

"No, I want to hear you scream when I bury my dick deep inside you."

I quickly stripped out of my clothes and made my way over to Abigail as I rolled the condom onto my dick. "Turn around— I'm fucking you from behind."

She quickly obeyed and before I even gave her a chance to say anything, I slammed into her hard and fast. She let out a scream. I needed to keep this raw. No emotions. I needed to forget.

Abigail began moaning immediately. "I love it when you fuck me. Yes! Harder. Do it harder."

I spent the rest of the afternoon fucking Abigail over and over until we both collapsed onto the floor, exhausted and dragging in breaths of air.

She turned and looked at me as she took in a deep breath. "That shit was worth the wait, baby."

I turned and looked at her as I smiled. Every time I closed my eyes, all I saw was Libby. *Fuck!*

Abigail got up and headed to her bathroom. "Can you stay?" I got up and made my way over to my clothes. I shook my head. "Nah, I have to get back."

She paused at the bathroom door and leaned against it. "I'm going to go take a shower. Want to join me?"

I laughed. "Abigail, my dick couldn't even function enough for me to take a piss right now. I need to get back." She shrugged her shoulders and winked at me as she headed into the bathroom. She called over her shoulder, "Your loss, cowboy."

I pulled my shirt over my head and walked over to the dresser. I grabbed my phone and saw I had missed calls from Will and Grace.

"Abigail, I'm leaving," I called out.

"Till next time!"

The moment I walked into the hall and shut her bedroom door, the guilt flooded my body and I felt like I couldn't pull in enough air to breathe. The temporary distraction of fucking Abigail had not been enough. Making my way down the stairs, I passed one of Abigail's roommates. She smiled at me as she whispered, "My turn next, cowboy?" I smiled back and picked up my pace. I needed out of that house.

Chapter Seven

Libby

I COULDN'T HELP but stare at Zach. We had been sitting at Starbucks for the last hour or so talking. The moment I first saw Zach, his light-blue eyes held me captive. We met through a mutual friend who introduced us. I wasn't looking to start dating anyone, but it finally hit me over Christmas break. Luke was never going to admit his feelings for me. Taking rejection after rejection was beginning to weigh me down.

"That's when my father decided to move to Austin."

Snapping out of my daydream, I smiled. Zach was handsome, not as handsome as Luke though. His dark-blond hair was always perfect. He dressed like he stepped out of a GQ magazine and he stood just a bit shorter than Luke. I didn't fit against Zach's body like I did Luke's. I looked down and away.

Luke.

"When do I get to meet your parents?"

Pulling my head back I asked, "What?"

Zach started laughing. "You seemed so lost in thought, Lib. I needed to say something to bring you back."

I giggled, reached across the table and hit his shoulder.

Zach leaned back and looked at me. His eyes screamed he wanted me, but I wasn't ready yet. I wasn't sure when I would be ready and if he would even be the one. I had been saving myself for Luke. Since I could remember, I wanted my first time to be with him. "I'm starved. How about Saltgrass?"

I nodded my head. "That sounds good." My phone beeped and I looked down to see I had a text from Alex.

Alex: Grace and I are in town.

Me: OMG! I want to see you!

I looked up at Zach and smiled bigger. "My two best friends from home are in town. Can I invite them and my brother to dinner with us?

Zach smiled. "Alex and ... Grace?"

The fact that he remembered Alex and Grace's names caused my stomach to jump. "Yes. Alex is dating my brother Will. Grace is Luke's sister."

Zach's smile faded a bit. "Luke? Who's Luke?"

I swallowed hard. I had failed to mention Luke to Zach. "I haven't mentioned Luke to you before? Are you sure?" My heart began pounding. *Why did I never mention Luke to Zach?*

Zach shook his head. "Not that I can remember."

I shrugged my shoulders. "He's another friend, from home." I let out a nervous chuckle. "My brother and Luke are room-mates."

Zach nodded his head. "Why don't you invite them all for dinner?"

Smiling weakly, I began typing out a text to Alex.

Me: Are you free this evening?

Alex: Yep! Why what's up?

Me: About to go to dinner at Saltgrass Steakhouse.

Alex: With who?

Me: A guy named Zach. We went out to a movie and will be heading to dinner soon.

Alex: A date. What about Luke?

Me: I can't wait for someone who clearly doesn't want the

same thing I want. Besides, he's been hooking up with that Abigail girl the last few months.

Alex: *What about what he said to you?*

Me: *He was drunk. I'm done waiting. Want to meet us for dinner?*

Alex: *Okay. Will went back to his dorm to get some clothes, so he could stay with me at the hotel for the weekend. Can we meet you there in half an hour?*

Me: *Sure! We're just talking at Starbucks. Make sure Grace knows!*

Alex: *Okay. See you soon, sweetie!*

I set my phone down and tried to push Luke from my mind. I smiled sweetly at Zach. "Alex, Will, and Grace will be joining us at the Saltgrass."

Zach's smile made my heart melt. He was beyond sweet to me and treated me like I was his world. We'd only been dating for a few weeks, but I loved that he hadn't pushed me into anything. He was taking it slow and that was what I needed.

Zach stood and reached his hand for mine. "May we stop by my dorm so I change first? I don't want your brother meeting me for the first time and I'm in running shorts."

I let out a nervous laugh. "He wouldn't care, but yes, we can stop by your dorm."

I sent Alex a text letting her know we might be a few minutes late since we had to stop at Zach's dorm.

We walked in and Zach looked around. I was guessing he was looking for his roommate. He turned and looked into my eyes. I let out a small gasp when he quickly pushed me against the door.

"Lib, I want to kiss you."

My breathing increased and I slowly smiled. "I'm not stopping you."

Zach leaned down and gently kissed my lips. I moved my

hand to the base of his neck and pulled him in more so he would deepen the kiss. His tongue ran along my lips and I opened up to him. His coffee and my tea mixed together as we got lost in the kiss.

Zach pulled away and rested his head against my head. "Libby, you have no idea how beautiful you are, do you?"

I closed my eyes and a memory of Luke instantly invaded my mind.

I WAS LEANING against the tree gasping for air. Luke and I had been paired up against Colt and Grace in the scavenger hunt.

"Did ... you ... get ... the ... plate?" Luke asked in between breaths. I smiled as I held up the sterling silver platter that had sat in Gunner and Ellie's china cabinet. Luke had distracted Ellie while I snuck into their formal dining room and took the plate. I had walked into the kitchen and gave him a look and quickly walked out the back door as I yelled good-bye to Ellie. The moment the door shut I took off running.

The smile that spread across Luke's face caused me to laugh. "Damn girl!" He grabbed me and pulled me to him as he picked me and spun me around. When he finally put me back down my body was screaming all kinds of weird stuff. I loved being in his arms. I loved him touching me. I loved ... him.

Luke reached over and took a curl that hung down in front of my eyes. He tucked it behind my ear as he whispered, "You have no idea how beautiful you are, do you?"

"LIBBY? ARE YOU okay?"

Zach's voice pulled me out of my memory. I smiled and nodded my head. "Yes, I'm sorry. I mean, thank you for the compliment. Sorry, I got lost in thought."

Zach tilted his head. I knew he wanted to ask me what I had

been thinking about but he didn't. "Let me go change."

"Okay. I'll be right here. Waiting. Um … here." I rolled my eyes and looked away when he chuckled. I wasn't sure why I felt so nervous. I guess it was being alone in his room with him that had me on edge.

Two minutes later he came walking out in jeans and a black shirt.

He reached for my hand and we headed to the restaurant.

The drive to the Saltgrass was lighthearted and fun. Zach had a wonderful sense of humor, but it was nothing like Luke's.

Ugh. Stop comparing him to Luke, Libby!

We walked in and the hostess pointed in the direction of where everyone was sitting. Zach leaned over and whispered in my ear, "I hope your brother likes me."

I glanced over at him and winked. "He's going to like you. Stop worrying."

As we walked up to the table, my smile quickly vanished when I saw Luke sitting there. I snapped my eyes over to Alex who mouthed, *sorry.*

I looked back at Luke and he mumbled something. I forced a smile and looked at Will. "Hey y'all. Um … Zach, this is my brother, Will and next to Will is my best friend, Alex." Zach reached out and shook Will's hand and then Alex's hand.

"It's a pleasure to meet you both. I've heard so much about the both of you."

Smiling, I turned to Grace. "This is my other best friend, Grace."

"Grace, it's a real pleasure. Lib has talked a lot about you."

I immediately saw Luke tense up. He looked pissed. Luke had been the first person to start calling me Lib. He was the only guy who ever called me that, besides Will.

Swallowing hard, I turned to face Luke. "Um … Zach, this is, um … Luke. Luke and Grace are brother and sister."

Luke reached out his hand and shook Zach's. Zach was about to talk when Luke started talking.

"Hey there, Zach. So, how long have y'all been dating?"

My mouth dropped open and I shot Luke a dirty look. Zach looked at me and I quickly smiled. "What? About two weeks now?"

I nodded my head. "Yes, almost three."

Zach pulled my chair out and I sat. The guys all sat after I did.

Luke glared at Zach. "What year are you, Zach?"

Will shot Luke a look of warning. Smirking, Luke looked back at Zach.

"I'm in my sophomore year," Zach replied with a smile.

"Where are you from?" Luke asked as Will cleared his throat.

I'm going to kick Luke's ass. I glanced at Grace and Alex as they just stared at Luke.

"With the twenty questions, I'd think Luke was the brother," Zach said with a laugh. Will and Luke both looked at Zach.

Shit. Shit. Shit.

Grace and I both let out a nervous chuckle as I said, "Zach, one thing you need to know is we are all very close. We grew up together. Will, Luke, and Alex's brother, Colt, have always been a bit … overprotective? Let's chill out on the questions, Luke. Okay?"

With the way Luke was staring at Zach, Zach should have dropped over in his chair. He slowly turned and looked at me as he barely said, "Fine."

Zach cleared his throat. "Well, to answer your question, I'm from Colorado Springs." I smiled as I looked at Zach.

"I love Colorado," I said.

Turning to me, Zach smiled and winked.

"So, what? No good schools in Colorado? You had to come to Texas?" Luke asked with sarcasm oozing from his lips. My mouth dropped open slightly as I glared at Luke. I couldn't believe how he was acting.

Zach glanced back over to look at Luke, his smile lessening a bit. "No. We have plenty of good schools. My father lives in Austin. I wanted to be close to him while I attended school. My mother passed away during my senior year of high school."

I sucked in a breath of air as did Grace and Alex. "I'm so sorry," the three of us said at the same time.

Looking at Luke, I saw him look down and then back up. "I'm really sorry to hear that."

"I'm sorry to hear that, Zach," Will said.

Zach smiled. "No worries. Thank you though. It's much appreciated."

Zach and I spent the rest of dinner mostly talking to Will and Alex. Luke's voice was driving me insane as I tried to focus on Zach and what he was talking to Will about.

"I'll show you around campus tomorrow, Sweat Pea, if you want," Luke said with a smile and wink to Grace.

Grace nodded her head. "Oh gosh, yes! I want to see everything Texas A&M has to offer."

I peeked over and watched Luke take a drink of his tea. I licked my lips instinctively and quickly looked away when he looked at me. Zach had reached for my hand that was sitting on the table. I quickly moved it down to my lap. I hated that I was trying to hide it from Luke. The feelings I was feeling now confused the hell out of me. It seemed like Luke was jealous. *Why would he be jealous?*

He didn't want me. He made that clear on more than one occasion. I closed my eyes and saw Luke's green eyes looking into my blue eyes.

"I love you, Libby. I've always loved you."

Quickly opening my eyes I saw Luke was watching me. My breathing increased as I remembered the night he told me he loved me. I needed away from him. Looking toward Zach, I asked, "Are we ready to head out?"

He turned and nodded his head. "Sure, if you are, Lib?"

Quickly standing up, I nodded my head. "Yep."

We walked out to the parking lot and I watched Luke kiss Grace and Alex good-bye. I longed for his lips to be on my body.

I shook my head to clear my thoughts. *Stop this Libby. Stop this right now. You're with Zach.*

Luke walked up to Zach and reached his hand out. They

shook hands while Luke said, "It was nice meeting you, Zach."

"Same here, Luke."

Turning to me, Luke captured my eyes. They looked sad. Heartbroken. I so desperately wanted him to beg me not to leave with Zach. I wanted him to take me in his arms and tell me he loved me. That he needed me.

"Lib, I'll see you around."

My eyes filled with tears as I nodded my head. I couldn't even say anything for fear of crying. I watched as Luke turned and walked off toward his truck. He pulled out his phone and began texting someone.

Abigail. He was probably going to Abigail. Looking away, I saw Alex staring at me. I gave her a weak smile before taking Zach's arm. "I'm not ready to end the night. Let's go dancing."

Alex and Will both shook their heads. "I'm tired, so I'm going to have to pass," Alex said with a smile.

Grace did a little jump. "I'll go with y'all!"

I smiled and gave Grace a high five. "Perfect! Let's go have some fun!"

Chapter Eight

Luke

I SAT ON the sofa and let out a sigh. Will and I had moved into the house our parents all chipped in for this past weekend. Libby declined to move in and I knew it was because of that fucker she was dating. My phone went off and I looked at it sitting on the coffee table. Abigail's name flashed across the screen. I rolled my eyes as I picked up the phone.

Abigail: *Hey baby. It's been a few weeks. I want a repeat.*

Hitting delete, I tossed my phone back down onto the coffee table. I hadn't been back to Abigail's house since the night I had dinner with Libby and her new boyfriend Zach. As soon as I left the restaurant, I sent Abigail a text and spent much of the night screwing her and trying to get Libby's face erased from my mind.

It hadn't worked. Every time I closed my eyes, all I saw was Libby. Every time I fell asleep, all I dreamed about was Libby. I stood and headed upstairs. I was going home for the weekend. The faster I got out of College Station and away from Libby, the better.

"WANT TO TELL me what's on your mind, Son?" my father

58

asked as we rode along in silence. I shrugged my shoulders and looked off to the west.

"Girl problems?"

I let out a husky laugh. "You could say."

Stopping his horse, my father cleared his throat. I stopped mine and turned her around so that I was facing my father. "You know, I've been your age once before. I kind of know a thing or two about this subject. I am after all married to your mother."

I let out a small laugh. "You and Mom have the most amazing love I've ever seen, Dad. The way she looks at you when you walk into a room." I shook my head. "The way you look at her when she walks into a room, it's magical."

My father smiled. "I do love your mother very much. She's my life. There isn't anything I wouldn't do for her."

My smile faded as I looked away. "You'd never hurt her."

"How do you know that?"

My head turned back quickly as I looked at my father. "What?"

He narrowed his eyes at me. "Do you think our love is perfect son? That we don't make mistakes? Hurt each other?"

"I know you would never purposely hurt Mom, Dad. You love her too much."

My father looked away as he said, "No. I'd never knowingly hurt your mother, but I have hurt her before. Deeply." His voice was filled with sadness as he turned to me. "There was a time that I thought I might have lost your mother forever. I had two choices. Walk away from her and never risk hurting her again, or stay and fight for our love. If I stayed, I knew I risked the chance of hurting her again, but our love was worth the risk. Love has a way of melting our defenses, Luke. You just have to know when to let those defenses fall."

I wanted to ask him what he did, but for some reason it didn't feel right asking.

"It must not have been that bad. She forgave you," I said quietly.

"She forgave me because she loves me, Luke. She knows

how much I love her. No one is perfect, Son. We all make mistakes. Sometimes we hurt the people we love in the process. That doesn't make us love them any less and that fear of hurting someone shouldn't stop us from loving them."

I felt the tears building in my eyes so I looked away. "What if you know the girl you love deserves so much better than you? Deserves so much more than what you can give her."

"Does she?"

Looking back I asked, "Does she what?"

He dropped his head and stared at me for a good thirty seconds. "Deserve better than you?"

I nodded my head. "I think so, sir."

"Have you given her the chance to decide that for herself?"

I was about to respond when we heard a horn honking. I looked over my shoulder and saw Gunner driving up in the ranch Jeep. He smiled big when he saw me. Coming to a stop, he jumped out of the Jeep and I quickly jumped off my horse. He walked up to me and pulled me in for a hug as he slapped the hell out of my back.

"Well, son of a bitch. Look who's home. Miss the ranch that much?" Gunner asked with a huge smile on his face.

Nodding my head and letting out a laugh, I replied, "Yes, sir. Very much so. I needed a weekend home."

Gunner smiled. "Colt know you're home?"

"Yes, sir. We've already made plans to go out this weekend."

Gunner placed his hand on my shoulder. "Good. Make sure you talk to him. He seems to have his head in his ass and I'm pretty sure it's about a girl."

My father let out a chuckle as I looked over at him. "Must be something in the air," he said as he started walking off on his horse.

SITTING ON MY tailgate, I kept my eye on Colt. Taylor had told us that Colt seemed to be drinking a lot in the beginning of the year until his football coach set him straight. One thing I noticed though, he couldn't keep his eyes off Lauren. I glanced over and saw Lauren sitting on a log laughing at something one of her girlfriends said. She looked up and caught me watching her. She smiled and waved. I waved back and grinned.

Someone bumped my leg and I looked to see Colt standing there. "My dad told you to keep an eye on me or something, Luke?" I smiled and let out a chuckle as I nodded my head. "I know he's worried about me, but I think he's more worried about Alex."

I looked over at Colt. "Alex? Why?"

Colt shrugged. "Probably the same reason we all worry about the girls."

I followed Colts gaze. "You ever talk to Lauren and get things straightened out?"

Colt lifted the Coke bottle to his lips and shook his head. He took a drink and then laughed. "Nope. She just pretends like we are the best of friends. She isn't dating anyone, but that's not very fair of me to be happy about that."

"How are things with you and Rachel?"

"I broke up with her." He turned and looked at me. "She wanted us to sleep together."

I pulled my head back and looked at him. "You broke up with her because she wanted to sleep with you?"

Colt let out a sigh. "No, I broke up with her because I walked in on her fucking another guy. She was pissed at me because I wouldn't sleep with her. I didn't want to sleep with her. I mean, I didn't love her. She deserved to have her first time be with someone who loved her and would cherish that moment."

I lifted the left side of my mouth into a smile. "So much like your damn daddy, you know that? Romantic bastard."

Colt laughed and then shook his head. "I guess, maybe it's because I want my first time to be with someone I love. Someone who I'll cherish the moment with."

My smile faded as I looked back out into the crowd. I'd never have that moment back. Lauren was now up and dancing with a few friends while they laughed.

"Yeah, you never get that moment back, Colt. Don't fuck it up like I did."

Colt turned and looked at me. I knew he wanted to ask me about it, but he didn't.

"If you could go back and change that night, would you?" Colt asked. I slowly turned and looked at him.

"In a heartbeat. If I could take away the biggest mistake of my life, I'd do it no questions asked."

Colt smiled weakly and nodded his head. "Why don't you just tell her, Luke?"

My heart instantly hurt. "Because she's moved on."

Colt looked back out to Lauren. "Why do they have to fuck with our heads and hearts so much?"

I closed my eyes and thought back to me kissing Libby in the rain. Opening my eyes I said, "They probably think the same thing about us."

Chapter Nine

Libby

ZACH WALKED UP and took me in his arms. "I'm really going to miss you, Lib."

I smiled and reached up to kiss him. "I'll miss you too, Zach." I stepped back and turned to shut my suitcase. I would be leaving soon to meet Alex and Grace in Austin. Then we were driving to the coast for spring break. The thought of being with Luke all week raced through my mind. I closed my eyes and took in a deep breath. I hadn't seen much of Luke at all. Will told me Luke spent most of his time working out or studying. According to Abigail, he spent much of his time fucking her. Any chance she had to talk to me, she was sure to tell me about their hook ups.

I hate her.

I jumped when Zach placed his hands on my shoulders. "Let me relax you, Libby." His hand slowly moved down my arm to my stomach. "Baby, you seem so tense."

My stomach clenched at the idea of Zach relaxing me. We had yet to have sex and Zach knew I was a virgin. I appreciated the fact that he was not pushing me. He did, however, manage to give me amazing orgasms with his skillful fingers. I closed my eyes and let out a moan. Zach slipped his hand around and into my panties. "Libby, let me make you come."

I dropped my head back against him and lifted my leg.

"Yes," I whispered as I let Zach push all thoughts of Luke from my mind.

Zach pulled me closer to him, feeling his hardness press against my body caused me to moan.

"You're so wet. Fuck you're so wet." Zach hissed as his fingers began to move in and out faster. I felt my body begin to quiver. Closing my eyes, I let it go. My orgasm ripped through my body as I felt my insides pulsing against Zach's fingers. He moved his lips to my ear and whispered, "I can't wait to make you mine."

My eyes sprung open and tears began to well up. If only I wanted to be Zach's. If only my heart didn't belong to Luke.

SPRING BREAK IN Port Aransas was beyond crazy. My parents, Alex's parents, and Grace's parents had beach houses here. All right next to each other. We had been coming to Port A for as long as I could remember.

Grace had her face buried in her phone as we walked along the beach. "So, what should we do tonight?" I asked Grace.

She shrugged her shoulders as she continued to look at her phone. "I don't know. Maybe we could ..."

Before I could warn Grace to watch out, she ran smack into a guy who had been standing there talking to his friends. Grace stumbled backward, but he grabbed hold of her before she lost her balance.

The smile that spread across his face instantly caused me to smile and Grace to let out a moan she surely didn't mean to let escape her lips.

"Grace?"

Grace's mouth dropped open in surprise. "Noah?"

Wait. What? They know each other?

Noah's smile turned to a grin. "At least this time I didn't knock you down." Grace giggled. I snapped my head and looked at her. Grace *never* giggled.

"I can't believe I ran into you again," Grace said as she bit down on her lower lip. *Holy hell.* Grace was into this guy in a big way. I cleared my throat and they both somehow managed to pull their eyes off each other and over to me.

Smiling, I held out my hand. "Libby Hayes, and you are?"

Noah took my hand and gently shook it. "I'm so sorry, Libby. Um, Noah, this is one of my best friends, Libby. Libby this is Noah. Ah ..."

Grace looked back at Noah and then back to me. "We kind of met a couple months ago and I never did get your last name."

Noah laughed and shook his head as he said, "My last name is Bennet. Grace and I had another run in, except last time I knocked her to the ground. You were with, Alex, that was her name right?"

Grace nodded her head. "Yep. Alex." Turning to me she said, "It was when Alex and I went to A&M right after Thanksgiving when all that stuff with Will and Alex was going on."

I smiled as I looked back toward Noah. "So are you here for a few days?" Noah asked.

"Um, yeah. Staying with our folks, we, um, we have a house down here," Grace said as she fumbled over her own words.

I smiled as I took it in. I'd never seen Grace not one-hundred percent in control. She was totally taken with Noah.

"What about you?" Grace asked, looking over Noah's shoulder at the four other guys standing there watching the whole scene play out.

Noah's smile turned somewhat wicked. As if an idea came to mind. "I'm staying at my folks place, but Mom and Dad stayed behind for this trip. It's just me, my brother and his two friends."

"Really?" Grace said with a bit of seduction to her voice. I slowly looked at Grace, thinking back to her saying she just wanted to hook-up with someone this week.

I looked between the two of them as they both just stared at each other. I cleared my throat before talking. "Grace, we're gonna be late for lunch."

Grace was pulled from her trance as she looked at me. "Oh yeah, right." Looking back at Noah she smiled. "It was nice running into you again."

They both chuckled and we began to walk off, but not before Noah grabbed Grace's wrist. "Grace, may I give you my number? Maybe we can meet up later or something."

Biting down hard on her lip, Grace nodded her head. "I'll text you it, what's your number?"

I looked away smiling, knowing Grace wanted to have Noah's number as well.

"512-555-2424," Noah said as he watched Grace type it in her phone. A few seconds later, Noah's phone beeped. He pulled it out of his pocket and smiled when he saw Grace's text.

"Now you have my number. I'll um, talk to you later then?" Grace asked as she began taking a few steps backward.

Noah nodded his head and winked at her. "Most definitely."

Turning around, Grace and I began walking back to the houses. "Oh my gosh, Grace Johnson. Who is he and why have I never heard about this Noah?"

Grace chuckled and brushed me off with her hand. "Honestly, I never thought I would lay eyes on him again. I ran into him as I was running after Alex, he knocked me down, helped me up and we exchanged names. That was it."

"Well he certainly remembered you." I turned to look over my shoulder. "And he is staring at your ass as you walk away."

Grace threw her head back and laughed. "Thank God I did some squats last week."

Grace's phone buzzed and she began reading a text message. The smile that spread across her face had been the first real smile I'd seen in the last few months. She looked over at me and winked. "Looks like I'll be getting laid after all."

My mouth dropped open. "Grace, I thought you were just saying that. Are you sure about this? You said yourself you don't really know this guy."

Grace looked behind her and I followed her gaze. Noah was now walking to his truck that was parked on the beach.

"Oh, I'm sure. I'm very sure," Grace said as she turned back around and walked with a smile on her face.

SITTING AT THE table, I glanced over to Grace. She had hooked up with Noah last night. When she got back, I could tell something was off. What I couldn't tell was if that something was bad or good. Her face was flush as she leaned against the door like she had just had the most amazing time of her life. She reached her fingers up to her lips and closed her eyes. She quickly changed and crawled into bed. I had tried to talk to her, but she said she was exhausted and we would talk the next day. She avoided talking to me about it all day. I was hoping she had talked to Alex at least.

Staring back down at my espresso-soaked brownie sundae, I began to pick at it. This was the first time in the last five years that Luke and I didn't share this sundae. I peeked up and saw him staring at me. I smiled weakly and his eyes lit up before he looked away from me. My heart dropped and I closed my eyes. I hated how my body reacted to him. I hated that the more I tried to push him out of my heart, the stronger he held onto it.

Alex sat next to me and bumped my shoulder. I smiled and looked back at my sundae.

Taking a bite, I looked back up, only to find Luke looking at me again as he began to talk. "I say we camp on the beach tonight. Throw up two tents and build a fire."

Lauren began to hop up and down. "Oh my gosh, yes!"

Meg smiled and said, "Totally sounds like a good time."

Colt talked about making s'mores as I watched Alex and Will exchange looks.

Turning to Taylor, Colt asked if she was in on camping.

She nodded her head and said, "I'm in. Sounds like fun."

Luke looked back at me. "Lib? You down for some camping?"

My stomach dropped as I thought how much I wanted to be

with Luke. Zach's voice popped into my head. I smiled weakly and nodded. "Why not. Sounds like fun."

Luke's eyes lit up before he turned and gently hit Grace on the side of her arm. "Grace? You down?"

"Hell yes, I'm down for that!"

Glancing around the table at everyone, Luke smiled. "Then, it's a plan. We're camping on the beach tonight." His eyes landed on mine and something happened. It was as if he was trying to tell me something but didn't know how.

Swallowing hard, I stood and threw my sundae out as I made my way outside. I needed fresh air.

I leaned against the railing and took in a deep breath. If he wanted me ... he'd take me.

Zach's words came back to me again.

"I can't wait to make you mine."

Chapter Ten

Luke

I GRABBED A few sticks and the bag of marshmallows and made my way over to the fire. I wanted to put this whole day behind me. The arguing with Libby, listening to her talking to Zach on the phone, and telling him how much she missed him still played through my memory.

Sitting next to Libby, I held out the sticks. "Grab a stick and roast some marshmallows, y'all." I took a marshmallow out for me and then asked Libby if she wanted one. She nodded and stared straight into the fire.

I put a marshmallow on her stick and handed it to her. "How is school going? I don't see much of you anymore."

Swallowing hard, Libby said, "It's fine. I hear you're busy, with other things."

I pulled my head back and looked at her. *What the hell is that supposed to mean?*

I turned and focused on the conversations around the fire. We laughed and talked about everything from school to how much Maegan hated the country life. When I said I would lock Taylor away if she was my daughter, everyone laughed. I glanced over to look at Libby and what little happiness I felt was gone the moment I saw her smile at her phone. She must have gotten a text from Zach. I watched as she stood and made her way out to the water.

"God, I need to get laid, again."

I jumped up and looked at my sister. "What? What the hell did you just say, Grace?"

Rolling her eyes at me, Grace said, "Please, don't even go there. How many girls have you hooked up with during the last two days we've been here?"

I glanced back to where Libby was standing. "None," I said as I turned back to Grace.

My sister shrugged. "Well, look at you. I'm impressed."

Glaring at her as she walked by, I wanted to know who in the hell she hooked up with in the last two days. I was going to kick their fucking ass.

Alex, Colt, and Will were all talking, but I tuned them out. Libby was no longer on the phone. I barely whispered, "I'm, uh … going to say good night to Libby."

Walking over to Libby, I stood next to her and looked out over the black ocean. "I miss you, Libby."

I felt her turn and look at me. "What?"

Looking back at her, I smiled. "I miss talking to you. Hanging out with you."

Libby quickly turned and looked back out over the ocean. "You miss hanging out as friends." I was about to say something when she laughed. She shook her head and looked at me. "You changed all that the night you kissed me. The night you told me you wanted more, Luke. Then …" She shook her head and looked down before looking back at me. "Then you just acted as if nothing ever happened between us. Do you have any idea how that made me feel?"

"Libby, I …"

She held up her hand. "No. I'm tired of arguing with you, of wondering why I was never good enough for you. I've found someone who does want to be with me. Someone who wants more than—friendship. Just like you found with Abigail."

I stood there stunned. "Abigail? What the hell does she have anything to do with this?"

Libby let out a nervous laugh. "Please, Luke. Don't play stupid. I'm tired of this. I'm done."

Turning on her heels, Libby headed back toward the tent. I so desperately wanted to go after her. I started after her before I stopped myself. She deserved someone who would never hurt her.

"I found someone who wants more than friendship."

I WALKED ACROSS campus in a daze. Every time I saw Libby with Zach, I felt sick to my stomach. This morning had been no different. Seeing the two of them walking together holding hands caused me to turn in the opposite direction and walk further than I needed to go. Thank God there were only a few more days left and the semester would be over.

Walking in, I shut the door and called out for Will.

I threw my backpack down on the sofa. Walking to the kitchen, I ran my hand through my hair and let out a sigh. My phone buzzed in my pocket and I pulled it out. I had a text message from my old girlfriend, Karen.

> *Karen: Hey there stranger. You up for pizza tonight?*
>
> *Me: Sure. Where at?*
>
> *Karen: Luigis? They've got live Jazz tonight.*
>
> *Me: Meet you there at six.*
>
> *Karen: Looking forward to it.*

I opened the refrigerator and pulled out a beer. Twisting the cap off, I tossed it onto the counter and made my way into the living room. I wasn't sure why Karen wanted to meet for pizza, other than to catch up. We had kept in touch and spoke once or twice every few months. Reaching down and grabbing my backpack, I threw it on the floor. I sunk down into the cushions and turned on the television.

I downed my beer and set it on the coffee table and leaned

back. Closing my eyes, I thought back to the last night of Christmas break, when Libby and I ended up alone together in my barn.

THE MOMENT I smelled her perfume, I stopped moving. I turned and looked at Libby standing in the middle of the barn. I began walking out of the stall when she held her hand up. She started laughing and I knew she was drunk.

"Lib? Have you been drinking?"

She nodded her head and stumbled. I dropped the rake and quickly reached out and caught her. I pulled her into my arms and helped her to stand straight.

"Don't let go of me, Luke," Libby said as she looked into my eyes.

I smiled and shook my head. "Lib, where have you been?"

She tilted her head and bit down on her lip, causing my dick to jump in my pants. "I's been drinking with Meg. We were drownin' our sorrows with Jack."

I nodded my head. "Baby, you're gonna be drowning in a hangover come tomorrow."

Her eyes lit up and she took a step forward, causing me to take a step back. "Why do you call me baby?"

"Um …" I looked around. Where the hell is Grace? "I won't if you don't like it, Lib." Libby's eyes lit up, even through the drunken haze, I could see her desire for me.

Libby stopped right in front of me. "I like it, Luke. A lot. More than I should. Just like I like you more than I should." Her eyes moved up and down my body and I was cursing myself for the thoughts I was having. I slowly licked my lips as Libby's eyes drifted back to mine.

The moment she placed her hand on me, my heart felt like it slammed against my chest. "Do you know what I want, Luke?"

Swallowing hard, I whispered, "A cup of coffee and some aspirin?"

Libby giggled and shook her head fast. "Nope!" she said popping the p. Moving my eyes down her body, I took in every inch of her. Those short blue jean shorts were begging for me to peel them off of her. I could see her hard nipples through the old Mason High T-shirt she had on. Her beautiful blonde hair was down with just the sides pulled back. "I want you, Luke. Since I could remember, I've always wanted you. I saved myself for you. Do you know that?"

Closing my eyes, I let out a moan as she pushed her body against mine. I opened my eyes and looked down at her lips. She smiled wide. "You want me, too. I feel your dick pressing against me, Luke."

"Libby …" I whispered as I placed my hands on her hips. "Not like this, Lib. Not like this."

Her hand moved up as it pushed through my hair. She grabbed a handful of my hair and leaned up on her toes. "Kiss me, Luke. Please kiss me. I want to remember what you taste like."

My heart was pounding in my chest. I placed my hand at the nape of her neck and leaned down, capturing her lips with mine. Libby wrapped her arms around my neck and moaned into my mouth. The kiss was passionate, yet gentle. Libby pushed herself into me more.

Pulling her lips from mine, Libby whispered, "Touch me, oh God, please touch me, Luke."

I moved my hand from her hip to her breast and cupped it in my hand. Libby's head dropped back. "Yes, oh God, yes."

"Libby, you drive me fucking mad with desire," I said as I pulled her head forward and smashed my lips to hers again. Libby began pulling my shirt off as I did the same with her. She stood before me in a pale-pink lace bra. My dick was so hard in my pants, and one painful throb after another reminded me of how much I wanted the woman who stood before me.

Pulling her bra down, I cinched her breasts up. I reached down and put one of her nipples into my mouth. I sucked and pulled on her nipple as Libby let out moan after moan. "Oh God.

Luke, I've waited so long."

Pulling my mouth away from her nipple, I lifted Libby up. She wrapped her legs around my waist and I carried her into a clean stall. I knew what I was doing was wrong. She was drunk. Very drunk. I didn't care though. I'd waited so long for her; I was tired of pushing her away.

I pushed my dick against her as I slammed her against the barn wall. "Libby, I want you so fucking much."

She smiled and looked at me. "Take me, Luke. Please take me."

I shook my head to clear my thoughts. "Baby, I don't want it to be like this. Not with you drunk, Lib."

"You can't hurt me this way, Luke."

I pulled back and looked at her. "What?"

She stared at me. Then, she laughed. "Don't you see, Luke? You always make me fall so head over heels in love with you. A dance in the rain. A soft whisper in my ear. Then you pull away. If we do this and I'm drunk, I won't remember. You can't hurt me, 'cause I won't remember."

I slowly let her body slide down mine as she leaned against the wall. I turned and walked out of the stall. Reaching down, I picked up her T-shirt. Turning around, I walked back over to her and adjusted her bra.

"Wh—what are you doing?" Libby asked.

"I'm sorry, Libby. I'm sorry for what I've done to you."

Her eyes filled with tears. "Even with me drunk, you still don't want me. Why?"

"I care about you, Libby. I don't want to …"

Libby quickly pulled her T-shirt over her head the best she could in her drunken state. She stumbled forward and pushed me as hard as she could. "I hate you, Luke Johnson. I don't want you to care about me! I want you to love me!" Libby shouted.

I grabbed onto her arms and looked into her eyes. "I love you more than you'll ever know, Libby." Libby sucked in a breath as I slowly let her go.

I pulled out my phone and called Will. "Hey, Will. It's me,

Luke. Can you come get Libby? She's drunk out of her mind."

Libby stood there and stared at me as tears rolled down her face. She slowly walked past me and out of the stall. She made her way to the end of the barn and sat down. She began crying as she said, "I hate you, Luke. I hate you ..."

THE DOOR SHUT and I flew up. "Damn dude, did you fall asleep or something?" Will asked as he walked in. I glanced around and saw the three empty beer bottles sitting on the coffee table.

"Ah ... yeah, I guess I did." I dragged my hands down my face. "Shit. I've gotta meet Karen for dinner." Glancing at the clock, I saw I only had thirty minutes to meet her.

"Karen? The girl you dated when you first came to A&M?" Will asked as I began sprinting up the stairs.

"Yeah!" I shouted back as I rushed into my bedroom and changed. Five minutes later I was back downstairs. I reached for my truck keys.

"Are y'all dating again?" Will asked as I grabbed a quick drink of water. I spun around and looked at him.

"What? No. She just said she wanted to meet up and talk. I have no idea what about. I haven't seen her in months."

Will nodded his head and smiled. "Have fun then."

I grunted as I headed out the door while Will laughed. I had a bad feeling this night was going to be anything but fun.

Chapter Eleven

Libby

ZACH AND I walked into Luigi's and I instantly felt the hair on my arms stand. I glanced to my left and saw him.

Luke.

Then I noticed the blonde sitting across from him. Her wavy hair fell just below her shoulders. She had the sides pulled up and her bright-red lipstick stood out like a sore thumb. She smiled and Luke's laugh moved through my body.

I felt Zach take my arm and begin leading me over to a table. I turned to him and smiled. "They have a jazz band here tonight," Zach said with a smile. He loved jazz. I personally could pass on it.

I sat down and let out a groan. Straight ahead was Luke's table. I looked away, but my eyes were drawn up again as I looked at the gorgeous girl sitting with him. *Who was she? Were they dating? What about Abigail?*

"Lib? Are you even listening to me?"

Zach's voice pulled me from my thoughts. I shook my head. "Sorry, I was lost in thought there for a second. Guess I have a lot on my mind."

Zach reached across the table and took my hand in his. "I'm here, Lib. All you have to do is talk to me."

Smiling, I nodded my head. I was constantly in awe of how Zach treated me. He was everything a girl could want in a boyfriend. Attentive, caring, an amazing kisser, and he'd do anything to make me happy.

He just wasn't Luke.

The waitress came and took our order. As we ate, Zach began talking about plans for this summer. He wanted to come to Mason and see where I grew up. I laughed. "There isn't anything really there. It's a really small town."

Zach gave me that panty-melting smile of his. "You grew up there; it's a part of you. That makes me want to know more about it."

My stomach dropped. I knew I was getting closer and closer to giving myself to Zach, completely. My eyes lifted and I saw Luke stand up and hold his hand out to the blonde. They made their way to the makeshift dance floor in the middle of the restaurant. I had somehow managed to keep my presence unknown to Luke. He began looking around once we sat down, but I hid behind my menu.

The band began playing "Let's Fall in Love" as Luke pulled the blonde into his arms and they began dancing. She dropped her head back and laughed and my heart was hit with a tinge of jealousy. Glancing back to Zach, I smiled.

"Want to dance?" The moment the words slipped from my mouth, I regretted it. I knew the only reason I was doing it was to try and make Luke jealous. Clearly he was enjoying himself though, from the smile on his face.

Zach stood and extended his hand for mine. "I'd love to dance with you, sweetheart." I gave him a weak smile. *Shit. Shit. Shit.* There were only two other couples on the dance floor. Zach walked up to the dance floor and spun me around and pulled me to him. I kept my eyes off of Luke and the blonde. I focused on Zach only. We danced in silence as he held me close to him.

I could feel Luke's eyes on me. One peek showed I was right. Luke smiled slightly at me and I gave him a weak smile in return.

The band finished the song and made an announcement. "We're taking a break, but please keep on dancing y'all. We've got some Frank for ya!"

Zach's phone started to ring. He pulled it out of his pocket and said, "Shit, I have to take this call, Libby. I'll be right back." Zach looked over my shoulder. "Hey, your friend Luke is here. Y'all should dance together."

"That's a wonderful idea."

My eyes widened in horror at the sound of Luke's voice. I spun around and saw him standing there. I looked around for the blonde. "She excused herself for a phone call."

My mouth dropped open slightly. I turned to say something to Zach, but he was already out the door. I felt Luke's hand on my waist and my breathing stopped.

Turning back around, I gave him a smirk as he held open his arms. Frank Sinatra's "It Had To Be You" began playing. Luke pulled me into his arms as we began to dance. I was terrified he would hear my heart pounding in my chest.

"How have you been, Libby?"

Taking in a deep breath, I was overcome with Luke's musky smell. I closed my eyes and tried to keep myself from burying my face into his chest. I looked into his green eyes. I slowly licked my dry lips and reached deep down into my stomach to find my voice again. Something about being in Luke's arms, with a stupid Frank Sinatra song playing, had me all weak in the knees.

"I've been um, fine. Busy with school and ..." My voice trailed off.

"Zach?"

I pulled my head back. "What?"

Luke smiled and said, "You've been busy with Zach?"

I looked back to the door, willing Zach to walk through it and take me out of my misery right now.

Glancing back at Luke I asked, "Who's the blonde? A new fuck buddy?"

Luke tensed in my arms as his smile faded. "An old girl-friend."

An old girlfriend? Hell I wasn't expecting him to say that.

I was sure my confused expression was priceless. "I started dating her beginning of my freshman year."

Anger consumed me as I looked away. "I guess that explains things."

"Excuse me?" Luke asked as we stopped dancing.

I let out a nervous laugh. "Why worry about the girl you kissed the night before you left for college when you can have something like that? Who cares if you left her wondering what in the hell she did wrong."

Hurt flashed across Luke's face and for one brief moment, I was glad he felt the same hurt I was feeling. I held up my hands and said, "You know what, I'm sorry I even said anything."

I spun around, but Luke grabbed my arm. "Wait," he said in a whisper.

I dropped my head and shook it. "Wait for what, Luke? Wait for you to get drunk again and tell me how you really feel and come on to me because that's the only time you're attracted me?"

"Me? What the fuck, Libby? You want to talk about getting drunk and coming on to someone? What about that night during Christmas break?"

I slowly turned around and looked at him. "What are you talking about?"

Luke threw his head back and laughed before he looked back into my eyes. "You really don't remember? You came into the barn and practically begged me to fuck you, Libby!"

My hands came up to my mouth as I stood there. I shook my head and moved my hands to my stomach. "Did we? Oh my God … please tell me we didn't? Oh God, no!"

Luke's smirk faded and it looked as if tears were building in his eyes. "Don't look so repulsed by the idea of being with me, Libby. Nothing happened. Glad to know the idea of being with me makes you feel sick though. I won't be bothering you again. Drunk or sober."

Luke took a step back and was about to turn around when I called out his name. "Luke, wait I didn't …"

"Libby? Is everything okay here?" Zach's voice stopped me in my tracks as I stood there and watched the blonde walking back in and up to Luke. She wrapped her arm around him and reached up on her tiptoes and whispered something into his ear. He looked down at her and gave her a slight smile as he nodded his head. They turned and walked back to the table where Luke pulled out his wallet and threw money down.

I tried to call out for him, but nothing came from my mouth. "Libby? What's going on?"

I turned back to Zach. "Nothing, I'm sorry. Can we get out of here now?"

Zach pulled his head back with a worried looked on his face. "Are you sure Luke didn't do or say something to upset you?"

Putting on my best fake smile I nodded my head. "I'm sure. If anything he just showed me how I'm ready to move on."

Raising his eyebrow, Zach asked, "Move on?"

Smiling, I took a step closer to him as I reached up and put my lips to his ear. "I'm ready, Zach."

Swallowing hard, Zach searched my eyes. The corners of his mouth rose in a smile as he took my hand and led me out of the restaurant.

My head was spinning. I needed to push Luke Johnson from my mind and heart once and for all and I only knew of one way to do it.

Zach walked me to the passenger side of the car and opened it. "Please, take me now, Zach. I need you now." Zach reached his hand behind my neck and pulled my lips to his. It didn't take long to get lost in his kiss as I pushed my fingers through his hair.

Yes. I am finally going to be able to move on.

STEPPING THROUGH THE door of Starbucks, coffee in hand, I began to head back to Hullaboo Hall, where my dorm was. I sighed in relief, knowing I was going to have some alone time finally. I had a one-room dorm, but next year I would most likely be moving into the house that my parents bought along with Alex and Grace's parents.

Zach had been all over me since I mentioned I was ready to go all the way with him. His father had called and needed him to come home for a family emergency, so he was gone that night I told him I wanted to make love. Then with finals, we had both been busy.

My phone vibrated in my pocket, reaching in I pulled it out.

> **Zach:** *I can't wait to see you sweetheart. I've been fighting a damn hard on for the last two days. I can't wait to be with you. I've been dreaming of this moment since you first smiled at me. I'll be there this afternoon.*

I swallowed hard and closed my eyes, only to run smack into someone. My coffee went everywhere. "Shit," I said as I knelt down and began picking up the books I dropped. When the person I ran into bent down, I knew instantly it was Luke. Glancing up, our eyes met. "I'm, ah, I'm sorry I wasn't paying attention," I said as Luke gave me a weak smile. His eyes were filled with sadness. I swallowed hard as we looked into each other's eyes.

"No worries. You seemed occupied with your phone." Luke handed me a book and I began wiping it, getting most of the coffee off. Luke had slowly stood and I began to stand as well, reaching for the spilled coffee cup. When I looked at Luke, I saw him looking down at my phone.

"Luke? Um, can I get my phone back?" Luke turned and looked at me. His eyes were filled with regret. He slowly handed me my phone, turned, and walked away. I pulled my head back in surprise and watched as he walked off. I slipped my phone into my pocket and headed to my dorm room.

Thirty minutes later there was a knock on my door. I swallowed hard and took another look in the mirror. My blonde hair was pulled up and piled on top of my head in a loose bun. I had on a Texas A&M tank top, sans bra, and short jean shorts. I spun on my heels and opened the door.

Zach's mouth dropped open as his eyes traveled up and down my body. "Jesus, you're breathtaking."

Zach moved into my room and shut the door behind him. His hands cupped my face as he pressed his lips against mine and pushed me against the wall. I moaned as his hand traveled under my tank top as he began to twist and pull my nipple.

Zach pulled his lips from mine, as he looked me in the eyes. "Lib, are you sure?"

The memory of Luke walking away from me this afternoon fueled my decision more. "Yes, I'm sure."

I need to forget. I have to forget. Please let this make me forget.

I CLOSED MY eyes as I lay next to Zach. That was not what I thought my first time would be like. It lacked passion and love. And something far more important, the man I wanted my first time to be with. I felt the tears begin to pool in my eyes. My mother's words of advice replayed over and over in my mind. If only I'd listened to them. I sat up and reached for my robe. "I'm going to take a shower."

Zach mumbled something as he lay there. Wrapping the robe around my body, I tied it and grabbed my phone as I made my way into the bathroom.

Shutting the door, I leaned against it and dropped my head back. "Oh God. What did I just do?" I whispered. I dropped down onto the cold tile floor and activated the screen on my phone. Zach's text message was on the screen. My hand slowly moved up to my mouth as I closed my eyes and thought about earlier when I ran into Luke.

Looking down, I read the text message again. Luke must have read it and that was why he turned and walked away from me. He knew I was going to sleep with Zach. Tears began to spill from my eyes as I quickly wiped them away, trying to contain my sobs. I closed Zach's message and opened up one to Alex. I was about to start typing a text to her when there was a knock at my dorm room door. I jumped up and quickly wiped away my tears. I opened the bathroom door and smiled weakly at Zach.

"Were you expecting a delivery or something?" Zach asked. I shook my head, fearing if I talked my voice would betray me. I opened the door and saw Luke standing there.

"Luke? What are you doing here?"

He shook his head and ran his hand through his hair. My heart began to race. "I need to talk to you, Lib."

He was too late.

He came too late.

"If you wanted to talk, you should have talked to me months ago." *Before I gave myself to another man, when all I wanted was to be with you.*

I closed the door more so that Luke couldn't see Zach, lying in my bed—naked.

"Libby, please just let me come in. I need to talk to you." His words were pleading and destroyed my already broken heart into a million pieces.

He let out a sigh. "Lib, just let me in … please."

I shook my head. "Now is not a good time, Luke. Can you come back later?"

"No, I'm tired of this, Libby. I can't take it anymore. I need to talk to you."

I closed the door more. "Later, Luke." Before I knew what was happening, he lifted his hand and pushed the door open and began walking in. I covered my mouth with my hand. I felt sick to my stomach.

"Oh, God," Luke whispered as he looked at Zach sitting up in my bed. Zach smiled slightly.

"Um, I believe she told you this wasn't a good time."

Luke turned and looked at me. I was frozen. I couldn't say a word as my heart pounded loudly in my ears.

Luke looked down to the floor and quickly walked out the door, quietly shutting it behind him.

He was too late. The moment I heard the door shut, I turned
and walked into the bathroom again. Soon my body was shaking with sobs as I sat on the cold floor and cried like I've never
cried before.

Luke …

Chapter Twelve

Luke

SITTING IN MY truck, I thought back to a few weeks ago when I had walked in on Libby and Zach. My stomach felt sick any time I thought about it. With everything that had happened with Alex and her attempted rape, Libby and I had pretty much ignored each other and focused on Alex since coming back to Mason.

Tonight was the barn dance at Mr. Banks' place and Grace pretty much forced me into going. She kept saying I needed to get out and socialize with people. I knew Libby would be there tonight and I dreaded seeing her. Will told me that Libby had broken up with Zach the same day she had slept with him for the first time. I knew by me rejecting Libby as much as I did, I was most likely the reason she pushed herself into sleeping with Zach. Knowing that Libby felt like she had made a mistake played havoc on my heart.

Opening the truck door, I jumped out and headed to the entrance to wait on Will, who had just pulled in. Will jumped out of his truck, and jogged around to the passenger side and opened the door for his cousin, Trish. Making their way to me, I held out my hand and Trish took it. "It's good to see you again, Trish. Are you ready for your first barn dance?"

She nodded her head in excitement. "Bring it on!" Shaking my head I laughed. Will, Trish, and I headed into the barn. I looked around and didn't see anyone else here yet. "Come on,

Trish. Let's show Luke what I've taught you so far. Trish chuckled as Will pulled her out onto the dance floor.

I felt a hand slip around my waist. I looked and saw Claire Montgomery looking up at me. "Hey, cowboy. Long time no see."

Tipping my cowboy hat, I smiled in her direction. "Claire, how are you doing?"

Smiling bigger, she winked at me as she said, "I'd do a hell of a lot better if you took me for a spin—on the dance floor."

Letting out a chuckle, I grabbed her hand. "Come on girl, let's two-step for a bit."

Claire and I fell right into step. I knew all I would have to do is take her to my truck and she'd let me fuck her senseless, but Claire was not who I wanted. She'd come in handy a few times, especially when she fell to her knees and would suck me off. Of course every time I let her do that, I was drunk out of my mind.

I spun Claire around as she laughed. Looking up, I saw Libby looking directly at me. Maegan, Alex, Taylor, and Lauren were all standing around looking out on the dance floor.

Fuck. I looked away and finished my dance with Claire. When the song ended, I excused myself and headed over to where Colt was talking to a few guys from his football team. He was talking about playing football with Texas A&M.

I turned when I heard Alex laying into Claire. Turning around, I stood there while Alex basically told Claire to fuck off and stay away from both Will and me. Claire pushed past Alex and me as she made her way out of the barn to leave.

Laughing, I brought Alex in for a hug. "Damn, little cousin. Where in the hell did that come from?

Alex giggled. "I guess I got tired of hiding inside my own body." I pushed a piece of Alex's hair behind her ear. I hated what she had gone through this past summer. I grinned and said, "Welcome back, Alex."

She grinned and said, "It feels good to be back. Hey, Luke?"

"Yeah?"

Clearing her throat, Alex asked, "Did Will tell you that Libby left Zach?"

My smile instantly disappeared. "Um—yeah, he did."

Alex placed her hand on my chest. "Stop hiding inside yourself, Luke. She's not going to wait forever."

Looking up, I saw Libby. She was watching Alex and me. She smiled weakly as I smiled back. "I know," I whispered.

A FEW WEEKS before school started back up, we all headed down to Port Aransas for a week. It felt great to get away and relax and it was the start to what we hoped would be an annual tradition.

"Libby, you can't play anymore!" Grace shouted.

Libby started laughing. "What? Why?"

Grace was throwing the volleyball up in the air. "You're too good."

I ran up and grabbed the ball. "Awe, is Grace pitching a fit 'cause she sucks at volleyball?" I rubbed the top of her head and she pushed my arm away.

"Fuck off, Luke. I swear, if you weren't my brother." I laughed as I jogged over and threw the ball to Alex. She served and Grace volleyed it back over as Libby jumped up and spiked it right in front of Colt. Maegan moaned and pushed Colt.

"Pay attention, Colt Mathews!"

Colt spun around and looked at Maegan. "I was, Meg. I can't help it if she's good."

Maegan rolled her eyes and crossed her arms over her chest. "I'd rather be tanning!"

Lauren laughed as she jumped up and down as if she was warming up. Grace turned and looked at Will, who was walking down from the house. "Hayes! Get down here. Your damn sister is kicking our ass!"

Will laughed as he started jogging. He ran up and grabbed Libby and threw her over his shoulder as Libby let out a scream. I chased after him. "Put our star player down!"

Will tried to turn but I grabbed Libby and attempted to take her from Will. He lost his balance and began falling, but not before I grabbed Libby and pulled her to me. I lost my balance and she fell on top of me.

She was laughing as she looked at me. "I'm having déjà vu," she said with a chuckle. I thought back to the day at the ranch when she had fallen on me. I loved having her in my arms. I smiled and winked at her. She pushed off of me and jumped up and clapped her hands.

"Let's kick some ass!" Libby shouted as she and Alex jumped and high-fived each other.

I SAT IN the pool house, attempting to catch my breath. Libby and I had gone running on the beach tonight. I tried five times to tell her how I felt. I tried like hell to tell her I loved her, but all I kept seeing was me sleeping with Karen. What if I hurt Libby again? What if I wasn't good enough for her?

You're hurting her now by pushing her away.

I was tired of the push and pull from the voices in my head. I needed to tell Libby how I felt about her, and the sooner the better, before I pushed her into another man's arms again. I stood up and pulled my T-shirt over my head as I opened the door to the pool house. Libby fell into my arms as she let out a small scream. I grabbed her and pulled her to me. Her breath caught in her throat and she looked at my bare chest. "Um ... I ... my ... um ..." She pulled her eyes from my abs and chest and looked into my eyes. "You have my phone still from our run earlier."

"Oh shit, yeah. Sorry!" I said as I reached into my shorts pocket and pulled out her phone. When I handed it to her, our fingers brushed together and my stomach dipped. Libby's mouth opened slightly and I knew she felt the same thing I did.

Smiling she turned and walked away. I pushed my hand through my hair and cursed. "Fuck me. I'm not going to make it through this week."

I SAT ON the beach and tipped back my beer as I finished it off. Setting it to the side, I looked out over the dark waters of the gulf. I closed my eyes and pictured Libby at the dance club. The sexy silver cocktail dress she wore tonight had almost every fucker in the club staring at her. I sat there and watched her dance with that built motherfucker for three dances before I got up and cut in. I was surprised when he stepped away without a fight.

I leaned back on the sand and closed my eyes. I could almost feel her warmth in my arms as we danced.

"YOU REALLY DO look beautiful tonight, Libby," I said as I held her closer to me.

Smiling, she looked up into my eyes. "Thank you." My hand was against her cool skin as I slowly moved it up and down her bare back. I wanted more than anything to press my lips against her sweat-shined skin. I could almost taste her on my lips.

The song we danced to ended and another one began. When it started playing, I had a hard time catching my breath. Cascada's "What Hurts The Most" was playing as Libby and I stared at each other as I held her in my arms. When the beat increased, we just stood there. Lost in each other's eyes. I wanted so desperately to tell her how much I loved her. How much I wanted her.

Libby's eyes began to fill with tears as she began to turn away from me. I grabbed her arm and stopped her.

"Libby ..." I whispered as I removed my grip from her arm. I didn't want to tell her how I felt in a damn nightclub. She turned and walked off as I stood in the middle of the dance floor.

Closing my eyes I sucked in a breath and blew it out. I'm always fucking hurting her. Always.

I WASN'T SURE how long I lay on the beach thinking, but I made up my mind on what I had to do. This whole time I had been pushing Libby away for fear of hurting her. What I needed to realize was that by not being honest with my own feelings—and fears, I was hurting her even more. Sitting up, I sucked in a breath of the salt air.

Standing, I wiped off the sand from my shorts and headed back to the house. Standing at the bottom of the stairs, my heart pounded as I lifted my leg and headed up the stairs. Each step felt like my legs grew heavier and heavier. The idea of totally opening up and telling Libby everything, only to have her walk away, scared the hell out of me.

Pushing my hand through my hair, I walked up to the bedroom where Libby was staying. I leaned in closer and heard her and Grace giggling. I raised the left corner of my mouth and smiled. Two of the most important women in my life sat on the other side of that door. Lifting my hand, I was about to knock when I heard Libby.

"If he loved me, he wouldn't be doing this to me, Grace. My heart can't take anymore."

The air immediately left my lungs as I heard the hurt in Libby's voice. Closing my eyes, I dropped my hands to my sides. By telling Libby the truth, I would be hurting her again and that was the last thing I wanted to do. My father's words flooded my mind. I had two choices and I knew which choice I was going to make. I turned and made my way back down the stairs. It felt like it took me forever to get to the pool house. I walked in and shut the door behind me.

Chapter Thirteen

Libby

I STOOD OUTSIDE the door to the pool house and listened closely. Taylor had come into our room and said Luke had been standing outside the door and was about to knock when he turned and headed back downstairs.

I wanted desperately to know what he wanted. He might have just wanted to talk to Grace. I placed my hand on the door and whispered, "Luke?"

Closing my eyes, I waited for his response.

Nothing. I reached down and opened the door slowly. The light from the moon lit up the room. I let out a gasp when I saw him sleeping. Making my way over to the side of the bed, I gazed down upon him. Smiling, I placed my fingertips to my lips. I wanted to feel his lips on mine more than anything. I took a few steps back and sat down in the chair and watched him sleep.

Maybe Luke couldn't move on from me sleeping with Zach? Was that the reason he was holding back? A tear slowly made its way down my cheek. I reached up and wiped it away. Would he ever be able to tell me how he felt about me? Or was there too much between us now?

Closing my eyes I slowly stood. I looked at Luke again before turning and heading back into the house. Quietly shutting the door, I walked to my bed. My phone had been charging on the side table. Picking it up I found Zach's name displayed on my screen.

Zach: *I've missed you Libby. Please call me.*

I inhaled a shaky breath. I'd given Luke so many opportunities to tell me how he felt about me. I wasn't sure what to do anymore.

Me: *Can I call you tomorrow?*

Zach: *I have a family function with my father but I'll text you when I can talk.*

Me: *Okay.*

Zach: *Night, Libby. I miss you.*

I closed my text messages and sighed. Dropping back onto the bed, I thought about Zach. Did I do the right thing by responding to him? Did I even miss Zach or was he a means to try and forget Luke?

I pulled the covers back and crawled under them.

Tomorrow. I'll decide what to do tomorrow.

THE DAY WAS spent just hanging around the house. Grace and I went for a run on the beach early this morning. If only I could keep running until I knew what to do.

I sat at the kitchen table and listened to Maegan, Taylor, and Lauren all talk about plans for next school year. I glanced up when I heard Colt's voice moving closer.

"I'm telling you, the system I designed will track all the vaccinations and send you monthly reminders. I just need to convince Scott to get on board with it."

Lauren sat up, her interest obviously piqued. "What about my dad?"

Colt had a bottle of water pressed against his lips. He slowly dropped it to his side. I guess he was shocked Lauren was talking to him after the knock-down fight they had last night. "Um—I thought you were never talking to me again?"

I rolled my eyes. *Oh gosh. Here we go again.*

"You mentioned my father, I was just curious about what y'all were talking about," Lauren said as she squared her shoulders. Lauren had every intention of taking over her father's breeding business someday. She had mentioned to Grace and me how her father felt she couldn't handle the business alone. Scott had felt that Colt had showed a great deal of interest in the horses and would make a great partner to take on the business with Lauren someday. Lauren had been livid the day she told us. In her eyes, she didn't need anyone to help her run her family's ranch.

Colt lifted the corner of his mouth. "What's the matter, Lauren? You afraid your dad is going to like one of my ideas?"

Lauren stood and walked to Colt. She pointed her finger at him and began poking him in the chest as she spoke. "If you think for one second I'm going to take a step back while you wiggle your way into my family's breeding business, you've got another thing coming, Colt Mathews. Stick with cattle, and leave the horses to me."

Colt's mouth dropped open and then he started laughing. "You're threatened by me? Why Lauren? What did your daddy say? Maybe that you couldn't handle it all on your own?" His eyebrow rose as if he knew something Lauren didn't, which caused her to ball up her fists.

Luke cleared his throat. "Who wants to go grab an early dinner?"

Maegan, Taylor, and I all shouted out, "Me!" Everyone could see the fight that was brewing between Colt and Lauren.

"You won't win, Colt," Lauren hissed through her teeth.

Colt smirked. "I didn't realize we had a contest going on, Lauren."

Lauren placed her hands on Colt's chest and pushed him. "Fuck you, Colt Mathews."

Colt grabbed her wrists, "You wish you could, Lauren."

Luke placed his hand on Colt's shoulder, "Alright, that's enough. Both of y'all just back the hell off each other. You're both in college and there is plenty of time to sort all this out. Let's get some dinner y'all." Luke pulled Colt back some and began to lead him out the door. He glanced at me and our eyes met. We both smiled weakly.

Luke mouthed, *After dinner?* I nodded my head. Luke had asked to talk to me earlier today, but I had been avoiding him all day. I was scared to talk to him. Not knowing what he was planning on saying to me. I walked up to Lauren and laced my arm with her arm.

"Come on, let's go get something to eat." Taylor walked on the other side of Lauren and took her arm in hers.

Swallowing hard, Lauren whispered, "I hate him."

Taylor and I both looked at her, as Taylor said, "No, Lauren, honey. I think you're fighting your feelings for him."

Lauren turned and looked at Taylor and then to me. She shook her head and whispered, "How can you love someone you hate so much?"

I stopped and took Lauren into my arms as she began to cry. Luke looked over his shoulder back at us as I motioned for him to keep going.

Maegan wrapped up Lauren and me in her arms. "We should have all signed in our blood not to fall for each other."

I looked into Maegan's eyes as she winked at me and then mouthed, *Talk to him, Libby.* Nodding my head I mouthed back, *I will.*

I STOOD UNDER the pier and looked out over the dark blue waters. The sun had already begun to sink beneath the horizon.

I slowly inhaled the sea air through my nose and then blew it out. I loved it down here. Something about the wind and the sound of the waves hitting the shore calmed my nerves and helped me forget.

Saving You

Dinner had been interesting. Colt and Lauren retreated to their corners. Then we all pretended everything was okay and back to normal. We were getting good at pretending.

I knew the moment he walked up behind me. I could feel his energy. I closed my eyes.

I can't do this anymore.

I'd never love anyone like I loved Luke, but my heart couldn't take the pain any longer.

He stepped closer, and my breathing increased. I longed for his touch, for his lips to softly brush against mine, and for him to whisper he loved me.

"Hey, Lib."

His voice made my heart drop and my stomach flip.

Taking a deep breath, I turned to face him. "Hey, Luke."

His smile was forced. Something was on his mind, like something was on mine.

I started walking along the beach, and Luke followed. My phone beeped in my pocket, and I pulled it out. It was Zach.

Luke let out a laugh, and I looked over at him. He was walking next to me but looking straight ahead.

"Do you remember the time we put salt in your mom's sugar container and Alex put three huge scoops in her oatmeal?"

Luke somehow always talked me into doing his crazy pranks with him.

Smiling, I nodded my head as I said, "Yeah, I remember."

Luke started talking about how he'd gotten grounded for that prank as I opened up Zach's text.

> ***Zach:*** *Libby, I'm so glad you texted me back. Baby, I understand you were confused, but I'm here. I'm waiting for you if you want to make this work.*

I quickly hit the Home button on my phone and pushed it back into my back pocket. My heart was pounding.

Shit. I shouldn't have responded back to Zach.

No, I did the right thing. Didn't I?

My head was spinning, and Luke was talking about damn

pranks.

I stopped walking and turned to him. I shook my head. "I really need to be alone right now, Luke. I have to think, and I can't think with you living in the past."

His smile dropped, and he nodded his head. I turned and started walking away from him.

"Libby, wait. Please."

The moment his hand touched my arm, I felt the most amazing rush sweep through my body. I almost wanted to whimper with the way his touch affected me. Zach's touch never did this to me.

I looked into Luke's eyes. He had the most beautiful green eyes. I could see why women melted when he looked at them. I quickly looked away.

I can't do this anymore. I can't.

My eyes burned with the tears I fought to hold back. "Luke, I can't stand here and pretend like nothing is wrong. Everything is wrong, and I ... I need to move on with my life, and I can't with—"

He held up his hand and shook his head. I stopped talking. His eyes searched my face and then moved to my lips. I instinctively licked them, and he snapped his eyes back up to mine where he searched them intently.

I held my breath and waited for what he was about to say.

"Libby, I have something I need to tell you."

Swallowing hard, my heart slammed against my chest. Was he going to tell me he was moving on? I didn't want to let him go. I didn't want to be with Zach. I wanted Luke. Closing my eyes, I inhaled a shaky breath.

Luke placed his hands on the sides of my face and my eyes opened. I frantically searched his face for a sign of what was about to come from his lips. My breathing picked up and I became acutely aware of everything around me. Ocean waves crashing at our feet as the warm water surrounded us. The smell of Luke's cologne filled my senses as the warm ocean breeze blew my blonde hair around. Birds flying over our heads searching for their evening meal.

"I love you, Libby. I've loved you for so long and I've been an idiot for pushing you away. If I could go back in time, I swear to God, Libby, I'd never hurt you. I'd tell you every single day how much I love you." Luke closed his eyes and slowly shook his head. He opened his eyes again and began softly moving his thumbs against my skin. I placed my hands over his and smiled as I felt my tears slide down my overly sensitive skin. "Libby, I've laid in bed at night and dreamed of feeling your soft skin against mine. Dreaming of my lips exploring every single inch of your body. I've wasted so much time trying to figure things out and all I've done is hurt you in the process. I'm tired of running, Lib. I'm tired of feeling like I'm drowning in a sea of doubt and fear. I want to figure this out—together."

A small sob escaped through my lips as Luke leaned down closer. His lips barely brushed against mine. "Please tell me I'm not too late, Libby."

I placed my hands on his strong arms and whispered, "Kiss me. Please kiss me so I know I'm not dreaming."

The smile that moved across Luke's face caused my knees to weaken. Was it finally happening? Was Luke finally giving himself to me and allowing me to give myself to him? He pressed his lips to mine as we moved our arms around each other. My lips felt as if they were on fire. My fingers pushed into his hair as he pulled my body closer to him. Our kiss started off slow and easy, but quickly turned into raw passion. Our tongues moved and explored each other as we kissed liked we couldn't get enough of each other. I wanted to crawl into his body and stay there forever. I was never going to let him go. I was never going to forget this moment.

Luke slowly pulled his lips back from mine and leaned his forehead against mine. "Libby," he whispered. His breathing was fast and short. "I'm sorry ... I'm so sorry it wasn't me."

Closing my eyes, I knew what he was talking about. "If I could go back in time, I would have never—"

Placing his lips back to mine, he kissed me again. It was

slow, passionate and filled with love. Pulling back some, Luke whispered against my lips, "Let me love you, Libby."

I let out a soft low moan, but then a thought occurred to me. The idea of Luke walking away caused my heart to begin beating harder within my chest. "I want you too, Luke. But my heart can't take it if you were to push me away again."

Time stopped the moment I saw the tear slowly begin to move down his cheek.

"I swear to you, Libby. I'll never walk away from us again. I want to be forever yours.

Smiling, I reached up and wiped his tear way. "Yes. Love me, Luke. Please."

Chapter Fourteen

Luke

LIBBY AND I walked back to the beach house. We stopped outside the pool house and Libby leaned against the door, smiling that smile that stole my heart so many years ago. "I feel like I'm dreaming, Luke. I don't want this to be a dream."

Placing my hand on the side of her face, I brushed my thumb against her cheek. "I promise you, you're not dreaming."

Smiling bigger, Libby bit down on her lower lip. I'd dreamed of making love to Libby for the last few years. I wasn't about to rush this. I wanted to erase all memories of her night with Zach. And the only way to do that was showering her body with love and attention. I reached down and picked her up as I pushed open the door to the pool house. Walking in, I kicked the door shut with my foot.

I slowly slid Libby down my body, making sure she felt how much I wanted her. Before her feet could touch the ground, I pressed my lips against hers and kissed her gently. "I'm going to love you all night long, Libby."

I saw the lump in her throat as she swallowed. Her lips parted slightly and I couldn't wait to have them wrapped around my dick one day. Today was not that day. This was going to be all about Libby. I was going to learn every square inch of her body. What she liked and what she didn't like. What made her toes curl and what made her body hum.

I glanced up and looked at the wrought-iron bed. My dick jumped at the idea of tying Libby up and fucking her senseless.

Not yet. Now was about making love to her. Making up for all the lost time.

"Libby," I whispered as I reached for her shirt and lifted it over her head as she raised her arms. Tossing her shirt to the side, I took every inch of her in. Her body was amazing. She had just the right amount of curves. Her muscular build was from years of running and hanging with us guys at the gym. Her breasts were begging to be sucked. I reached my hand up and placed it on her chest. Her soft cool skin beneath my hand rose and fell with each deep breath she breathed in. Smiling, I moved my fingertip along the edge of her blue lace bra. I cupped her breast and moaned when it fit perfectly in my hand. Rubbing my thumb across the lace fabric, I felt her nipple getting harder. She dropped her head back and moaned.

Reaching behind her back with my other hand, I unclasped her bra in three fast movements. She lifted her head and raised her eyebrow up at me. Smiling, I pressed my lips against her lips, sucking in her bottom lip as I retreated. Her bra dropped to the ground and she stood before me with the most perfect breasts I'd ever seen.

"Motherfucker," I whispered as I leaned down and began sucking and pulling on her right nipple. Libby's hands quickly moved to my head as she ran her fingers through my hair. When she stopped and tugged, I swore I had to fight coming in my pants.

My hands moved down her body as I dropped to my knees, my eyes looking at her perfectly flat stomach. My hands began shaking as I began to unbutton her shorts. Peeking up, I watched Libby as she chewed on her bottom lip. I knew she was just as nervous as I was, but wanted it just as bad.

"It's taking everything I have to go slow, Lib. I want to bury myself so deep inside you, you'll never forget I was there."

"Oh God," Libby whispered as her hands came up to her breasts. Pushing her shorts down, Libby placed her hands on my shoulders to keep her balance as she stepped out of them.

I looked back at her white lace panties. I could see through the lace to her bare soft skin. I pulled her panties down and just stared at her. "Holy hell," I whispered as I touched her and her body was immediately covered in goose bumps. Lifting her leg, I put it over my shoulder. "You're even perfect here, Libby."

Her hands pulled and tugged my hair. "Luke, I've never. No one has ever ..."

Looking up at her, I watched her fighting for air. "Never, Lib? I'm your first to do this?"

She nodded her head in a frantic gesture. Smiling I said, "Good," as I buried my face between her legs. Pushing my tongue inside her wet folds, I moaned. My dick was painfully hard. She tasted better than I had dreamed she would.

"Oh ... my ... God ..." Libby panted as my tongue continued to explore her. I needed a better look. I quickly pulled away, only to have Libby protest. "No ... wait!" she said as I stood and scooped her up. I put her on the bed and spread her legs open.

"I'm not going to last a minute inside you, Lib," I said as I pushed her lips apart and pushed two fingers in as she arched her back. "So damn tight."

"Luke, I can't ... please. I need to come!"

I smiled and began massaging her insides as I kissed along her inner thigh.

Libby's voice was cracking as she begged, "More. I need more!"

Leaning down, I brushed my tongue across her swollen clit. Libby's body jumped as she let out another moan. Her hands came down and pulled me closer to her as her hips began to move.

I didn't want to make her wait too long, especially since I planned on making her come over and over. All night.

I began to suck on her clit as I massaged her with my fingers. Her body shuddered as I felt her pulsing against my fingers.

"Oh God. Yes!" she screamed out as she began calling out

my name. I looked up and saw her watching me as she fell apart. The flush across her cheeks was the sexiest thing I'd ever seen in my life.

Son-of-a-bitch. She's watching me. I need to be inside her, now.

Her head dropped back as she attempted to come down from her orgasm. I didn't give her long to recover before I pulled my fingers out and dipped my tongue into her soaking wet hotness. I began fucking her with my tongue as I reached up and twisted and pulled her nipple.

She screamed out my name again as another orgasm ripped through her. Her hips rocked against my face and if my pants had been off, I'd be stroking my rock hard dick.

A little pressure on her back door and more attention to her clit with my tongue, flicking fast, and she was falling apart for the third time. Her body was so responsive to me. I was going to have fun exploring her.

"No ... more ... can't ... take it," Libby panted. I pulled away and watched her body come back to Earth. Her mouth was open and she was desperately attempting to breathe and calm her beating heart. I quickly stood up and began taking off my pants. Libby sat up. "No! Please, let me."

Oh hell. Please don't let me come the moment she touches me. Please.

Libby slid to the end of the bed and began unbuttoning my shorts. She looked up at me and smiled as she pushed them down. Looking back down, my erection sprung free and Libby gasped.

"Holy crap," Libby whispered. "I forgot how huge you were."

I chuckled and shook my head. Pushing Zach from her memory would be easier than I thought.

Libby reached her hand up and wrapped it around my throbbing thick shaft. She licked her lips as she stared at my dick.

Libby moved so quickly I couldn't stop her, she wrapped her lips around my dick and I jerked. "Holy fuck! Libby ... oh shit ..." My eyes rolled back as her tongue rolled around the top of my head. Libby moaned and I grabbed her head.

"Libby, I'm not going to last ... oh God ... Lib ..." She peeked up and sucked harder as she moved up and down my shaft. "I'm going to come, Libby! Fuck!" I shouted as my cum hit the back of her throat. She moaned and began taking it all in as she swallowed every bit I gave her.

My heart was pounding and my hands pulled at her hair. When she cupped my balls, another round of cum poured out of me. "Holy shit ... ahh." I dropped my head back as my whole body shuddered with the most intense orgasm I'd ever had.

Libby sucked and sucked until she got every last drop. Sitting back on the bed, she smiled as she wiped her mouth. "I've never done that before."

My knees buckled out from me and I dropped to the floor with her admission. Libby let out a small scream and dropped to the floor next to me. "Are you okay? Oh God. Did I do something wrong? Did I suck too hard or something?"

Turning, I looked at her. "You could never suck too hard, bite your tongue!"

Libby giggled and pushed me back. She crawled on top of me and began grinding against my dick.

"Lib, I need to recover. My dick isn't a super hero, baby."

Giving me a wicked smile, she continued to rub against me. "Really, cause that would be pretty awesome if he was."

I nodded my head. "Hell yeah it would."

She placed her hands on her breasts and began playing with her nipples. "What is it about you that makes me feel so brazen, Luke? I feel like I'm discovering another side of me and I want to know more."

My dick twitched back to life and Libby raised her eyebrows. Biting down on her lip, she pushed harder against me. "Do you like that idea? I want you to teach me things, Luke. Things that will give both of us pleasure."

My dick was growing harder and jumped as Libby rubbed against me. I couldn't believe I was getting hard again, especially after the powerful orgasm I had not even five minutes ago.

Lifting the corner of her mouth, Libby gave me a sexy grin. "Coming up so soon? What does that mean, Mr. Johnson?

Grabbing her hips I smiled and said, "That means I've died and gone to heaven, and my dick is a super hero."

Chapter Fifteen

Libby

MY HEART WAS pounding so loudly, I was sure Luke could hear it. My body felt alive, like never before. My first time with Zach was nothing like this. Luke and I hadn't even made love yet and I needed more of him. I had never desired something as much as I desired Luke. I'd never felt so wanton in my life.

I couldn't believe my actions or my words. I knew Luke was more experienced than I was, and I wanted to learn every possible way to please him. As I rocked against his body, his eyes closed. "You drive me mad, Libby." My stomach dropped and I smiled. Knowing I was driving him crazy fueled me along.

His hands landed on my hips. Stopping me from moving. I leaned down and sucked his lower lip into my mouth while he let out a long slow moan. I pulled back some. "Take me as yours, Luke. Please."

Closing his eyes, Luke cursed under his breath. Opening his eyes, I saw something in them. It was more than passion or lust. Far more than desire. It was love.

My eyes burned with the threat of tears. Four words from his beautiful soft lips and my tears fell freely. "I love you, Libby."

I slowly shook my head. Please don't let this be a cruel joke and I wake up with my hand down my panties. I barely spoke the words above a whisper. "I love you too, Luke."

He sat up and wrapped his arms around me as I wrapped mine around his neck. He got up and expertly carried me back to the bed where he gently laid me down. His eyes searched my body up and down. As if he was memorizing every detail of my body.

He walked over to his bag and dug through it. He pulled out three condoms and I raised my eyebrow at him. "Feeling lucky?"

He began to stroke his dick and I was shocked at how it turned me on even more—if possible. "I intend to make you mine, Libby. Over, and over, and over again."

A small moan escaped my lips as I whispered, "Okay,"

"Move up the bed, Libby." I scurried as fast as I could. "Lay down, baby. It's my turn to take care of you again."

I began chewing on my lower lip. I wanted him inside me and I didn't want to wait any longer. He crawled onto the bed and spread my legs apart, causing me to grab onto the blanket as I arched my back. He began kissing along the edge of my foot and I felt the orgasm beginning to build. *What the hell? He's just kissing me!*

Panting I mumbled, "Oh God."

His lips moved up my leg to my inner thigh. The feel of his hands softly gliding along my skin was more than I could take. I thrashed my head back and forth.

More. More. More.

He kissed slowly around the sensitive lips. His hot breath against my clit caused a rush of wetness between my legs. "Luke! Please! I'm so close ... oh ... I'm so close."

Luke began kissing around my stomach and slowly moved up. The moment his lips took my nipple and he bit down, my orgasm ripped through my body. I arched my back and began calling out his name as my hips gyrated and my body quivered.

Once my orgasm died out, Luke let off my nipple and looked at me. I was gasping for air. "Wow. Just—wow," I panted out as Luke smiled.

"Your body is so receptive of me, Libby." I nodded my head. I didn't want this evening to end. *Ever.*

"I was made for you, Luke."

His lips slammed against mine as he kissed me with everything he had. Our tongues danced and explored as our hands moved over each other's bodies. "Please, please don't make me beg for you. I need to feel you inside me, Luke. I need to have you. I need you to make me yours."

Sitting up, Luke grabbed a condom and ripped it open with his teeth. I smiled as I felt my core pulsing with greed as my eyes fell to his dick. I watched as he slipped the condom down his long thick shaft. His veins bulging as want and need pulsed through them.

He settled between my legs as he brought his lips back to mine. "Slow, Libby. I want to feel every inch of your pussy."

"Oh, God," I was shocked by how much I loved to hear Luke talk to me so raw. Could I do the same? Could I be so wanton as to express what I was thinking? "Luke—"

The tip of his dick pushed slightly into me. I wrapped my leg around his calves and attempted to pull him in further.

"Slow, Libby," he whispered against my neck.

Panting, I whispered back, "More. Luke, please give me more."

I closed my eyes as he pushed in a little deeper. My body was building again. Pushing in more I moaned as my body accommodated his size. Moving my leg up further, I pulled him in more. I inhaled a breath and decided to let my desire out. I wanted this moment to be like I dreamed of while lying in bed. "I need you to fill me deep, Luke. Now!"

Groaning, he pushed in hard and fast as I arched my back to him. "Yes!" I hissed between my teeth. Luke stilled as he filled my entire body. It burned like hell, but felt so amazing. I wrapped my legs around him as my fingertips moved lightly up and down his back.

"Libby. I've waited forever for this moment," he whispered as he lifted his head. Tears filled his eyes and my heart was forever lost to the only man I've ever loved.

Reaching up, I wiped a tear from his face. "Make love to me,

Luke."

Luke gently pressed his lips to mine as he tenderly moved in and out of my body. Whispering the sweetest words against my lips as he made love to me for the first time. My body began to shudder as the buildup was almost to the max. Pulling my lips from his I whispered, "I'm going to come."

One hard push in and I was off the ledge, as was Luke. We whispered our names against our kiss-swollen lips as we came at the same time. I would never experience a moment like this again. Nothing before and nothing after would ever compare.

LUKE AND I lay tangled up in each other as I moved my index finger lazily up and down his arm. His rhythmic breathing was calming. I don't think I'll ever be able to sleep soundly again unless he is wrapped in my arms. I could hear the sound of the waves as they crashed on the shore. Luke had made love to me three times, and with each time my orgasms grew more intense. He did as he said he was going to do—made me his, over, and over, and over again.

For me this was my first time. It was just as I dreamed it would be. With Zach, it had been awkward. Nothing about it felt good. He pulled out of me and finished himself off, even though he wore a condom. Nothing about that evening felt right.

Everything about tonight felt right. Smiling, I bit down on my lip. I wondered how long it would be before Luke moved past the romantic lovemaking and we got to explore each other more. Butterflies took off in my stomach as I thought about Luke doing naughty things to me.

"What are you thinking about, Lib?" His voice was low and tired sounding. And sexy as hell. "Your heart is pounding in your chest and your body temperature just got hotter."

I was shocked at how in tune he was with my body. "I'm thinking of—more."

Luke chortled. "I don't think I can. I'm exhausted, baby."

Smiling I shook my head. "I didn't mean more sex now; I'm talking about wanting more."

He lifted his head and looked at me. His eyes danced with delight. "More as in?"

Chewing on my bottom lip, I reached deep inside and found my courage. I've waited too long to be with him, there was no way I wasn't going to be honest and up front with him. "More, fun. Bedroom fun."

He narrowed his eyes and asked, "Explain further." I rolled my eyes. He knew what I was getting at, but he wanted me to say it. *Fine.* I wanted to play the wanton role, so here I go.

"I want to do other things. I mean, I loved ... *loved* what happened between us tonight and I want more of that. Lots more." Luke smiled that breathtaking smile of his. Green eyes lighting up at the mere thought of making love to me again.

"I just ..." I looked away.

Luke used his index finger and pulled my chin, causing me to look back into his eyes. "Keep talking, Libby."

Swallowing hard, I took in a shaky breath. "I want to do naughty things."

His eyes widened and lit up with raw passion. "Do you want me to tie you up and have my wicked way with you, Lib?"

My lips parted open. "Yes."

"Do you want me to use toys on you?"

I slowly nodded my head. "Yes. And I want to tie you up."

Luke sucked in a breath as he whispered, "Fuck me, Libby."

I licked my lips. "I want to do that too," I said between panted breaths.

Luke closed his eyes. "Libby, I only brought three condoms. I wasn't sure if—"

I put my fingers to his lips and began chewing on my lower lip. "I don't need it now. I just want to lay here and be with you. I've waited for so long to be in your arms. This feels so good. So right, Luke."

He leaned up and kissed the tip of my nose. "I love you, Libby." Smiling I pulled his lips to mine. It didn't take long before

we were lost in our kiss and Luke was between my legs, wringing out another orgasm with his magical lips.

Best. Night. Of. My. Life.

Chapter Sixteen

Luke

I SMILED AS I buttered toast for Libby and me. Grace walked into the kitchen and I glanced up at her. "Morning, baby sister!"

Grace stopped walking and stared at me. She tilted her head and a huge smile spread across her face.

"Holy hell," she said as she quickly walked over to me. She grabbed my face with both her hands and looked into my eyes.

"Jesus, Mary, and Joseph. You finally did it!"

I tried not to smile as I pulled back and looked at her. "What do you mean, Mom?"

Grace slapped me on the arm. She hated when I called her mom, but she was *so much* like our mother it was unreal.

"You and Libby. Finally! Y'all finally did it."

I heard someone gasp as I looked over Grace's shoulder to see Lauren and Maegan standing there. Lauren started jumping up and down as she covered her mouth with her hands. Looking at Maegan, she smiled and winked at me as she nodded her head.

Taylor walked between Lauren and Maegan. "Jesus, it's about time." Everyone looked at Taylor as she opened the refrigerator and took out the orange juice. "Make sure you bring her OJ. She loves it." Taylor looked up and glanced around to everyone. "What?"

I laughed and shook my head as I looked back at Grace.

"Yes, we are officially together." Grace bit down on her lip and nodded.

"Luke, I'm so happy. You two were made for each other and I'm glad you got your head out of your ass."

Meagan walked by and said, "That makes two of us. Dude, I was beginning to wonder if you were into girls."

Snapping my head over, I looked at Maegan. "What? Why the hell ..."

Lauren came skipping over. "Never mind, Maegan. You can't bring her toast!" Turning to Taylor, Lauren said, "Tay, you know what to do."

Taylor gave a thumbs up and began taking items out of the pantry. Grace grabbed a skillet and said, "I'll start the bacon while Lauren cooks her famous French toast."

Taylor put everything on the kitchen island as Lauren pushed me out of the way. "Luke, will you get the strawberries out and start washing them and cutting them please."

I looked at all four girls moving around the kitchen. "What are y'all doing?" They all stopped and looked at me. Grace pulled her head back and gave me a disgusted look. "Um, making breakfast so you can bring it to Libby. Duh. Romance bro, you've got to romance her."

I ran my hand through hair. "'Cause making love to her all night wasn't romancing her?"

Taylor, Lauren, and Maegan all let out a sigh and looked at me with goofy faces. Grace threw her hands up to her ears. "Oh gross. Yuck! My ears need to be bleached now, Luke! Blah!"

I laughed and pulled Grace into my arms and kissed her cheek. She looked up at me and smiled. "I really am happy for you both. She loves you so much, Luke."

I felt myself grinning like a fool. "I love her, too, Grace. I've always loved her."

Grace stood on her toes, kissed me on the cheek, turned around, and slapped her hands together and said, "Alright ladies. Let's do this!"

I CAREFULLY BALANCED the tray that carried two plates of French toast, bacon, fresh strawberries, two orange juices, and two cups of coffee. Grace walked with me and stopped right before we got to the pool house. She cleared her throat. "Luke, I just want to say one thing."

Turning, I looked at my beautiful baby sister. Her brown hair was pulled up into a ponytail and her green eyes danced with concern. "Please don't hurt her."

Swallowing hard, I felt my body tremble.

"I know you, and I know there was a reason you kept pushing Libby away. Please talk to her about it, Luke. I promise you if you don't, it will always be there, buried deep in your heart. You don't need that fear living in you."

I turned my head slightly, looking at my sister. "When did you become so smart on this stuff?"

Her eyes filled with sadness. "Because what I saw in your eyes, is what I see in my own eyes when I look in the mirror."

My heart dropped and if I hadn't been holding the damn tray full of food I would have taken Grace by the arm and walked her to the beach to talk. "Grace—"

She held up her hand and shook her head. "No, don't worry about me, please don't worry. I want you to be honest with Libby about everything. Your dreams, hopes, fears. All of it, Luke. You have to be honest about everything."

"I promise you, I'll talk to her." I looked toward the door and then back to Grace. "Grace, you know I'm always here for you. If you ever need to talk, or me to kick some asshole's ass, I will in a heartbeat."

Grace laughed and nodded her head. "I know you are and I love you for all of that. Right now, I want you to focus on that girl in there. I want you to know that you do deserve her love, Luke. The two of you were meant to be together."

I leaned down and kissed Grace's cheek. "I want us to spend

some time together alone before we leave, Grace."

Nodding her head, she smiled weakly. "We will. I promise." Grace walked up and put her hand on the doorknob to the pool house. "Right now, I just want you to romance the hell out of my best friend."

Laughing, I nodded. "I'll try my best."

Grace opened the door and stepped back. I winked at her as I walked into the pool house. I shut the door with my foot and smiled as I looked at my sleeping beauty. I turned and set the tray down on the table and made my way to the side of the bed. Looking at Libby, my breath was taken away by her flushed cheeks. I closed my eyes and prayed that I had made last night special for her. *Magical.* Opening my eyes, I watched as her chest softly rose and fell with each breath. I hope like hell I erased Zach from her mind, and heart.

I dropped to my knees and brushed my fingers through her beautiful blonde hair. When her blue eyes fluttered open she smiled immediately. I smiled in return and my stomach felt like I was riding on a rollercoaster. "Good morning, Lib."

Libby bit her lip before releasing it and whispering, "Good morning." She sat up and the sheet fell down, exposing her perfect breasts. I let out a moan as she giggled and pulled up the sheets. "Sorry."

I stood, leaned over and kissed her gently on the lips. "I have breakfast."

Her stomach growled. "Oh gosh! I guess all that activity last night worked up my appetite!"

Turning, I walked over and picked up the tray, and carried it back to the bed. I set the tray down, turned and grabbed one of my T-shirts and handed it to Libby. "I can't eat and look at your breathtaking naked body."

Libby's face flushed as she pulled the T-shirt over her head. My heart slammed within my chest. I loved how innocent Libby was, but at the same time she could tell me she wanted my cock to fill her.

Shaking the memory from my head, I adjusted my dick and

sat down on the bed across from Lib.

"Wow! Did you make all of this?" Libby asked as she took a sip of coffee and let out a long moan of satisfaction. I shook my head and laughed. "No. I was buttering you toast when all the girls came into the kitchen. Once they found out you and I were—well together. They jumped into action and began cooking up a romantic breakfast for you."

Libby laughed as she took a bite of bacon. "I think I just fell in love with you more."

Looking at her puzzled look I asked, "Why?"

She shrugged. "I don't know. Just knowing that you gave the girls credit for all of this when you didn't have to, just makes my insides all mushy."

"Huh, really?"

"Yep," Libby said, popping her p.

Taking a bite of French toast, I looked down at my food. "So what would you say if I told you I ran to the store this morning and bought something?"

Reaching for her orange juice, she raised her eyebrows. "I'd probably say something like, I hope you bought more condoms."

My dick jumped and my heart felt like it was about to leap from my chest. I dropped my fork and stared into her eyes.

"I'm no longer hungry," I whispered.

Libby set her fork down and lifted the T-shirt up and over her head. "I'm still hungry. For you."

I stood and moved the tray containing our breakfast so fast it made Libby giggle. A minute later I was naked and standing beside the bed. "Tell me what you want, Lib."

She pushed the cover off of her and rubbed her right leg up and down her left. "I want you, slowly. I want to feel you inside me all morning, Luke."

Slipping a condom on, I moved over Libby and settled between her legs. One slow, agonizing push in and I was buried balls deep inside the love of my life.

I moved our bodies to where I was sitting and Libby's legs were wrapped around me. "Are you sore, Lib?"

She nodded her head as she leaned down and pulled my lower lip with her teeth. "This feels amazing though." She slowly began to move as our lips found each other. The moment Libby came, she moaned into my mouth and I fought like hell to hold off my orgasm. Laying her back onto the bed, she spread her legs and wrapped them around me as I placed my hands on the side of her face and began to cover her face in gentle kisses as I made love to her for the rest of the morning. I had never in my life felt so at peace, yet so on fire. I would forever fight for our love. Forever fight for Libby.

Chapter Seventeen

Libby

THE HOT WATER poured over my body and relaxed my over-worked, sore muscles. I moved slightly and smiled. I was sore, but it was an amazing sore. Luke's stamina was amazing. The way he made love to me this morning for so long was the most romantic thing I could have ever imagined. The way he took care into giving me as many orgasms as he could was a pleasant surprise.

I reached over and shut off the water. I couldn't wait to tell Alex about Luke and me. She should be coming back soon from her night with Will. Grabbing a towel, I began to dry off as I thought about last night with Luke. My fingertips moved up to my lips, still swollen from Luke's kisses. I smiled as my hand traveled down my body to between my legs. I was sore as hell, but my body was so ready to take more of him.

Quickly drying off and changing into a Mason high school T-shirt and jean shorts, I walked out into the bedroom only to come to a stop. My eyes moved across five girls sitting on both beds. All dressed in tank tops and shorts. Each of them had their hair piled up on their heads in some fashion.

Alex was glowing. I glanced down and saw the engagement ring on her finger and smiled. To Alex's left sat Grace and Lauren. Maegan and Taylor were sitting on the second bed. "Oh my gosh, Alex! Let me see your ring!" I exclaimed as I made my way over to her.

She smiled and held out her hand. "Your brother did good, Lib," Maegan said. Holding the ring up, I let out a whistle. Alex pulled her hand away and gave me a look.

"I hear you have news for me, Miss Hayes," Alex said.

I shrugged and began drying my hair. "Um, not much has really been going on. I do have a date to get ready for though. A romantic walk along the beach and I believe he mentioned something about a picnic."

Lauren began bouncing up and down on the bed. "I knew Luke Johnson was romantic! I knew it! All three of those boys are."

Maegan looked at Lauren. "All three? Do we know something about Colt we aren't saying?"

Lauren's face flushed. "No. I mean, look at our fathers. They're all so romantic. Of course the boys would all be helpless romantics."

Grace laughed. "My poor father fucks up more than any man I know. I don't think my mother would use the word romantic in the same sentence as my daddy's name."

We all laughed as I sat and looked at my best friends. We had all grown up together. We shared secrets, we fought, we cried on each other's shoulders, and most of all—we loved each other more than anything. We weren't really friends. We were sisters.

Taylor looked at me and said, "So. Tell us everything!"

Grace looked at me and said, "Please don't say something like he has a big dick and you rode him all night. I don't think my ears could take it."

My hand covered my mouth to contain my laughter as Alex turned and smacked Grace. "Ew. I didn't need that visual." Alex's body shuddered as she looked back at me.

I dropped my hand and let the laugh escape. They were all staring at me. "Y'all don't really expect me to kiss and tell do you?"

"Yes. Yes we do, Isabella Gemma Hayes," Maegan said as

she dropped to the ground and moved in front of the other girls, pulling her knees up like she was ready for a story.

"Um ..." I looked at them and felt my face flush. "It was beyond anything I could have imagined.

"Was he gentle?" Taylor asked.

I nodded my head. "Very."

Grace looked at Alex as they exchanged a smile.

"Was it ... better than ... you know, Zach?" Lauren asked.

Smirking, I asked, "Zach who?"

We all laughed. Maegan leaned closer to me. "Okay I have to ask, Lib. Is he packing?"

"Oh Jesus H. Christ! You did not, Maegan Atwood!" Grace shouted.

I threw my head back and laughed. Grace turned and looked at me and pointed. "Don't answer that." Holding up my hands I shook my head. I looked at Maegan and winked as she giggled and Grace yelled. "I saw that, Libby!"

Alex raised her hand. "Me next!" She cleared her throat. "Was he romantic?"

"Yes. Very."

"Oh God, I can't wait," Taylor said with a sigh. Maegan turned and looked at Taylor.

"Ah, the hell you can wait baby sister." Turning back to me, Maegan wiggled her eyebrows up and down. "How many times?"

I bit my lip. "Including this morning?"

Grace moaned and dropped back on the bed. Maegan nodded her head. I barely got the words out of my mouth. "Four times, not including, other stuff we did during the night."

"Kill. Me. Now. Please!" Grace whined.

"Holy hell," Alex and Maegan said as Lauren and Taylor both looked at me with horrified looks.

"How are you walking?" Lauren asked.

I looked away and chuckled. Letting out a breath, I turned back to the girls. Grace was sitting up smiling like a fool. She acted like it bothered her, but I knew she was happy for Luke and me.

I shook my head and looked down before looking back up. "I came so close to giving up, but I honestly couldn't imagine my life without Luke in it." I swallowed hard as I looked down at my hands as I ringed them on my lap. "Even when we were best friends, I knew there was something more to our relationship. The way he would look at me used to make my stomach just flutter."

Lauren's smile faded some and I knew she was thinking about Colt. I was positive he made her feel the same way. She just wouldn't admit it.

"Then yesterday on the beach, he looked at me again and this time I saw something different."

Five voices all whispered, "What was it?"

Smiling, I looked at Grace. "Love. Pure love." I let out a small chuckle. "Finally, his head wasn't arguing with his heart."

"Did he tell you he loved you?" Grace asked.

I nodded my head. "On the beach. He told me he's always loved me and only me."

Lauren let out a dramatic sigh. "How romantic."

Maegan shook her head. "Four times. My God."

My cheeks burned with embarrassment. "Does it always stay this magical, Alex?"

Alex's eyes lit up. "Believe it or not, it keeps getting better. If you think his touch does crazy things to you now, just wait. The more you're together and learn each other, the more beautiful it becomes."

We all sat there for a few moments in silence before Grace jumped up and said, "Okay, well now I feel like I need to go for a run. I'm outta here y'all."

Alex jumped up and followed Grace out of the room calling out, "What? You said we were going shopping!"

Maegan stood and walked over to me. She leaned down and kissed my forehead. "I'm so happy for you both, I hope you know that."

I reached for her hand and nodded. "I do, Meg. I love you."

She smiled weakly. "I love you too, Lib." Turning, Maegan

made her way out of the room. Taylor and Lauren both stood up and walked closer to me. They dropped to their knees and I knew the questions were fixin' to come.

Lauren bit down on her lip and then asked, "Do you regret sleeping with Zach?"

I nodded my head. "Yes. I knew he wasn't the one and I used him to try and push Luke from my heart. It doesn't work like that and my mother even tried to warn me."

Taylor reached for my hand. "I want so badly to find what you and Alex have."

I placed my hand over her hand in mine. "Oh, Tay, it will happen, honey. Don't rush it. Wait for that one guy who's smile is going to light your whole body on fire."

"How do you know? I mean, how do you know when it's love?" Lauren asked.

I glanced back at Lauren. "I don't know how to describe it. Love seems to take its own sweet time. It doesn't take a straight path. It twists and turns, but somehow it finds its way to you. You have to learn to listen to your heart, but that's harder to do than it sounds."

"There were times when it seemed like you and Luke couldn't stand each other. How do you go from that to—this?" Lauren asked.

"I don't know, Lauren. Luke had made me so mad sometimes I wanted to spit in his face and kick him in the balls." I smiled and shook my head. "But then he'd smile at me—or look at me as if I was his everything, even when he wasn't trying to look at me like that he did. I guess that's why I waited for so long."

Taylor cleared her throat. "I'm going to be patient and wait for him. I'm going to wait for that smile that makes my knees weak and my stomach flutter with excitement."

"Do, Taylor. I promise you, it will be worth the wait."

LUKE AND I walked along the beach and talked about everything. We found a spot where there weren't many people. I turned and saw a huge mansion. "Um, I think this is a private beach, Luke."

We both looked around. There was no one around us. "Where is everyone? How far did we walk?"

I giggled and shrugged. "I'm not sure. I guess I was too lost in the conversation."

Luke scrunched up his nose and smiled. My heart dropped. It seems my heart was doing that a lot the last twenty-four hours. I watched as Luke placed the blanket down and then set the basket down. He took my hand and held it while I sat.

Luke opened the basket and took out two bottles of root beer and set them on the blanket. Placing two plastic plates down, Luke smiled. He opened a container and placed a croissant sandwich on each plate.

"It's chicken salad on a croissant. I know how much you love chicken salad."

Yep. There went my heart again. Dropping down to my stomach.

Reaching into the basket he took out two brownies and set them on the plates. "Where in the world did you get those?" I asked. Luke looked up at me and gave me the same smile I had been talking to Lauren and Taylor about early.

"Colt made them earlier and I stole them!" Luke said with a laugh.

I picked up the chicken salad sandwich and asked, "The sandwich?"

"I made them. My mom showed me a few years back when I found out they were your favorite."

Oh wow. Butterflies galore in my stomach.

"That is the sweetest thing I've ever heard, Luke," I whispered as I leaned over and kissed him on the lips.

The moment the chicken salad hit my taste buds I moaned. "Oh God. It's your mom's secret recipe!"

Luke nodded his head as he chuckled. "Mom said her recipe was your favorite." Nodding my head, I agreed.

Saving You

Luke's smile dropped as he looked out over the water. "Lib, I wanted to talk to you about something."

My heart began beating faster. *What if he regretted what happened? What if he wanted to take a step back?*

"O—okay," my voice sounded weak and that made me angry.

He glanced back at me and said, "I want to tell you what happened after I left to go to A&M."

Oh shit.

I had laid in bed and thought about why Luke had brushed me off for hours those first few months. Now I was going to get the answers I had longed for. I wasn't sure it really mattered anymore.

Chapter Eighteen

Luke

LIBBY BEGAN CHEWING on her index nail. Her eyes searched my face. It was as if she was debating whether she wanted to hear my reason for hurting her after that kiss. I cleared my throat and smiled weakly.

"Our friendship, Libby, has always meant so much to me. You were my best friend. You still are."

Libby gave me the sweetest grin.

"Will had said something to me not long after we shared that kiss under the bleachers. I was so confused about my feelings. I knew for a while my feelings for you ran much deeper than our friendship. That kiss brought it all up to the surface."

Nodding her head, Libby whispered, "Yes, it did."

"My head started playing games. I started questioning if the kiss was a mistake. I wondered if you had thought the same thing. What if we started dating and it didn't work—we would lose our friendship and that was the last thing I'd ever want."

Libby took my hand in hers.

"Once I got to A&M, things were so different. Will's words kept repeating in my mind. I couldn't stop thinking of what an ass I was for kissing you and then leaving. That's when I met Karen. It was only a few days after I got to school."

Libby sucked in a small breath. I looked away. "I thought I could push the kiss from my heart—with Karen."

"The girl from the Italian place?" Libby asked.

I nodded my head. "Yeah, but we were only together for a bit and then broke up."

Libby's eyes looked sad. "Was she—your first?"

Nodding my head I whispered, "Yeah. I went pretty far with Claire Montgomery once in high school, but not all the way. I kept thinking about—"

"Thinking about what?"

Looking into Libby's eyes, I attempted a smile. "You. It's always been about you, Lib. Even that night with Karen, you filled my mind and I tried so fucking hard not to think about you."

Swallowing, Libby looked away. "Abigail?"

"My poor attempt to push you out of my heart. I swear to you I haven't seen or talked to Abigail in I don't know how long. She was lying to you when she said we were together again, Lib. I swear to God."

Her eyes snapped back to mine as I searched them. I saw nothing but trust. Trust *and* love. "I believe you. I hate that she played a part in pushing me to Zach." Shutting her eyes she shook her head. "Luke, we've both wasted so much time and have done such stupid things. I don't want to waste any more time on the past. I want to focus on the future."

Pulling my head back, I looked at Libby with a surprised expression on my face. "Lib, you don't hate me? I mean I hurt you so many times."

Libby frowned. "I want to be honest with you too, Luke. Two nights ago Zach sent me a text. I was confused and not sure where things were going with us, so I sent him a text back. I told him I'd call him yesterday, but I knew Zach wasn't who I wanted. He was never who I wanted. It's always been you." She glanced down. "That day you showed up at my dorm." Shaking her head, she wiped a tear away. She slowly looked back up and our eyes met. "I'd give anything to take that back, Luke. Anything."

I lifted her hand to my lips. The sounds of the ocean rolling onto the shore made my heart take flight. Libby's eyes danced with regret. I never wanted to see that in her eyes again. "I'm going to love you so much, Libby, that you will forget that day with Zach. I'm going to make your body feel so incredible that you'll only know and remember my touch."

Wiping a tear away, Libby smiled. "You already made me forget him the moment you told me you loved me."

My heart dropped as I gazed into Libby's eyes.

Grinning bigger, Libby said, "As much as I love your mom's chicken salad, I'd much rather have you."

I glanced around. The beach was fairly empty, but it was still the middle of the afternoon. Looking over Libby's shoulder, I noticed the house. There was a deck and under the deck it appeared to be storage. The shutters were shut and locked, indicating that no one was occupying the house.

Standing up quickly, I reached for Libby's hands and pulled her up. I picked her up and threw her over my shoulder as she let out a scream. "Where in the world are you taking me?" She asked as she pushed herself up with her hands on my back.

"I want you, Lib. Now."

Giggling she said, "What? Now? Where, Luke? People are walking down the beach!"

I walked to the house and set Libby down. "Oh my God. We're trespassing, Luke."

I pulled her behind the wood trellis that separated us from the ocean and quickly pulled her shirt up and over her head. Her black bikini top was pushing up her perfect tits. "Fuck," I hissed through my teeth as I pushed her top up and began sucking on a nipple.

"Oh God," Libby gasped as her hands went to my hair and began pulling.

I reached down and pulled out a condom from my pocket. I pulled my lips from Libby's nipple and handed her the condom. "Take it, Lib."

Her hands were shaking as she reached out and took the condom. I wasn't sure if she was excited or nervous. Dropping down, I slowly began to pull Libby's shorts down. Her matching black bikini bottoms quickly followed her shorts. She lifted her legs out of her shorts and bikini bottoms and stood there as I moved my hands up and down her perfect legs. They were muscular from running and sexy as fuck. I pushed her legs apart and lifted a leg.

"Ahh ..." Libby called out as I swept my tongue over her hardened nub. I pushed two fingers inside of her and moaned with how wet she was. I moved my fingers in and out a few times and then stood up as I placed the fingers in my mouth and sucked on them. Libby's mouth parted open slightly as her eyes widened.

"You taste so good, Lib."

She bit down on her lip and closed her eyes quickly before opening them again.

"Lib, I always want you to know how much I love and adore your body." She nodded her head. "I never want to hurt you, so you have to promise me you'll always tell me if I do. Do you promise me, Lib?"

Nodding again, she held up the condom and smiled. "I promise you, Luke."

I quickly pushed my shorts down and kicked them off to the side, releasing my throbbing dick. I took the condom and rolled it over my shaft. I glanced up and saw Libby watching me as she ran her tongue along her bottom lip.

"What do you want, Libby?"

Snapping her eyes to mine, they danced with excitement. She chewed on her lip for a few seconds before her eyes changed. Excitement was replaced with lust. "I want you to fuck me, Luke. I want to feel what being with you in nothing but raw passion is like."

Swallowing hard and trying to keep my dick from exploding with Libby talking to me like that, I lifted her up as she wrapped her legs around me. I slowly sank her onto my dick. Inch by painfully slow inch.

She pressed her lips to mine as she panted out. "More. I want more."

When I was all the way in, we stood there for a few seconds.

I wanted to be buried inside her always. Our bodies felt connected. Each time with Libby it was more emotional than the last.

"Luke, you feel like heaven," Libby whispered against my lips.

"God, Lib. So do you, baby. I wish we could be like this forever." I pushed her against the house and pulled out of her a bit before moving back into her.

She let out a gasp and I looked into her eyes. "Promise me, Lib."

She frantically nodded her head. "I will! I will! More, Luke. I want it harder—faster. I want to feel that you were in my body with every step I take."

I gave her exactly what she wanted. With each pull out, I slammed back into her. Libby's moans of pleasure were hot as hell. Libby looked down and bit her lower lip. "Oh God ... Oh God ... that's so hot." I knew she could see my dick moving in and out of her body and I was so turned on I wanted to let go. "Libby, baby I need you to come."

Her eyes looked into mine. "I love you, Luke."

Pulling out almost all the way, I pushed back into her hard. She threw her head back and began calling out my name as I felt my own release explode. I lifted her and gently pulled out as I set her back down onto the sand.

Our breathing was out of control as Libby leaned against the wall with my arms on either side of her head as I attempted to catch my breath.

Libby finally smiled the most beautiful smile I'd ever seen. "That. Was. Amazing."

I laughed and nodded my head. "Sure as hell was."

"I want more."

My smiled faded as I stared at her. "W—what?"

She nodded her head and wrapped her arms around my neck. "Last night and this morning was more than I could have ever dreamed of. This though—this was beyond amazing. This was sexy as hell and I want to do this as much as we possibly can."

I let out the breath I was holding and smiled. Thank God she wasn't meaning she wanted to be fucked again, because my guy was exhausted from last night, this morning and our little fuck fest just now.

"I'm pretty damn sure I can arrange for a lot more fucking time in between the lovemaking."

Libby kissed my lips and quickly pulled them away. "I'm starving now!"

Libby and I quickly got dressed. Reaching down, I picked her up and carried her back out to our picnic. We spent the next hour eating, talking, laughing, and discussing the future—our future. Together.

THE COLD WATER ran over my head, causing me to let out a moan with the relief it provided from the heat. "Damn it's so hot out," I said as I wiped the sweat from my forehead.

"Welcome back home, son. One week at the beach and you turned into a pussy."

I turned and looked at my father and shook my head. "Pussy? I'm out here, aren't I? Where the hell are Colt and Will?"

My father shrugged his shoulders as he laughed. "I told them to take the day off."

My mouth dropped open. "What? Why in the hell would you do that?"

Looking over at me, my father winked. "I wanted to talk to you."

Hell. This wasn't going to be good.

Walking over toward him, I picked up the fence pullers. "About what?"

He grabbed the wire cutters. "Libby."

I stopped moving. I watched as my father went about his work as if nothing he just said should cause me to worry. He told Colt and Will to take the day off. He had me out here working in the damn heat of the day. He wants to talk about Libby. I began spinning around, looking for Josh. *Was Josh here?*

"What in the hell are you doing? What are you looking for?"

I spun around and looked at my father. "Is Josh here?"

My father lifted his eyebrow. "Should he be here, Son?"

I stared at my father. "Um, is that a trick question, Dad?" I looked around again before looking back at my father. Rolling his eyes, my father mumbled something under his breath. He threw down his wire cutters and walked over to the back of his truck. He opened the cooler and pulled out two beers. Tossing one to me, he motioned for me to sit down.

Beer. Alone time with my dad. Something was fixin' to go down.

"Dad, just come out and say it."

He popped open the beer and took a drink. "Tell me about you and Libby."

Walking over, I jumped and sat next to him on the tailgate. I couldn't help but smile. "Ah hell, Luke. I've seen that goofy-ass smile before."

Turning, I looked at him with a questioning look. He threw his head back and laughed. "I've seen it on my own face." Nodding, I tipped the beer back against my lips. "It sure took y'all enough time to get together."

My smile faded. "Yeah, that would be my fault."

Raising his eyebrows my father asked, "How so?"

I shook my head. "Where should I start? I was afraid of my feelings for Libby, so I acted like an asshole. I pushed her away and into the arms of another guy. I hurt her more times than I care to think about." Glancing at my father I asked, "Should I keep going?"

He smiled and let out a throaty laugh. "Apple doesn't fall far from the tree, that's for sure."

I chuckled. "I'm going to take that as a good sign though. Seeing how happy you and Mom are, Lib and I would be lucky to have a love like yours."

My father smiled and his eyes sparkled. Anytime I mentioned my mother to him, his eyes lit up. "May I offer you some advice?"

"Yes, always, Dad."

He took another drink of his beer and looked straight ahead as if he was recollecting something.

He inhaled a breath and slowly blew it out. "No matter how bad things seem to be, never give up on your love. Fight for it with all you've got, Luke. There were times your mother had me wanting to pull my hair out—many, many times."

I laughed as I took another drink of my beer. "I feel a 'but' coming."

Nodding his head, my father said, "Your mother saved me, Luke. I tell her all the time if it hadn't been for her love, I'm not sure what I would have done. Life without her is not an option."

Looking straight ahead, I let his words sink in. "I feel the same way about Libby. I think I've been in love with her for so long, the idea of actually doing something about it scared the hell out of me. I kept thinking if it didn't work out I'd not only being losing the love of my life, but I'd be losing my best friend as well."

Laughing my father shook his head. "It's like I'm listening to my younger self." Turning, he looked at me with a serious look. "Do everything in your power, Son, to never hurt her again."

Swallowing hard, I nodded my head. "Yes, sir."

He nodded his head and looked away. "I know you won't, because if I don't kick your ass first, I know Josh will."

I let out a nervous laugh. "Yeah, for some reason Josh scares the piss out of me now." My father threw his head back and laughed his ass off. "Trust me, someday, when you have a daughter, you'll understand."

My heart dropped to my stomach. I had never thought about kids before. *Ever.* That was the last thing on my mind. The idea of having a baby with Libby filled my heart with excitement. I smiled as I pictured Libby pregnant.

My father jumped off the tailgate and pointed at me. "No. Stop it right now, Luke Johnson. Right now."

I held up my hands in surrender. "Stop what?"

He kept pointing. "Don't you even picture it in your mind. I know what you're doing. I'm too young to be a grandfather and you have two more years of school."

My mouth dropped open. *How did he know what I was thinking?* Then I decided it was time to play with good ole Dad. I smiled when I looked at his shirt. My mother would flip if she saw it.

Lick it like a lollipop.

I chuckled inside. I got my love of crazy shirts from my father, that is for sure. I put on a serious face and dragged my hands down my face. "Sorry, Dad. It's just, it's gonna happen."

My father took a step back. Horror washed over his face. "I'm going to kill you, Luke Drew Johnson, if you say what I think you're fixin' to say."

I shrugged my shoulders. "The passion between us is too strong."

His mouth dropped open. "What the hell does that mean?"

Looking down, I kicked a rock. "We didn't want anything between us, Dad and well, I'm afraid you and Mom are gonna be a memaw and pappy sooner than you thought."

The beer dropped from his hand and he let out a gasp.

"W—what? Why in the hell would you think I'd want to be called—Pappy? I mean, Pappy?" I stood there shocked. He was more worried about the name Pappy than the possibility of Libby being pregnant.

I smiled as I walked over and placed my hand on his shoulder. "Yeah, you just look like a Pappy, Dad." He pushed my hand off his shoulder and turned and walked away. He was mumbling something, but I was trying too hard not to laugh so I couldn't hear what he was saying. I pulled out my phone and sent Libby a text.

Me: *Do you love me?*

Libby: *More than anything.*

Me: *Do you trust me?*

Libby: *With my life.*

Me: *Text my dad and say, Hey Pappy, what's up?*

Libby: *Okay … why?*

Me: *I told him you were pregnant and we are calling him Pappy!*

Libby: *What? HAHA! OKAY doing it now!*

Spinning around, my dad pointed to me. I slowly dropped my phone to my side. "Your mother and I taught you better. Always, always wrap your stick!" He pushed his hands through his hair as he let out a moan.

"I'm not going to be able to keep Josh from killing you. You know this, right?" He dropped his head back and looked up at the sky as he lifted his fist. "Why a boy? You did this to pay me back, didn't you?"

I looked up and laughed. "Yep, it's a blessing indeed."

"You think this is funny? Luke, you're going to start your life out struggling. And what about Libby?" His phone went off in his pocket and he pulled it out. The face he made caused me to smile bigger.

"What the fuck?" His head jerked up as his mouth dropped open.

"What's wrong?" I asked. He started walking toward his truck shaking his head. He turned and looked at me.

"Luke, you have to know that y'all are too young to be having a baby. I'm too young to be called Pappy, and Josh is going to kick your ass." He turned and showed me the text from Libby.

Libby: *Hey Pappy! How is your day going?"*

God I love her. Libby always went along with my pranks. No matter what the outcome was, she was always in. One hundred percent.

"Dad, it's a joke."

He began running his hands through his hair. "Oh God, Josh is gonna kill me. He's not only going to beat the shit out you, he's gonna beat the shit out of me."

I walked up to him and put my hands on his shoulders. "Dad, look at me. It's a joke. Libby's not pregnant; I've always wrapped the stick and always will." I frowned and made a face. "Well, I guess I won't always, but—"

Anger washed over my father's face. "Luke Drew Johnson. I ought to kick your ass now for doing that to me."

I laughed as he pushed me away. "Little bastard, you scared the hell out of me." Placing his hand on his heart he looked up and mouthed, *Thank you.*

Chapter Nineteen

Libby

I SAT ON the porch of Gram's house as I listened to my mother, Alex's mom, Ellie, and Grams, talk about life. Listening to them always made my heart soar. I glanced over and looked at Grams. She was talking about Gramps. Grams and Gramps were Alex and Colt's great-grandparents, but it felt like they were all of our grandparents. I can't even begin to count the number of times we have all sought them each out for advice.

"Garrett intends on taking me to Florida. Why in the world would I want to go to Florida? That man is crazy if he thinks he is dragging me away from my garden for two whole weeks."

I smiled as I glanced over to Alex. She was rocking away as she focused on the women surrounding us. She looked over to me and smiled as she shook her head.

"Grams, you'd have a lovely time in Florida," my mother said with a sweet smile.

Grams shook her head. "Heather darling, have you ever been on a plane with Garrett?"

Smiling, my mother shook her head. "No, I can't say I have, Emma."

Ellie started giggling. "Emma, tell them about the time Garrett passed out on the plane." Alex quickly turned and looked at her mother. "What? Gramps passed out on a plane?"

Grams slowly nodded her head and was about to say something when Gramps cleared his throat. I turned around to see, Gramps, Alex's dad Gunner, my father, Luke, Will, and Colt all walking up from the main barn.

"Why good afternoon, gentlemen," Grams said with a smile. "What a fine group of handsome men we have here. Isn't that right, ladies?"

Smiling, I looked each of them over. Good lord. It should be sinful to have six good-looking men all standing together like this. Gramps held his own with his blue eyes and gray hair. Gunner was beyond breathtaking and Colt was a mini version of Gunner. Except Colt had that ever present five o'clock shadow that fit him perfectly. Will was the spitting image of my father, handsome as hell. He smiled as he looked adoringly at Alex. My father smiled and winked at my mother, causing me to turn and look at her. When her face flushed I looked away. Their love affair, as she called it, seemed more on fire than ever before. Will and I had walked in on them last night in the kitchen. Of course they were just kissing, but Will declared to have the image burned forever in his memory.

Glancing back, my eyes locked onto the most beautiful green eyes. My heart fluttered and it felt as if the energy in the air changed. Luke was staring at me with the most breathtaking smile I'd ever seen. In less than a week, we'd all be heading back to school and the idea of living in the same house, waking up every morning wrapped in his arms, thrilled me beyond belief.

"Libby? Hello? Libby, darling are you even listening to me?"

I shook my head and turned to Ellie. "I'm sorry, Ellie. I was, um, lost in thought."

She smiled sweetly and then continued on. "We've made plans to have dinner with all of you before you leave. Tomorrow night, seven sharp at your parents' house. There are some—things we'd like to discuss with all of y'all. The idea of us buying the house in College Station was a good idea, but now that two of y'all are couples. We'd like to go over some ground rules."

I nodded my head and peeked over to Alex. Her face was flushed and she looked down. This wasn't going to be fun. It was sure to be awkward as hell. Gunner cleared his throat. "We've already chatted with the boys."

Luke let out a deep laugh. "Chatted? I wouldn't necessarily say threatening to end our lives is chatting." Alex stood up. "Daddy, you didn't!"

Gunner smiled. "Oh yes, I did. Two boys, four girls, all under one roof, what the hell were we thinking?"

My mother stood up, leaned down and kissed Grams on the cheek and then turned toward the guys. "We were thinking that they are all adults, we raised them right and that Will, Luke, and Colt will do nothing but always respect and protect our girls."

Gunner and my father both turned and looked at Luke. Daddy raised his eyebrow at Luke. "That was before Luke started dating my baby girl."

My mother slapped my father lightly on the chest. "Stop it. Come on, let's head on back. I've got a roast in the crock pot." Ellie kissed Colt on the cheek. "Don't be out too late; you leave to go back to A&M tomorrow."

Colt returned a gentle kiss on Ellie's face. He had to report to A&M a few weeks ago for football, but was home for a few days.

Taking my hand in his, Luke pulled me to him. "Want to go for a ride? I can saddle up a few horses." I nodded my head and smiled. I loved spending time with Luke. It was nothing like when we were best friends. It was a million times better.

"Gramps, Lib and I are going to take a couple horses for a ride," Luke shouted for Gramps to hear. Raising his hand, Gramps called out, "Have fun!"

Luke and I quickly walked to the barn and saddled up two horses and made our way onto one of the many trails that ran over the ranch. Since we were little kids we had been riding all over this property.

When we got a good ways away from the house, I looked at Luke. "So how horrible was my father to you?"

Luke looked over my way and gave me that naughty smile of his. "Let's see, he told me if I hurt you, got you pregnant, made your grades slip, slept in the same room as you, got you pregnant—"

I giggled. "You said that twice."

"Only because he said it like six times. After of course, he gave me the lecture about always using protection, making sure my number one goal was keeping you safe."

My eyes widened in horror. "Please tell me you're kidding?"

Luke pursed his lips and looked up. "Nope. I had to sit there with your brother on one side of me, who by the way, has also threatened to cut off my balls if I hurt you in any way. Yeah, with Will glaring at me from the side, your daddy came full force. Right out of the gate, he was telling me how he could kill me and make it look like an accident."

I covered my mouth, stopped my horse, and let out a moan. "Oh, Luke, I'm so sorry."

He stopped his horse and looked deep into my eyes. "I'm not, Libby. It just shows how much they love you. If Grace was to bring a guy home tomorrow, I'd take him out to the barn and show him how accurate of a shot I am. I have no problem spending the rest of my life in jail for having to shoot someone for hurting my sister. Or you."

Smiling, I glanced away. Sometimes Luke's eyes looked so deep into my soul it scared me. I heard him getting off of his horse. Looking back I asked, "What are you doing?"

Luke tied up the reins and let Starlight graze. "I want to kiss you."

I threw my leg over the saddle and jumped down. "Really? I'll take that kiss."

Luke reached up with his hands and cupped my face as he brought his lips to mine. He placed quick, soft kisses to my lips. "I love you, Libby. I love you so much."

The kiss grew deeper as he pushed me against Bear. The horse didn't budge. He stood steadfast in his spot. Luke's hand went under my shirt and pushed my bra up, finding my nipple. He began twisting and pulling it gently as he practically kissed my breath away. "Luke," I whispered as my hands went to his beautiful brown hair. I tugged on it as Luke let out a moan. "I want you, Luke."

His lips moved from my lips, down to my neck. My body was on fire, my core clenching with the idea of Luke filling my body to the max.

"Libby," Luke panted as he moved his hand from my nipple down. He was about to slip his hand into my pants when Bear took a few steps and caused us to lose our balance. I fell and Luke landed on top of me. I lifted my hips and pressed his hard dick between my legs. I was breathless. All those years of built up desire seemed to explode when we were near each other.

"Libby, I can't seem to get enough of you," Luke whispered against my lips.

"Get off of her, Luke. And for Pete's sake, help the poor girl up."

Luke pulled his lips from mine as we turned and looked up. Jeff and Ari were both perched up on horses. Ari was smiling as she looked down at Luke and me. I felt the heat move across my face as Luke's hard dick was still pressed against me.

"Nothing like your parents riding up on horseback to kill the mood," Luke said as he got up and held out his hand to help me up.

I started wiping grass off myself when Jeff laughed. "Jesus, I swear I'm looking at you and me, Ari."

Ari giggled. "I was just thinking the same thing."

I bit my lip and looked away. Jeff and Ari were like second parents to me. I was internally fist pumping Luke and I hadn't made it any further than kissing.

Ari jumped off her horse and walked over to me. She held out her arm and I accepted it as she began walking me away from Luke and Jeff.

"Wow, what we rode up on was some pretty hot and heavy kissing."

Smiling, I looked down at the ground. "Yeah."

"I have to tell you, Libby. I don't think I've ever seen my son walking on cloud nine like he has ever since y'all came back from the beach. I've never seen him so happy."

My eyes snapped over to Ari. "Really?" I asked.

She chuckled. "Really. I've also never seen such a glow on your face."

My heart stopped. *The practical joke. Oh Shit. Did Luke ever tell Jeff he was kidding?*

"I'm not pregnant, Ari. I swear. It was a joke Luke wanted to play on Jeff and I went along with it. I swear to you that we always use protection when we have sex." My hand went up to my mouth as I gasped. "Oh God. I just told you we have sex all the time."

The corner of Ari's mouth rose. "You didn't say *all* the time."

I moaned. "Um ... well no it's not like we're having sex *all the time.*" I giggled nervously. "Just whenever we can make it happen and—" *Oh God shut up, Libby. Stop talking.*

I stopped walking and placed my hands on my knees as I bent over and inhaled a deep breath. "Where is the closest rock?"

Ari leaned over and looked up at me. "Libby, take a deep breath and stand back up, sweetheart."

I did as she said. "Ari, I'm so sorry I didn't mean to say all that. It's just. Well, to be honest with you, sometimes this just feels like a dream." I wrapped my arms around myself as I thought about the last few weeks with Luke. The romantic picnics, the passionate lovemaking in the bed of his truck, the long walks along the river just talking. "I never thought in my wildest dreams love would be so, amazing!"

Ari chuckled. "It is pretty amazing, isn't it?" Ari motioned for me to sit down on a rock next to her.

"To be in love with your best friend, and to share such—" I looked over at Luke's mother and blushed.

She smiled and said, "Go on."

"Well, to share such passionate moments with him where he just sweeps me off my feet. I don't want it to ever end. Please tell me it never stops being this way."

Ari pulled back and made a funny face. "My son sweeps you

140

off your feet, huh?"

Smiling, I nodded my head. "All the time."

"Really? He must have learned that from me!"

We both giggled as Ari took my hand. "It never ends, darling. Sure, that new love phase wears off, but the key is to keep it alive. Even after all these years when, Jeff walks up behind me and wraps his arms around me, my stomach just drops."

I sighed as I listened to Ari talk about her and Jeff's love. "And the smile. Oh lord, Jeff has this smile that I swear about drops me to my knees."

"Yes! Luke does, too. I feel butterflies when he smiles at me like that. It's like I'm his ..."

"Everything."

Ari and I both threw our heads back and laughed when we spoke at the same time.

When we finally stopped laughing, I took in a deep breath. "May I ask you something, Ari?"

Ari looked into my eyes with nothing but love. "Of course, Libby. I'm always here for you, sweetheart."

I began chewing on my lower lip. "Did you ever feel scared? What I mean is, by your love for Jeff. Did it ever scare you? I love Luke so much it scares me. I keep wondering if the floor is going to fall out from underneath me or if he is going to change his mind and leave me. I've tried to push these stupid feelings away but the thought of losing him—I don't think I could stand a day in this world without him."

Ari looked away quickly and then slowly turned back to me. Her eyes were filled with tears. She wiped a tear away and squeezed my hand. "First off, Luke is one lucky son-of-a-bitch to have a woman like you love him."

I felt the tears building in my eyes as Ari smiled at me. "Yes, Libby. I was scared to death and I still am. There are days that Jeff will be gone and I won't see him and I feel like I will burst if I'm not in his arms soon. It doesn't have to be sexual, Libby. It's about sitting next to a fire while he holds you in his arms and talks about his day. When you walk into a room and he looks at you and his smile lights up like his whole day just got brighter. His unexpected touch ignites your body on fire and all you want is for him to kiss you like it's your last kiss. The feeling of him making love to you and you're so overcome with love that it brings you to tears."

I felt my tears rolling down my face. "Yes," I whispered.

"Love is a crazy emotion, Libby. Hang on, baby girl." Ari chuckled. "Hang on for dear life!"

142

Chapter Twenty

Luke

I SET THE last box down in Grace's room and collapsed onto her bed. "Holy hell, Grace. Did you bring everything you own?"

Giggling she fell onto the bed next to me. "I thought about it, but decided not to."

I smiled at my baby sister. "Are you happy, Sweet Pea?" Her smile faded but she quickly plastered on a fake one. "Of course I am, Luke. I'm glad we are here together. I hated UT with a passion. I think I'm really going to like A&M."

Nodding my head I said, "I think you will. Plus, I can keep my eye on you."

She reached over and slapped my arm. "I'm a big girl you know. The cherry was popped a few years back." Grace jumped up and headed toward her closet.

I sat up and balled my fists. "You know, Grace, you can't say shit like that to me. It makes me want to kill someone."

She looked over her shoulder and winked. "You know what I think is funny?"

I shrugged my shoulders. "What?"

"That Alex moved most of her stuff in here, and Libby moved most of her stuff in Lauren's room, yet they have no intention of ever staying in their rooms." Grace used air quotes around the word rooms.

I smiled. "We'll try to keep it down for you since my room

143

is right next to yours."

Grace's mouth dropped open as she stared at me while I backed out of the room with a smile on my face. "I hate you, Luke Johnson. I hate that you just put that in my head!"

I turned and headed back downstairs to help Lauren with her stuff. I thought back to the night our parents all sat down and talked to us about our living arrangements.

WE ALL LOOKED at each other as our parents sat across from us. Gunner and Ellie were holding hands. Josh and Heather were sitting on the sofa with Heather snuggled into Josh's side. My father and mother were sitting on the love seat. Dad's arm was wrapped around my mother and they both oozed love.

Gunner spoke first. "Since Colt is going to be in the dorms because he's playing football, we have decided to go ahead and just stick with the one house. Will, Luke, y'all will still have your rooms and the girls have decided to bunk up together."

Heather spoke next. "Libby and Lauren are bunking together and Alex and Grace will be in the fourth bedroom."

Josh was staring at me, kind of like how Gunner was staring at Will. I swallowed hard. Surely they had to know that was not how this was going to play out.

Josh cleared his throat. "One thing y'all need to know is we're not stupid. Will, Alex you're engaged." Turning, Josh looked at Libby and then me. Libby squeezed my hand tighter. "Luke, Libby—you're dating each other and I get that. Just know if anything happens, Luke, I will hunt you down and hurt you."

I SHUDDERED JUST thinking about the look in Josh's eyes. Lauren walked up and handed me a box. "Here ya go!" She turned and skipped back to her car. I smiled as I turned and headed back into the house. Alex was coming down the stairs when she stopped and smiled at me.

"Hey!" she said with a smile.

She looked beyond happy. "Hey there, little cousin."

She had a worried look on her face as she looked over my shoulder. "Are you nervous about living with Libby?"

I tilted my head and looked at her. "No. Are you nervous about living with Will?"

She quickly nodded her head. "What if I snore? Or worse yet, fart in my sleep or something."

I busted out laughing. "Fart in your sleep? Holy hell, I was not expecting that comment, Alex." Rolling her eyes, she let out a sigh. "Alex, do you love Will?"

She smiled sweetly. "More than anything, Luke."

"I know for a fact he loves you more than anything. I also know that if you do happen to—fart in the middle of the night. He's still going to love you."

Alex wrapped her arms around me as I held Lauren's box to the side. "I love you, Luke Johnson. Take care of Libby."

"Oh, I intend to," I said with a smile.

"I AM SO full I think if I sneezed I'd bust open. I never want to eat pizza again!"

I laughed as I looked over at Libby sprawled out across my bed. My dick jumped at the idea of making love to Libby tonight. Finally, we were together. I couldn't wait to fall asleep every night with her in my arms and wake up every morning tangled up together.

Libby rolled onto her stomach and rested her chin on her hands. "You know what I'm most excited about?"

"What are you most excited about, baby?"

Wiggling her eyebrows up and down she purred, "Falling asleep wrapped up in your arms. Having your heartbeat lull me to sleep every night." She got up onto her hands and knees and slowly moved closer to me as she licked her lips. "Making love to you any ... time ... I ... want."

Letting out a moan, I stood and moved over to the bed. "Lib, you drive my body crazy do you know that?"

She smiled sweetly. "And you drive my body equally crazy."

I ran my hand through her blonde hair and gave it a tug back, exposing her neck to me. I ran my tongue along her neck as she let out a moan and whispered, "Luke."

Libby pulled back and looked at me, desire filling her eyes. "I want you so much, but I'm so full and I don't think I could move an inch."

Chuckling, I leaned over and kissed her lips. "Thank God. I'm so tired from moving all of y'alls boxes I could pass out right now."

Libby giggled. "I say we get naked, crawl under the covers, and get some sleep."

I took a step back and pulled my shirt over my head. "That sounds like a plan."

Libby and I stripped out of our clothes and crawled into bed. I was about to doze off when she jumped out of bed. The nice thing about this house was each bedroom had its own private bathroom. I watched as my naked girl made her way to the bathroom. "Where are you going, Lib?"

She called out from the other room, "I forgot to brush my teeth!"

Two minutes later she was running and jumping into the bed. Under the covers she went and threw her leg over me.

"I love you, Luke."

Kissing the top of her head, I held her closer. Everything about this moment was perfect. We didn't have to be making love to be connected. We just needed to be together. Libby, wrapped up in my arms was the most amazing thing in the world to me. My heart about burst with the amount of love I felt for this woman.

"I love you more, Lib."

Saving You

PICKING UP MY pace, I walked faster. Classes were done for the weekend, I wanted to get home, change into something warm, and feel Libby in my arms. The first few weeks of school kept everyone busy. We hardly ever saw Colt, but tonight was a home football game and we were having a small party at our house. It seemed like the only way we could get Colt to come over. He pretty much stayed away for fear of running into Lauren.

Opening the door, I walked into the house. Looking around I tossed my backpack onto the sofa and made my way into the kitchen. Grabbing an apple, I bit into it and headed for upstairs only to find Libby sleeping peacefully on the bed.

I couldn't control the wicked thoughts moving through my mind. We had the house to ourselves. I quickly got undressed and walked over to my side of the bed. Reaching into the drawer quietly, I pulled out a condom and set it on the side table. Libby's breathing alone caused my dick to harden within seconds.

She had on a tank top and pink lace boy shorts panties. I slowly moved on to the bed and began to slip her panties off. She mumbled something and rolled onto her back. *Perfect.*

I skillfully slipped her panties off without waking her up. Poor thing was exhausted. Alex and Grace spent most of last night trying to talk Libby into dropping one class. She took a full load and a few weeks in I could see the stress building.

I ran my hands softly up and down her legs, slowly pushing them open. Libby stirred. "Luke," she whispered. Smiling, I pushed her legs open more and began kissing the inside of her thigh. Libby had gotten waxed and her soft smooth lips were begging to be kissed.

I moved closer and Libby moaned. Spreading her lips open I dipped my tongue into her sweetness. Libby's body jerked and her hands grabbed my hair. "Oh God!" she called out. I peeked up at her and watched as her chest rose and fell with each breath. "Luke, you have no idea how much I need you."

147

Pushing two fingers inside her, I began working her as I moved my tongue to the hard bud. All it took was a few swipes of my tongue and Libby was moaning into her pillow. I could feel her pussy pulsing against my fingers as I worked her into another orgasm, this one must have been stronger because her whole body began to shake and she begged me to stop.

I covered her body in sweet kisses, making my way up her stomach to one nipple. I began sucking on one as my fingers twisted and pulled the other.

"Yes, feels so good," Libby whispered.

I looked up at her and smiled. "We're alone."

The naughty smile that spread across her face caused my dick to feel like it was going to explode. "Can we play?" she asked in the most innocent voice.

Jumping up, I reached into the side drawer. I had bought a vibrator for Libby, but hadn't showed it to her yet. I reached in and grabbed the blindfold and the ties. I held them up as Libby's lips parted and she let out a soft moan. "I'm going to tie up your hands baby, blindfold you and make you come so hard you'll be screaming."

Licking her lips she nodded her head slowly. Libby and I had fucked a few times, but I hadn't had a chance to really play with her and I couldn't wait.

"Lift your hands above your head, Libby."

She quickly lifted her hands above her head. "Wait, what if someone comes home?"

Glancing at the clock I smiled. "Nope, we've got about two hours before anyone gets here, thanks to you skipping your afternoon classes." I winked and she blushed.

"I was so tired, Luke. I had to come home and nap."

"No worries, baby." I tied up her hands and was about to put the blindfold on her when her eyes widened.

"What are you planning on doing to me?" she asked as her chest rose and fell with anticipation.

Placing the blindfold over her eyes, I whispered against her lips, "I'm going to rock your world, baby."

I stood and looked at Libby. Her body was beyond beautiful. I wanted to make her come over and over before I buried myself deep inside her.

Turning, I walked out of the bedroom. "Luke? Luke! Where are you going?" Libby called out.

"I need something from the kitchen," I said over my shoulder.

I couldn't help but laugh when I heard Libby say, "Oh holy hell."

I LAID ON the bed, my breathing became more and more erratic, as I wondered what Luke was going to do.

What in the hell did he need from the kitchen?

I pulled on the restraints and for one brief moment I began to panic. Then I heard Luke running back up the stairs. I giggled thinking about him running through the house naked. The door to the bedroom opened and my core immediately clenched as my body anticipated the pleasure that was about to happen.

The bed moved. He must have sat down. I jumped when I felt his tongue moving across my nipple. Oh God. *He is going to tease me, I know it.*

Then, I felt something cold against my nipple. Goose bumps covered my body and I let out a long moan as his hand moved down my stomach and between my legs. His lips grazed my neck as he whispered, "So wet. Are you ready for me, Libby?"

If I thought I was turned on before, I was beyond turned on now. My body felt as if it was on fire. The need to touch him, see what he was doing, was driving me crazy.

"Yes. Luke, so ready!"

The ice moved along my chest and made its way to my other nipple. I arched my back at the feeling.

"I love your body, Libby. I love how I can touch you and you instantly react with pleasure."

I thrashed my head back and forth. "Luke, please let me touch you. I have to touch you!"

He chuckled as he began kissing down my chest. He removed the ice and began sucking on my nipple as his fingers moved painfully slow in and out of my body.

"More! I want more, please, Luke."

His kisses moved down my body. "Yes," I hissed through my teeth. I loved when Luke went down on me. The orgasms were toe curling.

He stopped kissing me and positioned himself between my legs again. Then his mouth began its assault and I screamed out. The feel of his hot breath mixed with cold confused me at first, until I realized he had the ice cube in his mouth.

"Oh ..." I moaned out.

Then I felt nothing but cold. He was using the ice cube to play with me. The intense cold was both painful and pleasurable. "Luke, w—what are you..." I couldn't even form words in my mouth. I felt my orgasm beginning to build. "Yes! Yes! I'm so close to coming, oh dear God."

Then everything stopped. The cold was gone, his hot breath was gone, his fingers pulled from my body.

No! No, no, no, no!

My head thrashed back and forth in frustration. "Why did you stop? I was going to come. Luke!"

I could feel him moving around, but he wasn't saying anything to me. I wasn't sure if that turned me on, the not knowing what he was doing, or pissed me off.

Then, I felt him position himself across me. He was just above my chest. My breathing picked up as I felt him move his dick across my lips. Licking my lips in anticipation of taking him.

"Open your mouth and take me in, Libby."

I did what he said and moaned when I felt his hard dick fill my mouth. Something about this was hotter than hell and I could feel the pressure building again and he wasn't even touching me anywhere. He pulled out and pushed back in as I moaned.

"Motherfucker, this is so damn hot," Luke whispered as he moved in and out of my mouth. My tongue swirled around him, and as he pulled out, I sucked harder.

I wanted to watch. I wanted to see his face. Luke moaned as he fucked my mouth slowly. I moaned again and this time Luke took himself all the way out. "I don't want to come yet, Lib."

Panting I said, "I do!"

Moving off of me he got off of the bed. I pulled on the restraints. "Please tell me you're not going back down to the kitchen."

Laughing, he settled back onto the bed. "No baby, no more trips to the kitchen."

I felt something wet. He was pouring something on me, lubricant? I felt something rubbing against my sensitive nub. I stopped moving, trying to concentrate on what it was.

Oh my God. He has a vibrator. He's going to use a vibrator on me.

I pulled on the restraints as I attempted to get the blindfold off by moving my head around. My breathing was crazy erratic. I could hear my heart pounding in my ears.

"Something tells me you like vibrators, Lib."

"Luke, oh God stop teasing me."

"I like teasing you, Libby. I love watching your body react to all of this."

"Come, I need to come or I'm going to die!"

Laughing, Luke kissed my inner thigh, then turned on the vibrator, causing me to jump and arch my back.

"Yes! Please, Luke. Don't make me beg."

I couldn't believe how I sounded. I didn't care. I felt so wanton and I wanted to be fucked. At this point I didn't care if I was fucked by the vibrator or Luke, I needed to come.

Luke slowly began pushing the vibrator in a few inches and then he would pull it out. "Jesus, that looks good."

"Luke!"

Then again, this time he went a little bit deeper before he

pulled it out again. He repeated the process two more times. "Luke! Fuck me with it already!"

The vibrator was all the way in and Luke turned it on high. My back arched and my orgasm rushed through my body as he began to work the vibrator in and out.

I started calling out his name and then began mumbling incoherently. I had never experienced such an intense orgasm. My body was still trembling when Luke pulled the vibrator out. The sound of something tearing had my body working itself up again. I knew what the sound was. Luke was sheathing himself with a condom and my body would soon be filled with him.

"Luke, yes, I need you so badly. I want you."

He began teasing me with his tip. I lifted my hips to get more of him. "How much do you want me, Lib?"

I was starting to feel dizzy. My mind was racing as I thought about nothing but Luke pushing inside me. "I need you so bad."

He pushed a little ways in and then pulled back out. "How. Much. Do. You. Want. Me?"

I attempted to lift my body higher. "Gah! So much. So, so much! I can't take it any more. I have to have you inside me, now, Luke!"

He pushed in hard and fast, filling me completely. It was a mix of pleasure and pain.

Luke dropped his body on mine as he moaned and then pulled out. *Fuck! Not again!*

He reached up and pulled the blindfold off. It took me a few seconds to get my eyes adjusted to the light. He was looking down at me with lust filled eyes and my heart slammed against my chest. "Roll over onto your knees and hold onto the head-board, Libby."

I quickly moved, well, as quickly as I could with my hands still tied up. My arms were crossed as I held onto the head-board. My body shuddered as his hands moved across my ass. He pushed his finger against me and placed his lips against my skin. "I'm going to take you here someday, Libby."

Moaning I dropped my head. "You're trying to kill me."

Luke placed his hands on my hips, positioned himself at my entrance and asked, "How do you want it, Libby?"

Looking over my shoulder I smiled. "I want it all."

He pushed inside me in one movement, causing me to scream out and grab onto the headboard tighter.

"Ah, I'm so damn deep this way."

I pushed back against him. I needed him to move. He took the signal and gripped my hips tighter and began pulling out and slamming back into me. The feel and sound of his balls hitting me was beyond amazing. "Yes! Harder!" Sweat was beginning to cover our bodies as Luke gave me what I asked for.

Luke continued to thrust into me over and over until my orgasm hit me. I screamed out his name as I felt his dick grow bigger, pulsing with the need to release inside of me. Leaning over he grabbed my breasts and called out my name as we came together.

Luke's arms were wrapped around my body as my senses finally came back to reality. I didn't remember him pulling out of me, or untying my hands, or even laying down on the bed.

"Libby, every time we're together it's like the first time. You're so amazing."

Smiling, I ran my fingers lazily up and down his arm. "You're amazing. You take my body to ultimate pleasure and back. That was—incredible." My eyes felt heavy as I slowly let myself fall back asleep in the arms of the man I loved more than life itself.

GRACE AND I sat at the bar in the kitchen and looked out into the living room. Will and Luke had decided to throw a party, but for no particular reason other than to see Colt. I watched as Luke and Will talked to a few football players. Alex was standing next to Lauren as she drooled over the sophomore quarterback, Bruce. Colt was leaning against the doorjamb, talking to a few football players. I noticed he kept looking over to Lauren.

"Good lord, there is so much potential dick in this room; it makes my girly parts all excited."

I snapped my eyes back to Grace. "What? Potential dick?"

She nodded her head as her eyes scanned the room. "Yeah, look at some of these guys. I'd be willing to take a smaller dick just to be able to look at their handsome faces while we f—"

"Stop! Oh my gosh, Grace. When did you become a whore?"

She threw her head back and laughed. "Please, Libby. I have no intentions of hooking up with any of these guys, or any guy for that matter. But I can fantasize, can't I?"

I tilted my head and decided to try and approach the subject of Noah again. Alex and I tried to talk to Grace this past summer but she wouldn't talk about him at all. "Have you heard from Noah?"

Grace looked at me with a surprised look on her face. Her eyes looked sad for a brief moment before she frowned slightly. She looked back over the dance floor. "No."

"He hasn't tried to contact you after y'all hooked up over spring break?"

Grace turned her head and shook it. "Nope."

I had the feeling Grace wasn't being honest. "Weird, cause I ran into him a couple days ago."

Grace quickly looked back at me. "What? You ran into Noah? Where?"

I smiled slightly. "I was walking across campus and there he was. Walking straight toward me with that *drop my panties and take me on-the-spot* smile of his."

Grace narrowed her eyes at me. "You can't talk about another guy like that, not when you're with my brother."

I bumped her shoulder. "I believe those were your words when you came back from seeing him again this past summer when we were all at the beach."

Grace's mouth dropped open. "How did you know? Wait— you knew I met up with him again?"

"Not until you got toasted our last night at the beach and told me and Alex. You ran into him when you were running on the beach and he invited you back to his parents' house and y'all ..." I looked up like I was thinking. Looking back at Grace I smirked and said, "Y'all got all sweaty again."

Grace turned and looked straight ahead. "Noah asked me how you were. Said he has texted you a few times and hasn't heard back from you. Why are you ignoring him, Grace? You really acted like you liked him that night."

Still staring straight ahead Grace answered. "I was drunk." She looked into my eyes. "I'm not opening myself up to be hurt again, Libby."

I pulled back and saw the fear in Grace's eyes. "What is it about you Johnson kids? Grace, you'll never know unless you open up and let him in. He's a really nice guy and I think—"

Grace stood up. "Don't think, Libby. He was nothing but a good fuck. That's it and that's all he'll ever be. A guy like Noah Bennet does not want a girl like me."

I stood up. "What does that mean? A girl like you? You're amazing, Grace. You're beautiful, smart, and can get any damn guy you want."

Grace chuckled as she shook her head and looked away. "Not this time, Libby." I watched as Grace walked to the living room. Two guys were standing there talking. One was blond and the other had light-brown hair. He must have been a football player because he was built and had an amazing body. He pushed his hand through his hair as Grace walked up and held out her hand. She smiled and that was all it took—he was putty in her hands. Luke and Will had hired a DJ who was set up in the backyard. Grace took the guy's hand and began leading him outside.

I let out a sigh and closed my eyes. My arm tingled and I quickly opened my eyes to see Luke standing there. "Dance with me, Lib?"

Biting my lip, I nodded and placed my hand in his. We made our way through the living room, formal dining room, and then through the game room. When we walked out back I glanced around for Grace. She was wrapped up in the arms of the guy she walked out here with. "I Put a Spell On You" was playing and it was pretty clear Grace had indeed put a spell on the poor guy dancing with her.

Luke pulled me into his arms and began singing to me as I looked into his emerald-green eyes. Leaning down, Luke sucked in my lower lip with his teeth as I let out a moan. When his lips pressed against mine and our tongues danced together, I was lost. I soon forgot about Grace and Noah and focused only on the incredible urge to be lying in bed, wrapped in Luke's arms.

"I CANNOT BELIEVE I'm letting you talk me into this!" Libby whispered.

I laughed and glanced to her. "Why are you whispering? No one is home, Lib."

Libby shrugged her shoulders as she helped me put the clear plastic wrap over Grace's toilet. "I don't know."

Chuckling, I pulled the clear wrap tight. We stood back and looked at our work. Smiling, we looked at each other and gave a high five. I reached down and grabbed the wrap. We made our way out of the bedroom. "What time is Grace due home?" I asked as we made our way back downstairs.

Libby smiled. "Any minute! I didn't know it was so late."

We made our way into the kitchen and I was brought back to the time when Libby and I talked Will into trying to fly off the barn. It hadn't taken much convincing and we had Will believing if we attached homemade wings he would be able to soar in the sky and land softly to the ground.

One broken arm later, Libby and I were both grounded for a month. I would sneak out at night and take my bike over to her house. Climbing up to her window, we would sit on the roof of the porch for hours and talk.

Peeking over to Libby, I watched as she pulled out a watermelon and began cutting it up. Glancing up she smiled. "Want some watermelon?"

I nodded my head and sat down on one of the barstools we had at the kitchen island. "Do you remember the time we got grounded for talking Will into flying off the barn?"

Libby's eyes met mine. She smiled so big it caused me to laugh. "I remember the time you talked *me* into talking my brother into soaring through the air." She shook her head. "Poor, Will. He broke his arm and we were all so afraid to tell my mom."

I watched as Libby moved across the kitchen. My heart began to beat stronger in my chest. *She's mine. She's finally mine.*

Taking in a breath, I slowly let it out. "Do you know what I remember most about that time?"

She continued to cut up the watermelon and put it into a bowl for us. "Will threatening to hurt you every single time he saw you?"

I chuckled. "Nah, that was funny though. I bet if we brought it up to him he'd still be pissed." Libby giggled and nodded her head. "I remember sneaking out and coming to your house in the middle of the night. Tapping on your bedroom window and sitting under the stars, talking for hours."

Libby stared into my eyes, smiling softly. "I remember that too. I used to lay in bed and pray so hard you would be there that night. Then, I'd hear you tap on my window and I would get giddy at the idea of sitting next to you on the roof. I remember if your body brushed against mine, I would get the silliest feelings in my stomach." She looked down and then back at me. "I still do."

Pushing the stool back, I walked over to Libby. Placing my hands in her hair, I pulled her head back and pressed my lips to hers. The kiss was passionate—filled with love, as we kissed each other like we hadn't seen each other in days. I pulled back some and whispered against her lips. "I loved you then, Libby."

Closing her eyes she barely spoke, "Never stop loving me, Luke."

"Never," I whispered as I picked her up and set her on the counter. I was about to take things further when the front door opened. Closing my eyes, I said, "Shit."

Libby laughed and leaned over and kissed my lips. "If you were about to do what I think you were, we can sneak down here later tonight and you can make it up to me!"

I picked up her hand and kissed it. "I love you."

Biting on her lip, Libby whispered back, "I love you more, Luke."

"Never," I said as I shook my head and helped her back down. Grace walked into the kitchen and glanced over at us. "What's up, bitches?"

Snapping my head over to Grace, I looked at her. She opened the refrigerator and grabbed a Diet Coke. "I have a huge test to study for. Y'all want to grab some dinner later?"

I could tell Libby was having a hard time holding back her laughter. She always was the weak one on the team when it came to keeping a straight face. "Sure. We can grab something if you want."

Grace looked at me and tilted her face. "Why are you looking at me that way?"

I shrugged. "Because you're beautiful, and I'm lucky to have you as a sister?"

Grace's mouth dropped open. "Oh God. Y'all are pregnant and need me to be there when you tell Mom. I knew it. The way you two go at it like rabbits. I admit I thought this was going to be Alex and Will, but I'm not surprised. Mom and Dad are going to be pissed. Dude, wrap the stick!"

Libby and I just stood there stunned. Finally, Libby spoke. "I'm not pregnant, Grace."

"Why does everyone keep telling me to wrap my stick? I wrap my damn stick!"

Grace took a step back. "Oh. Sorry." Turning on her heels, she headed into the living room and then up the stairs. I turned to Libby. "Shit, all these people talking about you being pregnant is starting to freak me out!"

Libby laughed. "You know I'm on the pill, Luke, so stop freaking out."

Turning, I looked at her. For one brief moment, I wanted to sink my dick inside her and feel what she would feel like without a condom on. Raising her eyebrow she looked at me with a knowing look.

"Wrap the stick, baby," she said with a wicked grin.

I was about to suggest the one thing I swore I would never do, when Grace screamed out. "Luke! You son-of-a-bitch!"

Libby's hands went up to her mouth as I smiled bigger. "I guess Grace had to go potty!"

WALKING OUT OF the library, I stopped dead in my tracks. Libby was standing there talking to Zach. The smile on her face as she talked to him caused knots in my stomach. *Why the fuck is she talking to him? Had he contacted her again?*

Libby and I both had classes in the science building and would meet here every Monday, Wednesday, and Friday before going to lunch. I began walking toward them. As I got closer, Libby threw her head back and laughed. I balled my fist and tried to stay calm, even though I wanted to pound Zach's face into the ground.

Libby looked up and smiled bigger when she saw me walking up. I attempted to smile, but I was sure it came across as fake. Her smile lessened some as I came up and stopped. Glancing over to Zach, I looked at him and then back to Libby. "What's going on?"

Libby shook her head slightly. She obviously could tell I was pissed. "Um, nothing I ran into Zach and he was telling me about his hunting trip with his father last weekend. Their Jeep got stuck in the mud and ..."

I turned and looked at Zach. If this asshole thought he had any chance with Libby ever again, he had another thing coming. "You do realize she's with me, right?"

I felt the heat move through my body. I wasn't even sure why I was feeling jealous. I trusted Libby. I just didn't trust the little bastard standing here smirking at me.

Zach's smile faded and was then replaced with a smirk. "You feel threatened by me, Luke? That doesn't say a lot about your relationship with Libby."

Libby sucked in a breath. "Zach!" She then turned and looked at me. "Luke, stop this. We ran into each other and were catching up."

"I don't feel threatened by you, I just don't trust you."

Libby stepped in front of me. "Stop this. Zach is a friend and that's all." I could feel the hurt wash through my body. *Why would she continue a friendship with him? The man who stole what was mine.*

Looking at her I frowned. "I see, why lose a friendship that holds so many memories. Is that it, Lib?" Turning around, I began walking off. I heard Libby suck in a breath and I knew it was a shit move on my part. Seeing Zach reminded me that he took Libby's virginity, not me. He had her first. He had what should have been mine.

By the time I got back to the house, I was pissed more at myself than anything. I let jealousy get the best of me and I hurt Libby. After I promised her I wouldn't hurt her. Taking out my phone, I saw I had text from her.

> **Libby:** *I'm sorry it hurt you to see me talking to Zach. I was only trying to be polite when he walked up and said hello to me. I'm leaving class early.*

I saw I had another text. This one was from my buddy, Roy. He had been my best friend my freshman year of college. He liked to party and was what I had needed to drown out memories—and feelings.

> **Roy:** *Whippets this afternoon. Don't say no. One beer, Luke. Just come and hang out and have one beer.*

The last thing I wanted to do was go out, but I needed to get out for a bit and clear my head. I looked back at Libby's text. I sent Libby a text and then another to Roy.

162

Me: I didn't mean what I said. I'm sorry, Lib. I need to clear my head. Going to Whippets to meet Roy for a beer. I'll be home later.

Me: Hey Roy. I'm on my way but I'm only staying for one beer.

I quickly changed clothes and headed back down the stairs and to my truck when my phone beeped. I looked to see Libby had sent me a text back.

Libby: Luke we need to talk.

I instantly panicked. My fear of Libby leaving me slowly invaded my mind. I attempted to push my fears aside. I wasn't sure where this fear was coming from, Libby saying she wanted to talk to me only caused me to think the worst.

THE MOMENT I walked in and saw Roy and Gus, I smiled. I walked to the table and held out my hand to Roy. "Long time," I said as Roy and Gus stood up and shook my hand. I sat and smiled at the waitress as she brought over a Blue Moon and set it in front of me. Glancing up, I smiled at her. "You read minds?"

She laughed and said, "Nah, your buddy told me when you got here that's what your flavor was."

She turned and walked away. "And she is my flavor. I've been working on tapping that for the last few weeks," Roy said as his eyes followed the waitress while she walked back to the bar.

Shaking my head, I laughed and tipped the beer back, taking a drink. Looking around I saw a few people I knew. Gus slapped me on the back. "So what in the hell have you been up to, Luke? We haven't seen you around the last year."

I shrugged. "Trying to focus on school. Taking extra credit hours to finish up early so I can get to work."

Roy nodded his head. "Who's the blonde you've got on your

arm all the time?"

My heart dropped slightly. Knowing I acted like a dick again to Libby had me pissed off at myself and wishing I hadn't headed over to the bar. One beer and I was out of here and back to my girl. Smiling, I said, "Libby. My girlfriend."

"Dude, she's fucking hot," Gus said as I snapped my head over to him. He threw up his hands. "Not that I'm looking."

"We're having a party this weekend. Why don't y'all stop by?" Roy said as he looked over at Gus. Glancing back and forth between the two of them.

"I think I'll pass. We have plans this weekend." Looking over Roy's shoulder I saw Karen. A guy with dark-brown hair had his arms wrapped around her. She looked my way and when she saw me she smiled. We each gave a wave. I stood and looked down at Roy. "I'm going to go say hi to Karen."

Roy spun around in his chair. "Tell her we said hey. Miss seeing her at the parties, too. Heard she was engaged."

I looked down at Roy and then back up to Karen, "No shit?"

Nodding his head and turning back to the table he said, "No shit."

Slapping Roy's back I said, "I'll be right back."

Karen smiled bigger as I made my way over to her. Karen was the only other girl I had ever had feelings for. She never knew she had taken my virginity. I never told her because in my mind I had pretended that night I was with Libby.

Did I ever truly have feelings for Karen? She was a great listener. She knew how to party and have fun. And she taught me how to please a woman in more ways than I would have thought. It was almost as if I was a little project for her. Someone she could play with and teach.

Walking up, I stopped in front of her. The huge bastard who had his arms around her must have been her boyfriend. "Hey there, cowboy! How have you been?" The guy dropped his hold on Karen and she walked up and kissed me on the cheek.

"I've been good. How have you been?" I asked as I extended my hand to the guy. "Hi, Luke Johnson."

Smiling he took my hand and shook it. "Mark Overton. It's a pleasure to meet you. Karen has mentioned you a few times."

I pulled my head back and looked at Karen. "Really?"

Mark smiled and nodded his head. "Yep, Karen mentioned y'all dated for a few months when you were a freshman? Is that right?"

I was surprised Karen would have shared that with him. We hadn't dated that long and most of time I was drunk. "Well, Karen didn't really see the better side of me I'm afraid. I was pretty much either in class or drunk."

Mark laughed. "Dude, wasn't that freshman year for all of us? I can't wait to get out of school." Mark looked down at Karen and smiled sweetly. Karen glanced back at me and held up her hand. The giant oval diamond sparkled in the lights of the bar.

"I heard from Roy. You're getting married huh?"

She nodded her head enthusiastically. "I am. I finally found one who could tame my wild ways." Reaching my hand out, I shook Mark's hand again. I turned and gave Karen a hug. "Congratulations, sweetheart. You deserve to be happy."

"Thank you, Luke." She squeezed me tighter and then said, "There is a girl shooting me daggers. I'm gonna guess it's your girlfriend."

Karen pulled back and leaned into Mark. I knew she was doing that to show she was with another man. Turning, I saw Libby standing there. I smiled and she gave me a weak smile in return. I waved her over. *Why is she here?* Shit. She was either really pissed at me or she was going to tell me we were over. Either option had my heart slamming in my chest.

She walked up to me and smiled politely at Karen and Mark. I leaned down and softly kissed her lips.

"Libby, this is Karen and Mark." I knew Libby knew who Karen was, and I was prepared for her to lay into me. Here I jumped all over her for talking to her ex and she walks in and sees me hugging mine.

"Karen was telling me that her and Mark are engaged." Libby looked at me and then back at Karen. Smiling, she extended

165

her hand.

"Congratulations on your engagement," Libby said with a smile.

I knew Libby must have really wanted to talk to me if she had come here. I reached my hand out to Mark again. "I'm going to take off, but congratulations again. I'm happy for you both."

Karen smiled and hugged Libby. She whispered something into Libby's ear and then pulled back. "I'll see ya around." Lifting my hand in a good-bye wave I said, "See y'all."

I took Libby's hand in mine and led her over to Roy's table. "Let me say good-bye to Roy and them." Libby pulled me to a stop.

"Luke, I don't want to interrupt your time with your friends. I didn't like how we left things and I don't want us fighting over Zach of all things."

I searched her eyes. "You're not breaking up with me then?"

Libby's mouth dropped open. "What? No! Why in the world would you think that, Luke?"

Pushing my hand through my hair, I let out the breath I was holding. "The stupid hurtful thing I said to you. God, Libby I swear I didn't mean it. I don't know what came over me. I acted like such a dick and I turned around and did the same thing. I saw Karen and said hello to her."

"And hugged her," Libby said.

"Lib, it meant nothing."

Libby placed her finger over my lips. "Luke? Will you do something for me?"

My eyes searched her face. "Anything."

Libby looked into my eyes. "Dance with me?"

Slipping my hand around the base of her neck, I brought her lips to mine. I kissed her with as much passion as I could. Everyone started yelling out and Libby giggled. The blush covering her cheeks was sexy as hell.

I took her hand again and headed over to Roy. "Hey guys, I'm taking off." Roy and Gus both stood up. "You're not going to introduce us to your girl, Johnson?"

Turning, I looked at Libby. Smiling I said, "Libby, this is Roy and Gus."

Libby didn't even have a chance to say anything before I was pulling her out the doors.

She gave me a seductive look and asked, "Where are we going?"

"I'm taking you dancing, and then to a hotel and making love to you all night."

Shutting her door, I turned and jogged to the driver's side.

Libby giggled. "Where are we going dancing?"

Glancing over to Libby I winked. "You'll see."

Ten minutes later I pulled into the parking lot of an HEB and parked. Pulling out my iPod, I found the song I was looking for.

"Luke, what in the world are we doing?" Libby asked as she raised her brow.

I rolled all my windows down and jumped out of the truck. Jogging over to Libby's door, I opened it and held my hand out for her. She gave me the sweetest smile as she placed her hand in mine. I helped her down and let my eyes take in every inch of beauty.

Reaching up, I pulled her hair down and watched it as it fell along her shoulders. "You're beauty leaves me speechless, Lib. I want to make love to you all night."

Watching the blush move across her cheeks I leaned down and brushed my lips over hers. Pulling back I smiled. "Give me two seconds."

Libby chuckled as I jumped back in my truck and hit my iPod. I shut the passenger door and took her hands in mine as Blake Shelton's "My Eyes" began playing through the speakers of my truck.

Libby's eyes lit up as I pulled her body closer to mine. "Luke ..." she whispered.

Libby and I began dancing slowly in the middle of the parking lot. She pulled back slightly when I started singing the song to her. I watched a tear begin a trail down her gorgeous face. I placed my hand on the side of Libby's face as I wiped the tear away with my thumb. "Are you happy, Lib?"

"I've never been so happy in my life, Luke."

Pulling her lips to mine I stopped just short of a kiss. "I love you."

"I love you, Luke.

Thirty minutes later, I had Libby wrapped up in my arms as I kissed her soft lips and pushed inside of her.

We spent the entire night tangled up in each other's arms.

ALEX GRABBED MY arm! "Go, Colt, go!" she screamed as we all jumped. Colt had the ball and was headed for a touchdown.

"Damn it, Colt run!" Luke yelled out. When Colt crossed the goal line, Alex and I began hugging and jumping. I turned and Luke took me in his arms as I kissed him. Alex turned and kissed Will. It was an A&M tradition to kiss the guy next to you after a touchdown.

Luke pulled back and smiled. "Damn, Colt has got to be making Gunner one proud daddy!"

I nodded my head and watched as they kicked the extra point. Everyone on the sidelines was still congratulating Colt. He had quickly become the star wide receiver for A&M. This was the second touchdown he scored today and we were only in the second quarter.

Will and Luke high fived each other as I pulled out my phone and sent Lauren a text.

Me: *Did you see Colt?!*

Lauren: *I did! Did you see Bruce?!*

Ugh. I rolled my eyes. Lauren was now officially dating Bruce, the A&M quarterback. She had been pretty friendly with him ever since we had that party at our place. She talked to him almost all night and if they weren't talking they were dancing. I swear Colt watched them the whole evening.

    Me: Yep. But I like watching Colt more!

I waited for a response. Nothing. I let out a sigh and looked out over the field. "What's wrong, Lib?" Luke asked.

I shrugged. "Lauren. This whole Bruce thing isn't sitting right with me."

Luke frowned. "Yeah. Colt didn't take the news of the two of them dating very well. Will said Colt got trashed and the coach had to have a talk with him."

I shook my head. I hated to see the same thing happen to Colt and Lauren as what Luke and I did. This stupid cat-and-mouse game was crazy insane. Alex and I had tried to talk to Lauren about it. Her response was she wanted to have fun. She didn't need a man to help her. I was pretty sure it had something to do with her dad. Lauren seemed to think he didn't have faith in her to run the business. Him bringing Colt on as a partner when he graduated was throwing Lauren off big time.

I shook my head to clear my thoughts. I turned to Alex and asked, "Are we all driving home together for Thanksgiving?"

Alex looked over my shoulder, then looked at me. "Um, sure."

"Okay, cause I think it would be easier if you, me, Luke, and Will all just drove in one vehicle. Unless y'all had plans?"

Alex wasn't paying attention to me. I snapped my fingers in front of her. "Hello? Earth to Alex? Turning back to me she smiled and then asked, "Who's Luke talking to?"

Turning, I saw Karen. She was standing on one of the seats on the bleacher below us. Luke was leaned over talking to her. Her hand was on his arm as she said something into his ear. That same zip of jealousy rushed through my veins as when I saw the two of them dancing that night at the Italian restaurant, then again at Whippets when they were hugging. I looked back at Alex. "That's Karen. Luke's ex-girlfriend."

"Huh. Wonder what she wants?" Alex asked as she kept her eyes on Karen.

I looked back and Karen saw me looking. She smiled and dropped her hand from Luke's arm. "Hey, Libby! How are you?" Peeking at Luke, I noticed he was already back into watching the football game.

"I'm doing well. How about you?"

"Couldn't be better. I was just telling Luke that I wanted to invite y'all to the wedding. I'd love to have you both there."

Uh-huh. Sure you would.

Smiling politely, I nodded. "Of course. We'd love to be there."

She smiled sweetly and her fiancée walked up and wrapped his arm around her. She looked into his eyes and I couldn't help but smile. Guilt raced through my body as I watched them exchange a kiss.

Looking back at Luke, Karen reached up and tapped his arm. "We'll see y'all at the wedding then?"

Luke nodded quickly and then went back to watching the game. I chuckled at how stupid I had acted a few seconds ago.

Karen waved good-bye as I lifted my hand and returned the gesture.

Karen jumped off the seat and made her way back through the crowd. I looked up at Luke. "I have no idea why she came up and invited us like that, Lib. I swear I haven't talked to her since that day at Whippets."

I placed my hand on the side of Luke's face. "Stop. Luke, I trust you and I know you'd never do anything to hurt me."

He leaned down and brushed his lips across mine. Everyone started screaming as Luke and I looked down at the field. Colt was also a punt returner and he was taking off toward the goal line—again. Seconds later, I was kissing Luke again to celebrate the touchdown.

MY PHONE BEEPED as I reached into my riding boot and took it out. Grace, Alex, Meg, and I were all out riding. It was Christmas break and I was so glad we all got to hang out together.

I rolled my eyes when I saw Karen's name. Ugh. I was quickly beginning to hate her.

"If looks could kill, whoever sent that text should be dead right about now," Maegan said with a laugh.

I let out a grunt. "It's Luke's ex, Karen. She all of sudden wants to be my best friend. I can't stand to even look at her at this point. All she does is remind me of the fact that she had Luke before me."

Grace groaned. "Tell her to back off, Libby. I mean, she's getting married, so I don't think she is a threat."

"I know she's not a threat and I know she really wants to be friends. I'm going to have to explain to her why it's hard for me to be friends with her," I said as I shoved my phone back into my boot.

We continued on the path toward the river. Maegan let out a sigh and said, "I just love it here."

We all came to an abrupt stop. We watched as Maegan's horse kept walking on. She finally stopped and turned around. "What's wrong?" she asked.

"You said you loved it here. Are you feeling okay?" Alex asked.

Meg laughed as she shrugged her shoulders. "I just—wish I was home." Her eyes filled with tears. "I hate school. I hate everything about school."

Grace, Alex, and I all slipped off our horses. Alex reached Maegan first. Maegan jumped off her horse and began crying as Alex took her in her arms. Grace and I looked at each other. I don't think I've ever seen Maegan cry in my entire life. Alex ran her hand up and down Maegan's back gently. "Maegan, what's wrong? Please talk to us."

Maegan pulled back and wiped her tears away. "Oh gosh, I'm so sorry I broke down like that. It's been a rough year." She turned and sat on a fallen tree. It was the first time I noticed how tired Maegan looked. More like she looked defeated.

Alex bent down in front of her and pushed Maegan's red hair behind her ear. "Meg, talk to us."

Grace and I each took a seat next to Maegan on the tree. Swallowing hard, Maegan started talking. "My whole life, my father has done nothing but compare me to Taylor. I don't think he even knows he does it. He always tells me I can do better. Make better grades, be a better example to Taylor, make them prouder. I feel like I can't make any mistakes and then there is—"

Maegan stopped talking and tears began rolling down her face. Putting my arm around her I asked, "There's what, Maegan?"

Maegan let out a small laugh. "I guess when you leave high school you think you leave all the mean girls behind." She shook her head. "That's not the case. I've got these four girls that hate me. I don't know why. They don't stop, ever. I can be walking to class with someone and they will do whatever they can to make my life miserable. They would bump into me and knock everything out of my hands. Spreading rumors about how I'll give guys blowjobs at frat parties or in my dorm room. I haven't even been to a single party this year for fear of some guy coming on to me." A sob escaped her lips. "Last year I had guys walking up to me asking me to make arrangements to give them head! I finally stopped leaving my dorm room unless it was to go to class."

Grace cursed. "Maegan, why don't you knock the fuck out of those girls?"

Maegan laughed. "At one party, I ended up beating the shit out of a girl who called me a redheaded whore. The only thing it did was bring me more grief. My parents asked if I was doing drugs, and oh man, I wasn't setting a good example for Taylor. It isn't worth it. So I try to ignore it."

Alex grabbed Maegan's hands. "Meg, you have to talk to your parents about this."

She nodded her head. "I know I do. I was hoping this year would be better. The bullying happens less often. I feel like I've lost myself though. I don't even know who I am anymore. I'm chasing after that girl I used to know and she might not be there

173

anymore."

Alex wiped a tear away. "I still think you need to talk to your parents. At least get it out in the open with your dad."

Nodding her head, Maegan leaned over and kissed Alex's forehead. "I promise I will. Come on let's ride. The only happy time I have is with you girls and I don't want this to turn into a sad sappy afternoon."

LUKE AND I walked hand in hand as I pulled my sweater tighter around me. "Are you cold, Lib?"

"I'm chilly, but I'm okay," I said as I watched Luke search my face. He pulled off his sweatshirt and pushed it over my head. I laughed as I pulled it on. My senses were overtaken by his scent. My libido instantly kicked in. "I miss you," I said as I gave him a seductive smile.

"Damn, Libby. I miss you, too. I want to hold you in my arms. I can't even sleep without you next to me."

I giggled. "I feel the same way. I could hardly fall asleep last night."

Luke stopped and turned to me. "Do you have any idea how happy you make me, Libby?"

My eyes filled with tears. "Tell me."

His smile made my knees shake. "I think I'm my happiest when we are together at night. When I have you wrapped in my arms and you're starting to drift off to sleep. Your breathing starts to slow and I know at that very moment you feel safe in my arms." Luke placed his hand on the side of my face and brushed his thumb across my skin, causing a trail of fire behind it. "Then when you walk into a room. The energy changes and I can't seem to pull my eyes from you. You smile and my world rocks off balance. Your touch brings out feelings I never thought I would experience. Your love—has me excited about our future, Libby. I dream about it all the time. I dream of long walks along the river, snuggling up next to a fire with you in my arms, my hands on your belly feeling our baby kicking."

A sob escaped my lips as my heart pounded in my chest. I'd never felt such happiness in all of my life. I wanted to pinch myself to make sure I wasn't dreaming.

"I don't think I could ever put it in words how happy you make me, Libby. More than I ever imagined."

Swallowing hard, I reached up on my tippy toes and kissed him. This man. This man would forever be mine. No one or nothing would ever take him from me.

Ever.

MY EYES SNAPPED open and I laid still. *What is that noise?* I sat up and looked around.

I pushed the covers back and that's when I heard the pebble hit my window. I smiled and jumped out of bed. I opened my window and looked down to see Luke. "What are you doing?" I whispered.

Smiling that naughty smile of his, Luke began climbing up the side of the house—like he did so many years ago. He quietly walked over to my window and winked at me. "I thought you might like to lay on the roof and watch the stars with me. I can't sleep."

"Luke, it's Christmas Eve!"

He nodded his head. "I know. What a better night to watch the sky? We might even see Santa!"

I giggled as Luke took the screen off my window and set it to the side. He put his hand out for mine. "Oh wait! I need a blanket." I turned and grabbed my quilt and blanket. Luke helped me out the window and then helped me to spread the quilt down on the roof. We lay down and covered up with the blanket.

"Oh wow. Look at the stars," I whispered.

Luke pulled me closer to him. "I don't think I've seen such a clear night before."

"Yeah," I whispered as I looked at him. Luke turned to me and the moon was shining back at me through his beautiful green eyes. "I love you, Luke Johnson."

Before I knew it, Luke was on top of me, while kissing me passionately as he helped me to remove my sleeping shorts. I reached down and moaned as his hard dick fell into my hand as he pushed his sweatpants down. His hands moved up my shirt and he moaned in delight when he was met with no bra. He began twisting and pulling my nipple as he continued to kiss me senseless. My hands soon found his hair as I grabbed and pulled as Luke teased me with his tip.

"Libby," he whispered against my lips as I pushed my hips to him. Silently begging him to take me. Luke placed his elbows down and took my face in the palm of his hands. He slowly pushed into me as we looked into each other's eyes. I wanted to close my eyes and moan in pleasure but our gaze was locked onto each other. Luke pushed in all the way and bit down on his lip before he pressed his lips to mine.

Slowly, passionately, Luke made love to me as he kissed me softly and tenderly. I didn't want this moment to end.

"Luke, you feel amazing," I whispered as he pulled his lips from mine.

"Libby, oh God Libby. I love you, baby. You feel—" His eyes closed as he pushed in more. His eyes opened quickly and I was pretty sure we both realized why it was feeling so amazing. Luke didn't have a condom on.

"Lib—"

I shook my head. "Please don't stop. *Please.* I've never in my life felt so complete as I do this very moment."

Luke reached down and sucked my bottom lip into his mouth as I moaned. "Love me, Luke."

"Oh God, Libby." He pulled out painfully slowly and pushed back in. Repeating the heavenly process over and over as I felt my body tingling with the build of my orgasm.

"Luke, I'm going to come," I whispered as I looked into his eyes.

He began to move faster as his dick started to swell and he hit the spot over and over.

Luke's eyes lit up with a passion I'd never seen before. "Libby. I'm going to come." When I saw the tear roll down his face, I sucked in a breath. I was so overcome by the moment that my emotions took over and the tears began to spill. Luke never stopped looking into my eyes the entire time we came together. When he finally stopped moving, I could feel him still twitching inside me. I reached up and wiped his damp face. "I don't want to move, Lib. I want to stay connected to you like this forever."

"Don't move," I whispered against his lips as he leaned down to kiss me. Luke pulled back slightly. His green eyes capturing my blue eyes.

"Marry me, Libby."

Chapter Twenty-Four

Luke

THE WORDS WERE out of my mouth before I could stop them. I didn't want to stop them. I wanted to be with Libby for the rest of my life. I wanted to experience this type of moment as much as I could.

I searched Libby's face for her reaction. When she smiled and the tear rolled from her eye I knew her answer.

"Yes," she whispered as her eyes landed on my lips. I leaned in closer. The moment our lips touched something amazing happened. It felt as if our love exploded. I began moving my dick inside her again.

God. It felt amazing to make love to Libby with no condom on. I couldn't believe I was getting hard again. Libby wrapped her legs around me and squeezed. I stopped moving as I pulled my lips from her lips.

"I don't think I've ever felt so loved in my life, Luke."

I smiled and kissed her nose. "Good."

Then she began chewing on her lower lip. "As much as I want to repeat that amazing moment, I want something else—more."

My dick jumped as I pulled out and rolled off of her. I reached down and pulled up my sweatpants as Libby quickly put her sleeping shorts back on. She stood up and grabbed the blanket.

"Where?" she asked.

Smiling, I said, "Let's just get to my truck and we'll figure it out." Libby started back to her room. I grabbed her quilt and shook it off and threw it into her window. Stepping into the room, I stopped dead in my tracks.

Holy shit.

I was pretty sure my life was about to end. Josh was leaning against the doorframe of Libby's room. He looked at Libby and then me. His body was tense, even though he tried to appear as if he was standing there casually. "What are y'all up to?"

Libby snapped her head over to me and I looked at her as I swallowed the lump in my throat. My stomach instantly felt as if it was in knots. "Um, just watching the stars like we used to when we were little," I said as Libby nodded her head. I felt the beads of sweat starting to form on my forehead. *How long had he been there? Did he hear us? Did he know I just made love to his daughter, on his roof?*

Looking away, I frowned. That didn't even sound right.

Josh took in a deep breath and blew it out. "Okay, so you were watching stars. What are y'all doing now?"

"Daddy, why are you up here?" Libby asked.

"I woke up and couldn't sleep. I was heading up to my office when I heard a noise from your bedroom. I opened the door to see you sneaking back in your window."

Libby and I both let out the breath we were holding. He hadn't been there that long. Libby let out a nervous laugh as Josh looked over at her. "We were actually going to go for a drive."

Now, it was Josh's turn to laugh. I cleared my throat and looked at Josh. "Josh, um, Mr. Hayes, um—" I pushed my hand nervously through my hair. *What did I call him now?*

He tilted his head and gave me a smile. He knew I was nervous and he was enjoying this a little too much.

"Sir, I'm not sure what to call you anymore," I said.

"Josh is fine, Luke."

Nodding my head, I asked, "May I please speak with you in

private sir, um, Josh, sir?"

Libby smiled and looked away.

Josh chuckled and he motioned for me to head on out of the room. I began walking out, but quickly turned and kissed Libby on the lips fast. "In case I don't make it back alive."

She giggled and slapped me on the chest. "Stop it!"

I made my way out of Libby's bedroom and followed Josh to his office. The moment we walked in, I was transported back to when I was younger and Will and I used to play in here. I smiled at the memories.

"I would think if I just got caught by my girlfriend's daddy sneaking into her bedroom window, I wouldn't be smiling while standing in his office," Josh said with a shit-eating grin on his face.

"I was thinking about being younger and Will and I playing in here. We loved to be in here. The smell of your wood desk was my favorite thing."

Josh's face relaxed and he smiled as he sat behind his desk. I sat and pulled deep down inside for my courage.

"I'm not really sure where to start with this, so I'll just come right out with it." Josh leaned back in his chair. Bastard looked intimating as hell.

"I love, Libby, sir. I love her with all of my heart and I've loved her for as long as I can remember. She's my best friend. I want to give her the world, Josh." I stopped talking and took a deep breath. "I'd like to ask for your permission to marry, Libby."

Josh sat there for a few moments and just stared at me. "Do you know how much I love that girl?"

I nodded my head. "I can only imagine, sir."

Josh closed his eyes and smiled, as if remembering something. "I'll never forget the first time I held Libby in my arms. I thought her mother stole my heart." He shook his head and opened his eyes. Tears filled them and my heart dropped to my stomach. "Libby stole my heart the instant she looked into my eyes. I made a vow that day, Luke. I vowed to protect her forever. Oh, I knew someday a guy would come along and she would steal his heart like she did mine."

I smiled and nodded my head.

"I dreaded that day to be honest. She was my girl. My little girl and she deserved so much. No guy in my eyes would ever live up to what I thought she deserved." He smiled at me as I moved about in my seat. "Then I saw the way you looked at her one day. The way you look at her, follow her as she moves about the room. I see how much you love her. You both grew up together. The two of you got in more trouble together than I think all the kids combined."

I laughed as I shook my head. "She is a good partner when it comes to pranks."

Josh tossed he head back and laughed. "You don't have to plead your case with me, Luke. I already think of you as a son. I'd be honored to have you as my son-in-law." I was pretty sure the smile on my face was a big goofy-ass grin. I stood and reached my hand out to Josh. He stood up and shook my hand. "I just have one request."

I nodded my head and held my breath as I waited to hear his request. "Yes, anything."

"Don't ever have sex on my roof again with my daughter. If I ever catch you in my daughter's room again, I'll hang you from a rafter in the barn. By your balls."

I fell back into the chair. My breathing picked up and I felt like I couldn't get in enough air. Swallowing hard, I looked at Josh. "You knew?"

Josh tilted his head and looked at me. "Someday son, when you become a father, you'll understand. You become acutely aware of things. I knew the moment you both crawled through that window. All it took was the look on your faces to know what the two of you were up to."

Nodding my head I stood up and turned to leave. "Oh, and Luke?"

Turning back around I asked, "Yes, sir?"

"I'm not sure where the two of you were planning on going,

but I think it's pretty late for a drive. Don't you?"

I wanted desperately to say no, but I did what I was raised to do. "Yes, sir. It's pretty late. I'll go say goodnight to Libby and head on home."

Josh grinned.

Heading down the hallway, I smiled. I had asked Josh for permission to marry Libby. I asked Libby and she said yes. Now I just needed to get the ring and make it official.

Tapping on Libby's door lightly, I pushed the door open. She was sitting on her bed with her legs crossed. She glanced up from a book she was reading and smiled. Biting her lip, she jumped up and walked to me. "I take it we're not going on our drive," she said as she jetted her lower lip out in a pout. "Was it bad?" She looked my body up and down, as if making sure I wasn't hurt in any way.

I shook my head slowly and kissed the tip of her nose. "It could have been worse. Will could have been in there as well." Libby let out a chuckle. "I did however ask for your hand in marriage."

Her smile grew into a beautiful grin. "What did he say?"

"He said he would be honored to have me as his son-in-law." Libby jumped into my arms and smashed her lips to mine as she repeated over and over, "I love you, I love you, I love you!"

Josh walked by and cleared his throat. I slowly set Libby back down and kissed her softly on the lips. "Merry Christmas."

"Merry Christmas, Luke. Will I see you before we head over to Alex and Colt's house?"

"Yes. I have something for you," I said.

Libby wiggled her eyebrows up and down. "I have something for you too, we have to be alone though for you to open it."

"Hmm, I'm intrigued."

Libby whispered, "You should be."

Groaning, I closed my eyes then opened them. "Goodnight, baby. Sleep good. Love you."

"I will, you too. Be careful driving. Love you back."

I started to walk through her room. Climbing through the window, I walked out onto the roof.

"Luke! You could have gone through the house," Libby said in a hushed voice. Looking around, I shrugged. I climbed off the roof and began walking down the drive to my truck. I couldn't wipe the smile off my face, even if I wanted to.

Libby's going to be my wife.

LOOKING THROUGH THE clear glass, I was no closer to picking out a ring than I was an hour ago. Glancing to the entrance, I saw Grace walking in. I couldn't help but smile. She commanded attention the moment she set foot through the doors. The salesman was all over Grace like a fly on shit. She was in her element. Anything to do with shopping and she was all over it. I called her twenty minutes ago in a panicked state.

Grace smiled and pointed to me as she turned to the guy who looked to have been about our age. The salesman nodded and began walking with Grace toward me. "Hey there, big brother. So wedding ring shopping are we? When were you going to tell me?"

"I thought Libby would have said something to y'all."

Grace's smile faded and her mouth hung open. I reached across and closed it with my index finger. "That bitch."

"Hey don't call my fiancé that!" I said as I turned back and looked at the engagement rings. Grace grabbed my arm and turned me toward her.

"You asked Libby to marry you? When? Oh my gosh, Luke. This is so exciting."

I chuckled. "Christmas Eve, while making love to her."

Grace scrunched up her nose. "Ew, but also sweet and romantic. Do Mom and Dad know?"

I shook my head. "Josh and Heather do. I asked for Libby's hand." Grace placed her hand over her heart. "Man oh man, did Mom and Dad do right with you."

I gave her a gentle push on the shoulder. "Help me, Grace. There are so many. They are different sizes, shapes, colors. I have no clue."

Turning around and looking down Grace sighed. "Well, first off, Libby is a simple girl so you want to keep the ring fairly simple. Do you want to go with a diamond or something different?"

"Different like how?"

"Like what Gunner did with Ellie. Ellie's engagement ring is a sapphire. You don't have to do a diamond."

Smiling an idea occurred to me. "The yellow diamond."

Grace pinched her eyebrows together. "Yellow diamond?"

I grabbed her hand and led her over to the other side where I saw the ring that immediately caught my eye when I first walked in. I had thought of Libby right away. The pale-yellow color reminded me of her. Libby's smile was like the sun's rays—bright and radiant. My ray of sunshine. It was her light that saved me in the first place.

Walking to the counter, I pointed to the light pale-yellow diamond. Grace brought her hand up to her mouth and drew in a gasp.

The saleswoman approached. "I had a feeling you'd be back to this diamond. I saw your eyes light up when you first saw it." I glanced to her and smiled.

Grace dropped her hand and sighed, "It's breathtakingly beautiful." Turning to me she smiled. "This is so Libby, Luke."

Nodding my head, I agreed. "I know. It reminds me of the sunlight, which reminds me of, Lib."

The saleswoman smiled and began telling us about the ring. She took it out and set it on a black velvet board. The contrast made it more beautiful.

"This diamond is a cushion cut yellow diamond. It is just over one carat in size. The two side diamonds are oval diamonds. They are approximately half a carat each. They are all set in a platinum band."

Grace picked up the ring and slipped it onto her finger. Smiling Grace looked up at me as she handed the ring to me.

Saving You

"Luke, it's perfect. You didn't need me after all."

Chuckling, I said, "I would have never have come back to this ring if you hadn't said something, Grace."

I watched as tears began to fill Grace's eyes. I frowned. "Grace, what's wrong?"

Shaking her head, she laughed. "Nothing, it's just that I'm so happy for you and Libby. I'm glad y'all finally got your shit together." I leaned over and kissed my sister on the cheek. If only I believed that was why she had tears in her eyes.

Taking another good look at the ring, I knew it was the one. Handing it back to the saleswoman, I said, "I'll take it."

Her eyes widening in surprise as she asked, "Don't you even want to know how much it is?"

"No matter how much it is, Libby is worth every single penny. This ring is perfect for her, I don't care how much it costs."

She checked the sales tag and peeked up at me. "This ring is fourteen thousand dollars."

"Holy sheets," Grace said. I pulled out my wallet and handed her my American Express card.

Grace bumped my shoulder and smiled. "Had I known you were rich, I'd have hit you up for that Coach purse I wanted for Christmas."

The sales lady walked back over to us and handed me my card. "Grace, can I ask you something?"

"I don't know, can you?"

Rolling my eyes, I sighed. "I hate when you do that. May I ask you something?"

Smirking, she nodded her head. "Have at it."

"Why is a girl as beautiful as you not dating anyone? You mentioned last summer about fighting your own fears."

Grace began chewing on her lower lip. "Talk to me, Sweet Pea. Please."

Grace looked down as her eyebrows pinched together as if she was thinking of something. "I did meet someone."

Smiling, I tilted her chin up. Looking into her eyes I saw nothing but sadness. "And?"

Swallowing hard, I watched as a tear slowly moved down my sister's face. My entire world stopped. I was going to kill the motherfucker if he hurt my sister. Keeping calm, I waited for her to say something. It felt like time was moving in slow motion as I waited for Grace to talk.

"We had an amazing connection, but, I—I pushed him away. I said some awful things to him, Luke. I didn't mean them at all. I saw the hurt in his eyes. I won't ever let myself be hurt again by someone and I didn't know what to do. I was scared by how I felt and I panicked. Now, I think I've lost him forever."

Closing my eyes, I pulled her into my arms as she began to cry. I've never seen my sister cry. Ever. "Shh, it's okay, Grace. We'll fix it. I promise."

She shook her head as she pulled away. "You can't. He's getting married."

Chapter Twenty-Five

Libby

LUKE HELD ME in his arms as we stood and talked to Roy. Roy had thrown a party to celebrate how well the football team did this season. Luke said Roy used any excuse to throw a party. I looked around and saw Colt leaning against the wall smiling politely at a few girls who were talking to him. Colt had an amazing season. Smiling, I watched as he charmed them with his handsome good looks, dimples, and sky-blue eyes.

I turned and saw Lauren walking in with Bruce. He did not seem like the type she would be with. He was cute that was for sure. Dark-brown hair, amber-green eyes, backward baseball cap that made him even cuter and a pretty rocking body. Bruce couldn't hold a candle to Will, Colt, or Luke's body. Turning, I looked at Luke. My eyes traveled down his body. He had on Wrangler jeans that fit him oh so good, a tight, blue T-shirt that hugged his muscles in that perfect sexy way. His messy brown hair had that just-fucked look and he was sporting a three-day stubble.

Oh lord. The way his body made my body hum with desire was unreal. Chewing on the inside of my cheek to get my libido under check, I looked back at Lauren. I frowned as I watched Bruce lean down and kiss her. I prayed to God she hadn't given herself to him. Bruce didn't seem like the type who would wait patiently. They had been dating for three months now.

Luke sighed. "Shit, Colt should probably find someone soon. It looks like Lauren has."

Turning around, I looked at Colt who was glaring at Lauren and Bruce. Before I knew it, he grabbed one of the girls and brought her out to the dance floor. My mouth dropped open at the way he was dancing with her. "Oh my gosh, Luke. What is Colt doing? He looks like he's about to crawl into her pants," I said, looking at Luke.

Looking back at them, Colt's hands were all over the girl and she was just as bad. Her hands were on his ass, pulling him closer to her. The moment their lips touched, I let out a gasp. "No. Oh gosh, Luke. He's gonna turn into a man whore!"

I turned away. I couldn't watch him anymore. This was the fourth girl I'd seen him making-out with in the last two weeks. Will and Luke had a party last weekend and I watched as Colt made out with one girl in a corner and then leave with another girl.

Luke grabbed my hand and led me across the dance floor. "Where are we going?" I asked.

"I need fresh air."

Luke walked over to his truck and dropped my hand. He ran both hands down his face and let out a sigh. "What's wrong?" I asked.

Turning to look at me, Luke shook his head. "Colt's headed down the wrong path and I have no idea how to stop him. I'm afraid he is going to do something stupid and make a mistake that will cost him his future. Have you talked to Lauren? What is going on with the two of them?"

"I know Lauren has feelings for Colt. The summer before their senior year I guess they spent some time alone, things got a bit heavy and they ended up making out pretty good. Lauren said she practically begged Colt to take her, but he wouldn't, not in his truck. He told her he wanted it to be special."

Luke smiled slightly. "Good. I'm glad he stopped it."

I nodded my head and continued. "A few days later, Lauren was riding with her dad. You know Lauren wants nothing more than to take over her father's breeding business. Horses are that girl's life. She told Grace and me that she had some great ideas, but Scott wouldn't listen to her. He told her she needs to go to school, get her degree and then they would talk."

Luke nodded. "Okay, keep going."

"When Lauren and Scott got back from their ride, Colt was at the barn waiting on them. He asked to talk to Scott. Said he wanted to work there for his senior year and expressed an interest in breeding. Scott asked Colt why he wasn't interested in the cattle ranch. Colt said that was yours and Will's thing. I guess Colt had been helping your dad, Jeff, a lot more on the horse side of things."

Luke rubbed his chin. "Yeah, Colt's always been more interested in the horses than the cattle."

Letting out a sigh, I dropped my head back and then looked at Luke. "Colt had an idea for Scott. Scott listened to it and loved the idea. Offered Colt to come work for him. Lauren was furious. She was already upset and planted it in her head that Colt didn't want her. Now she said she feels like she is competing against Colt for a position in her dad's business. Lauren thought Colt was leading her on to get closer to Scott."

Luke frowned. "Colt would never do something like that. Surely Lauren knows that. Has she talked to Colt or Scott about it?"

I shrugged. "Grace and I told her she needed to. That time when Colt opened up about his feelings for Lauren and she blew him off, that was the same day Scott offered Colt to come work for him."

Luke's shoulders sank. "Jesus, our little group, I swear. It's a good thing we ran out of boys for Meg and Taylor."

I giggled and nodded my head. Walking to Luke, I placed my hands on his chest. "I want to go home."

Luke's eyes lit up. "Your wish is my command, Lib."

Opening the passenger door to his truck, I jumped in. Luke leaned in and kissed me quickly on the lips before shutting the door. Making his way around the front of his truck, he waved to someone. Looking I saw it was Colt. He was walking up to Luke, and he was alone. That was a good sign. They spoke for a few seconds and Luke shook Colts hand. I watched as Colt made his way into the parking lot.

The door opened and Luke got in. "Colt's heading home. Alone."

I let out the breath I was holding. "Good."

Luke pulled out of the parking lot and looked over at me. "Did I tell you? I bought you a new toy?"

Squeezing my legs together I whispered, "Hurry home."

OPENING MY EYES, I squinted from the sun shining through the window. I stretched and moaned softly. Luke had his wicked way with me last night and I was relishing in every succulent memory. His lips softly kissing my body, his mouth on my mouth, his unbelievable ability to make love to me, and make it feel like the first time every time.

Smiling, I placed my fingertips to my lips. His stubble felt amazing on my body last night, but I was sure I would pay for it today. Pushing back the covers, I walked into the bathroom. One look in the mirror and I knew I had been thoroughly fucked last night. Closing my eyes I hugged myself, then pinched myself.

Nope. Still not dreaming.

Brushing my teeth and throwing my hair up in a ponytail, I turned and walked back into the bedroom. I put on my favorite comfy clothes, and a pair of fuzzy socks. Rubbing my hands down my arms, I made my way downstairs. I had no clue where Luke had snuck off to, especially on such a chilly morning.

As I walked down the stairs, my nose was filled with the smells of coffee, bacon, and pancakes. I reached the bottom step and stopped. Luke was in the kitchen with Lauren. They were cooking and dancing together to Dan + Shay's "Nothin' Like You". Smiling, my heart filled with more love for this man.

The way he was making Lauren smile and laugh spoke more than any words could.

Walking over, I sat on the bar stool as Luke gave me a quick wink. "I talked Lauren into making her famous pancakes."

I raised my eyebrows and smiled bigger. It was nice to see Lauren with a smile on her face. She had seemed sad lately. "What are your plans today, Lauren?" I asked as Luke set a cup of coffee down in front of me.

Lauren sighed. "Study. Then study some more."

Looking at Luke, my stomach fluttered when our eyes met. I quickly looked away. If I kept looking at him, I was going to pull him back upstairs. Grace came walking into the kitchen and let out a whispered good morning. Pouring her coffee Luke kissed her on the cheek. "Good morning, Sweet Pea. Hope you slept good." Rolling her eyes she took a sip of coffee and glanced over to me. I smiled and she pulled her coffee from her lips.

Giving me a wicked smile, Grace pointed to me. "Jesus, Mary, and Joseph. You got some serious action last night, didn't you?"

Gaping my mouth open, I moved about uncomfortably in my seat. Widening my eyes, I looked at her. "W—why do you ask?"

Grace threw her head back and laughed. Shaking her head she took another drink of coffee and moved around the island, she came and sat next to me on the stool. "Let's see. You have that just-fucked glow about you. Your skin looks chafed, and by the looks of big brother's stubble, I'd dare say the rest of your body looks the same way."

Luke smiled bigger as I felt my face warm. "Gesh, Grace." I looked away from her and saw Lauren grinning from ear to ear.

"I'll take that as you had a nice evening. Lucky bitch," Grace said as she reached over and grabbed a piece of bacon.

Grinning, I looked into Luke's eyes. "I would say it was more than nice."

"Aww," Lauren said as she clapped and smiled. "I love y'all together!"

Grace made a gagging sound. "Ew. Gross."

Giggling, I said, "You brought it up."

Sighing, Grace nodded her head. "Touché, that I did. What's the plan for today?" Grace asked, looking directly at Luke.

"I have a huge test to study for so I'll be staying home today," Lauren said as she jetted her lower lip out in a pout.

Luke shrugged his shoulders. "Lib, what are we doing today?"

I bit on the inside of my cheek as I attempted to control my desire. "It's chilly out. I'm down for hanging out at home. Maybe watch a few movies."

The smile that spread across Luke's face was infectious. I smiled and looked at Grace. "What are you doing today?"

Grace was still staring at Luke. The look on her face confused me. It was as if she was expecting Luke to say something. Luke looked back at Grace and gave her a knowing look. "Staying home and movies sounds perfect, Lib." Glancing back at me he winked. "We can cuddle under the covers all day."

"That sounds like a damn good plan," Will said from behind me. Turning I saw him and Alex walking toward the kitchen holding hands. "Alex, you down for a movie marathon?"

Alex seemed pleased with the plans Will had made for them. She walked into the kitchen and gave Luke a kiss on the cheek and then hugged Lauren. "That sounds like heaven actually. I'm so tired of studying and doing homework. I want a day of doing nothing."

Lauren sighed. "Shit. Okay, I'm gonna study for a few hours and then I'll join y'all."

Luke held up his hands and stood in the middle of the kitchen. "Now hold on a minute. I don't know if there's going to be enough room in Lib and mines bed for all of y'all."

Laughing I shook my head as Grace stood up. "I'm thinking the living room, big brother. Let's do oldies!"

Everyone groaned. Grace placed her hands on her hips and tilted her head. "Oh come on you pussies. We haven't watched an old movie in forever." She walked around the island and put her coffee mug in the sink then rubbed her hands together as she gave a wicked smile. "I'm gonna head upstairs and see what I've got. I'm pretty sure I have *Bringing Up Baby*." Grace clapped, causing everyone to jump. "How about each of us brings one movie a piece?" Grace said with a smile.

"Sounds like a good plan," I said as I hopped off the stool and headed to make myself a plate of Lauren's pancakes.

I peeked back over my shoulder at everyone. I couldn't wait for today. A day of nothing, but spending time with the ones I loved so dearly.

Reaching down, I pinched my arm as I giggled.

Chapter Twenty-Six

Luke

WALKING OUT OF my last class for the day, I let out a sigh. I was exhausted, tired and wanted to go home and sleep for the entire week of spring break. I had been busting my ass the last two and half years so that I could try and graduate early. That meant taking at least twenty-one hours or more a semester. I was beginning to regret it. Especially, if it meant I would be graduating and Libby would still be in school. Smiling, I thought about Lib's degree. She thought she wanted to be a teacher. Then she changed it to law, then nursing. Now she was back at not knowing what she wanted to do.

Will, Colt, and I all were pursuing degrees in rangeland ecology and management. The goal was to someday take over the Mathews Cattle Ranch. Colt had his sights set on horses, but still wanted to help manage the ranch. My father and mother's side of the business, which was mostly training horses, was where Will held the biggest interest. He had also begun to have an interest in racehorses.

My phone buzzed in my pocket. Pulling it out, I saw I had a text from Grace.

> **Grace:** *Are you ready?*
>
> **Me:** *No. Scared shitless*
>
> **Grace:** *Why? She's already said yes!*

Me: Still scared. What if she doesn't like the ring?

Grace: She will. Is everything ready to go?

Me: Yep. One week of camping alone with the love of my life.

Grace: HAHA the only reason y'all want to go camping is so you can keep having sex! Can't have sex at the coast with Mom and Dad there!

Me: You know me so well. Are you sure you want to stay at home all week alone?

Grace: Yeah. I need some quiet time. Besides, I'm not going to be alone. Colt's staying home. I don't think he can take the idea of being around Lauren. Things between them are starting to heat up more and not in the good way.

Me: Yeah, I know. I'm heading back to the house to finish packing up. Love you.

Grace: Make sure you pack the ring! Love you the most!

Pushing my phone back into my pocket, I made my way back to the house. Thinking about this week had my heart racing. I had talked Libby into going on a camping trip to Colorado Bend State Park. It would be a week of nothing but kayaking, biking, hiking, and fishing. And it would mean we would be alone in a tent for five nights. My stomach had that crazy flutter at the thought of making love to Libby any time I wanted.

Grinning like a fool as I walked, I thought about last night. Libby knew how to make me crazy for her in bed. I would never get tired of making her come, over and over again.

SPREADING LIBBY'S LEGS apart, I buried my face. She let out a low moan from the back of her throat as she pushed her hands *through my hair and moved her hips against my face.*

"Luke, I'm so close," she whispered as I flicked my tongue against her sensitive clit.

Reaching my hand up, I began playing with her nipple. Her body began to tremble and I knew she was close. Arching her back, Libby let out a shallow moan and came hard and fast. Moving up her body I covered her in soft kisses. My mouth found hers and we soon got lost in a passionate kiss. I loved that Libby didn't mind getting a taste of herself after oral sex. Every time she would moan, my dick would harden to an almost painful state. "I need you inside me, Luke."

Pushing in, I tried to be slow. I wanted to enjoy the feel of Libby's warm body. Pushing balls deep, I stayed still for a moment and just felt her. I had sworn I'd never have sex with someone and not wear a condom, but that all changed the night on the roof when Libby and I made love. Being with Libby without any barrier between us felt so right. We had both talked after that night and decided since Libby was on the pill, neither one of us wanted me to continue wrapping my stick.

"Luke, move please!" Libby whimpered as she lifted her hips to gain friction. I pulled almost all the way out, leaving only my tip inside her. Pushing back in fast and hard, Libby cried out. Slamming my lips to hers, I pulled out and pushed back in harder with each stroke. I could feel my build up and I wanted to make Libby come again. Swiveling my hips, I hit the spot that had Libby digging her nails into my back and whispering my name. I quickly grabbed her body, lifted her as she wrapped her legs around me and held her in my arms as I got ready to come. "I love you so much," I whispered as my balls tightened and cum rushed to my dick and exploded inside her.

Libby melted in my arms as we whispered each other's names against kiss swollen lips.

PULLING UP TO the state park I peeked over to Libby. She was grinning like a little girl on Christmas morning. I parked and we both got out of the truck and made our way into the park office. Checking in, the young girl behind the counter greeted us with a warm welcome. "Welcome to Colorado Bend State Park. My name is Lindsey. Let's get you all checked in."

After a few minutes of talking, Lindsey gave us our campsite number. "I gave y'all number sixteen. It's at the end and on the riverside. It's pretty private."

Libby blushed as I chuckled and said, "Thank you! This is a special camping trip for us." The young girl smiled as she looked at Libby.

Once we got to the campsite and checked everything out, we began setting up. I put the tent up as Libby took care of setting up the picnic table with the stove and eating supplies.

Libby was wiping her hands on her pants as she looked at the fire-pit. "We need to buy firewood because it's gonna get chilly and I want a fire." I walked behind her and wrapped my arms around her. She placed her hands on my arms and kept talking.

"I totally want to go on the Gorman Falls Trails. Then I think we should take the bikes and do the canyons trail." Spinning around she looked into my eyes. "Then, tonight we should find a place where we can lay under the stars.

"And make love?"

Libby's lips parted and her skin flushed. I could feel the pull of desire already building. I reached up and pulled her hair down from her ponytail. Her blonde hair fell and hugged her shoulders. Her blue eyes lit up as she searched my face, before they landed on my lips. I placed my hand on the side of her face as I rubbed my thumb gently back and forth across her silky skin.

"Do you have any idea how beautiful you are, Libby?"

Enticing eyes found mine. "Do you have any idea how you make me feel?"

Brushing my lips across hers, I spoke in a soft voice. "Tell me."

197

The tear rolling down her face caused my breath to catch. "Like a princess."

"My goal in this life is to make all your dreams come true, Princess, Libby."

Placing her hand over mine, a sob slipped from her lips. "You already have."

My hand slipped behind her neck as I pulled her to me. My lips crashed to hers. Running my tongue along her bottom lip, she opened to me and I dipped my tongue into her mouth. Our tongues danced together as our hands moved across each other's body. I wanted her. I needed her.

Barely pulling my lips back, I panted into her mouth. "Must. Break. In. Tent."

I reached down and picked Libby up as she giggled. "Luke, people are gonna know what we are doing!"

I quickly looked around as I made my way to our tent, carrying Libby in my arms. "Who gives a shit. I don't know these people."

Dipping down, I made my way through the unzipped opening and gently set Libby down on the thick-ass air mattress I bought. I turned and zipped the tent closed. Libby looked around. "This isn't camping! This is better than our mattress at home."

I wiggled my eyebrows up and down. "The best part is, when I fuck you senseless it won't make noises."

Libby sat up and pulled her shirt over her head. My eyes looked at her perfect breasts.

"Let's test it out."

I don't think I've ever gotten undressed so damn fast in my life. Libby was pulling her yoga pants off, but not fast enough for my liking. I grabbed her delicate lace pink panties and pulled. They fell apart in my hands as I moaned.

"Roll over, Lib. I want you from behind."

Grinning, Libby flipped over. I dropped onto the mattress causing Libby's whole body to jump. She laughed as I gripped her hips. "God, Libby. I want to take your ass so damn bad."

She looked over her shoulder, eyes on fire. "Luke, I'm going to come the second you push in."

I pushed my fingers inside her, only to find her wet and ready. Rolling my eyes practically in the back of my head, I let out a moan. "Always so ready."

I pushed my tip barely in her as she hissed, "Yes. More."

One quick push, I was thrusting in and out of her. It wasn't going to take me long to come. Libby was holding on for dear life as I pounded her relentlessly.

Looking at her ass, I took a chance. I pulled out and buried my fingers inside her again, coating them with her silky desire.

"Luke!" she called out frustrated. I smiled as I pushed back into her. "Yes. Harder, Luke. Harder!"

The beads of sweat building on our bodies was a turn on itself. I pushed my fingers against her ass as she jumped. "Yes! Luke, *please.*"

Oh hell. I've gone to heaven.

I pushed my finger into her ass and Libby moaned as I felt her clamp down on my dick and finger as she came. "Oh hell," I whispered as I felt my cum pouring into her. I closed my eyes as I continued to move inside her. I'd never had such a long orgasm before. I pulled my finger and dick out at the same time and Libby collapsed onto the mattress. I dropped down next to her, trying to catch my breath and clear my head. It felt as if I was in a fog.

"That was hot and I want to do that again," Libby said as she rolled on her side and draped an arm over me. I laughed and held her close to me. It didn't take long before we both relaxed completely and fell asleep.

Chapter Twenty-Seven

Libby

LEANING MY HEAD back, I felt the warm sun against my face. Luke had laid a blanket out after we had biked the canyon trail. It felt good to not do anything. I was sick of school. I thought back to my conversation with my mother during Christmas break.

"LIBBY, YOU KEEP changing your major and you'll never finish school."

Rolling my eyes, I sat. "Mom, I hate college. I have no idea what I want to do." Looking down at the floor I let out a chuckle. "Actually I do know what I want to do. I want to do what you do."

My mother stopped rolling out the pie crust. She smiled and leaned against the counter. "Come again?"

I stood and held out my hand as I looked around the kitchen. "This, Mom. I want this. I want to be a wife and mother. I don't want a career where I go in and sit in a drab office."

She pinched her eyebrows together. "You need an education, Libby."

My shoulders dropped. "I know that, Mom, and I'll get one, but can't I just get a business degree or something. Maybe accounting. I love numbers and I was actually helping Ellie do the

200

books last summer for the ranch.

Raising her eyebrow, she pursed her lips out. "Ellie did say you helped her a ton and actually organized her books better than she ever had." Smiling, I felt a spark of hope for the first time in a few years.

I jumped. "Oh Mom, do you think Ellie would teach me? I mean, I could even help Daddy with his books. I know how much you hate doing it."

She laughed and nodded her head. "I certainly wouldn't argue if you took that job over." I walked over and hugged her. "Talk to Ellie. See what she recommends as far as classes go."

Jumping up and down I fist pumped. "I love you, Mom!"

"WHAT ARE YOU thinking about, baby?" Luke asked as he placed his hand on my stomach. Everything fluttered in my stomach and I smiled. Turning my head, I peeked at him through my hand that was shielding the bright sun.

"Our future."

Luke smiled so bright my breath caught. "Do you feel like going for a hike after lunch?"

Nodding my head, I sat up. Our site was pretty secluded, even though we were just off the trail. Looking around I noticed for the first time there was hardly anyone camping. "I can't believe how hardly anyone is here. It's spring break. Where is everyone?"

Luke stood. "I know it's weird. It's dead here. Should make our hike later more romantic." Wiggling his eyebrows, I scrunched my nose and held my hand out for him to help me up.

"I'm starved. Let's go make some lunch."

LUKE AND I sat at the picnic table eating a sandwich when an older couple came walking up. We both smiled as we stood up and made our way to them. I held out my hand.

"Hello, how are y'all today?" I asked as the older gentleman shook my hand. He had the bluest of blue eyes. I turned to the older lady and was taken aback. She looked familiar to me.

"Hello, how are you young wipper snappers doing this afternoon?" she asked as she looked at me and then at Luke.

Luke reached his hand out and shook the older gentleman's hand first, followed by his wife's.

"We are doing wonderful. It's crazy how hardly anyone is here," Luke said.

The older gentleman looked around. "Indeed, it is rather quiet. Make sure to stay on the trails. Don't wander off. Bring those silly phones as well."

"I hear you can take pictures with them," the older lady said with a giggle. Luke and I chuckled.

"Yes, you can take really good pictures with them. I'm Libby Hayes, this is Luke Johnson."

Smiling, the older couple looked at both of us. "Mr. and Mrs. Lambert."

I pulled my head back in surprise.

Mrs. Lambert sucked in a breath and quickly let it out as she clapped her hands together gently. "Well, we should be moving along. The fresh air is wonderful. Keeps you young and healthy, but gets Mr. Lambert sleepy."

Luke extended his hand again, "Mr. Lambert, Mrs. Lambert, it was a pleasure. Enjoy the rest of your afternoon."

I shook my head and smiled. "It was a pleasure. Have a wonderful day."

Mrs. Lambert grinned and nodded her head while Mr. Lambert stepped up to Luke. "Watch your step hiking son and keep an eye out."

They turned and began walking away.

Luke and I stood there and watched them.

Finally, Luke broke the silence. "That was weird. We didn't mention going for hike."

Wrapping my arms around myself, I nodded. "What's even more weird is their last name. My mother's maiden name is Lambert."

Luke glanced over at me. "Really? That is weird." Turning back, he shrugged his shoulders. "Let's hit that trail. I want to make it to the falls with plenty of time to get back before it gets dark."

Walking back over to the tent, Luke ducked inside as I stood there and watched the Lamberts until I couldn't see them anymore. A strange feeling washed over my body.

Making my way back to the campsite, I grabbed my phone from the picnic table. It was at eighty percent. I shoved it into my back pocket. Luke came out of the tent and smiled. He handed me a sweatshirt. "In case it gets chilly by the falls." I took the sweatshirt and wrapped it around my waist tying it.

"I don't think I'll need it, but just in case," I said. Grabbing two bottles of water, Luke and I began walking. Peeking over at him, he seemed nervous as hell. "Is everything okay? You seem nervous?"

Giving me a nervous chuckle, Luke pushed his hand into his pocket. He pulled it out and ran his hand through his hair. "Nah, it's all good here."

Looking ahead I smiled.

My heart began racing. I couldn't wait to tell him. I almost told him when we were laying on the blanket, but I decided I would tell him when we got to the falls.

Grinning like a fool, I held onto Luke's hand as we made our way to the trailhead.

Chapter Twenty-Eight

Luke

LIBBY AND I walked along the Gorman Falls trail hand in hand. I must have checked six times to make sure I had the ring in my pocket. I attempted to calm my nerves. I had no idea why I was nervous. I'd already asked her once and she said yes, so I was pretty sure her answer would be the same.

Libby sucked in a breath and pointed. "Luke, oh my gosh, there it is!" I looked straight ahead. I heard the water before I saw it. Then the falls came into view. It was perfect.

"It's beautiful," Libby whispered as we drew closer to it. We walked to a clearing that had a perfect view of the falls. The rocks surrounding the falls were covered in moss. The green was bright against the clear water falling all around it. Spring flowers were beginning to pop up everywhere and the smell was amazing. Peeking over, I watched as Libby took the scene in.

Libby smiled and shook her head. "I've never seen anything so beautiful. I don't think this day could get any better. This is the perfect spot to share—"

Reaching into my pocket, I pulled out the ring box and fell to one knee. I took Libby's hand in mine and cleared my throat. Libby turned and the moment she saw me on my knee she stopped talking. Her left hand came up and covered her mouth.

"I remember sitting in your kitchen one day and your father walked in. He leaned down and kissed you on the cheek, then turned to your mother and greeted her with the sweetest kiss I'd ever seen. I think I was about sixteen at the time. I'll never forget what he said to her."

Libby moved her hand and wiped away her tears. "What did he say?"

I gazed into Libby's beautiful blue eyes. "He told her she was the most beautiful woman he'd ever seen. Then he kissed her and whispered against her lips, 'I'll love you forever plus infinity, princess.'"

Libby let out a small laugh. "He's always called her princess."

I nodded my head. "I know, and they've always mentioned loving each other for infinity, but it was something about that moment. It was different. I never understood what it was until the first time I made love to you."

Biting on her lip, Libby began to sob. "It was different because in that moment, I knew I wanted that with the girl who was sitting next to me. She wasn't only my best friend; she was the most beautiful girl I'd ever laid eyes on. The girl who made my heart stop with the sound of her voice."

Dropping her hand, I opened the ring box. Libby let out a gasp. "Oh my goodness." Both hands came up and covered her mouth as tears streamed down her face. "It's beyond beautiful."

Inside I was fist pumping and thanking God she liked the ring. "I saw this ring and immediately thought of you, Libby. The color just reminds me of you. Sunshine. You are the sunshine in my life every single day. You warm me, make me feel so loved, and so very blessed to call you mine. Your light is like the ocean. It kept pulling me to you when all I wanted to do was run away. You led me back to you when I was so scared of my feelings. I promise you, Libby. I will never leave your light again. Ever."

Falling to her knees Libby cupped her hands on my face. "I love you, so very much."

"And I love you, baby. So very much. I want nothing more than to make you my wife."

Libby dropped her hands and looked down at the ring and then back into my eyes. "Isabella Gemma Hayes, would you do me the honor of becoming my wife and lifelong side-kick in pranks?"

Her smile grew bigger on her face and she let out a short chuckle. "Yes, and yes!"

I took the ring out of the box and reached for Libby's hand. I slipped the ring onto her finger as Libby gazed upon the ring. Libby threw her arms around me and kissed me. I could kiss her forever.

Pulling back, our eyes met. "I've never been so happy in my entire life. Pinch me so I know I'm not dreaming."

Placing my hand behind her neck, I brought her lips back to mine and gently bit her lower lip before sucking it into my mouth as she let out a long low moan from the back of her throat.

Standing up, I took her hands in mine. "Come on, I want to climb to the top. Colt said the view is amazing."

Libby and I began walking along the trail and climbing further up. A few times, I stopped and reached back to help her up and over rocks. "Are we still on the trail, Luke?"

Looking around, I called over my shoulder. "It looks like it. Damn thing is steeper than it looks."

"And taller!" Libby called out. "If I scratch my new ring, it's your fault."

Laughing, I made my way over rocks. Finally, making it to the top I saw the trail. "Shit. We must have gotten off of it somewhere along the way."

Libby walked up next to me. It took us longer to hike up to the top than I thought it would. It was already getting late. My plans of taking Libby against a tree may have to wait. Walking along another trail I cut across to get to the other side. The view looked better. Looking back to check on Libby every now and then to make sure she was still right behind me. "Doing okay, Lib?" She gave me a thumbs up and said, "Yep."

"Be careful, it's a steep drop off on this side. Let's get to the right trail and then we'll start heading back down."

Libby smiled. "Okay."

I glanced up to see where the trail was and quickly looked down when I heard something. A rattlesnake sat on the rock I was about to step on. I kicked a rock, causing it to hit the snake. It lashed out but thankfully toward the direction of the rock and not me. I jumped back and my foot landed right on the edge of the cliff.

Shit! I felt the rock slip and I knew I was going to slip right with it. I tried to find something to grab onto. Libby screamed out my name as I began to go over the edge. Trying to ride it down on my ass, my foot hit a boulder, causing me to tumble forward. The moment my head hit the rock I felt the pain. It was almost more than I could bear. One more hit of my leg on something and I heard a crack and let out a scream. The pain moved up my leg and my body instantly felt cold. I couldn't tell what hurt worse, my head or my leg. Yelling out, I could hear Libby above me screaming. All I could think about was the snake. When I finally came to a stop, I looked up. Using all my strength, I yelled out, "Libby! Rattlesnake, get out of there."

Everything started to get blurry. I could barely hear Libby calling out my name. I heard her scream again and I tried to turn in the direction of her voice. She was sliding down the trail on her ass. She stood up and began limping as she made her way over to me.

She fell down next to me as she began crying harder. Her face had dirt on it and I could make out the trail her tears were making. "Oh God, Oh God, Luke. Your head is gashed open and—" She looked down at my leg and let out a gasp. My right leg was throbbing. Her hands covered her mouth as she began crying harder. "There's so much blood! I see your bone; it's sticking out of your shin." She snapped her head back to me as she shook her head quickly. "Luke! I don't know what to do!"

Swallowing hard, I tried to talk, but the pain was unbelievable. My head was killing me and everything seemed to be clouding over. "Call ... for ... help."

Libby quickly stood and reached into her back pocket. When she pulled her phone out her mouth dropped open. She began shaking her head as she screamed out, "No. No. No! It's broke! Oh my God, my phone must have broken when I slipped and fell."

I held out my hand and Libby fell to her knees again. Luke, "I'm so sorry. I'm so sorry!"

"It's okay baby, we have to hike out of here, but I need you to stop the bleeding."

Her eyes widened in horror. "How do I stop the bleeding? I don't know how to stop the bleeding."

Taking in a deep breath. "A tourniquet, Lib. You have to make a tourniquet. Use your belt baby."

Libby pulled her belt off. "Put it above the open wound and get it as tight as you can."

Libby began placing the tourniquet on. Her eyes moved to mine. "How do I get it tight without hurting you?"

"Just get it as tight as you can."

Libby closed her eyes and pulled the belt as tight as she could. I bit the inside of my cheek and tried like hell not to call out.

"That's as tight as I can get it, Luke." Standing up she looked down. "You've lost so much blood." Placing her hands over her mouth again, she began crying. "Oh God."

"Baby, I need you to find the biggest stick you can, but watch for snakes. I need to get up so we can hike out of here.

Her eyes widened in horror. "You can't hike out of here, Luke."

Standing, she began screaming. "Help! Somebody help us!" She started to walk toward the trail. She had blood running down from her knee and she was limping.

My head hurt so damn bad. *I'm so sleepy.* I glanced over to Libby. Everything was starting to get blurry. "Lib, help me up."

Libby came running back over with a giant stick. "I found this."

Getting next to me, Libby wrapped her arms around me as

I held the stick in one hand and wrapped my arm around her shoulders. Somehow I got up. "See, I told you. We're gonna get out of here and find help."

"Did you not bring your phone, Luke?"

Shaking my head I whispered, "No." I felt pain everywhere as we began making our way slowly back down the trail. I couldn't put any pressure on my broken leg and tried hopping. Every move shot pain through my body.

Everything started spinning. "Luke, the road wasn't that far. Maybe a half a mile. We took the longer trail, we can make it."

Everything went black. "Lib, wait. It's all spinning. Everything is black."

I felt Libby move as she guided me somewhere. "There's a fallen tree. Can you sit on it, Luke?"

The temperature must have been dropping. The wind picked up and was blowing. "Libby, the cold front is moving through early."

I started shaking. "I need to lie down."

Libby placed her hands on my face. "Look at me. Luke, please look at me." I slowly opened my eyes and saw her beautiful blue eyes.

"Libby. My head hurts, and my leg ... the pain."

Glancing down she let out a small gasp. "Your bleeding picked up again. We need to get help, Luke. Libby pulled her sweatshirt off of her waist and began putting it over my head. "Put this on, it will warm you up."

Standing Libby screamed out, "Help! Please someone help us!"

Bending down she looked into my eyes. "I'm not going far. I'm going to walk a little ways to call out for help. I promise, I'm not leaving."

"I'm so tired."

Quickly wiping her eyes, she shook her head. "You can't go to sleep. Please don't go to sleep. You hit your head, Luke. Promise me you won't go to sleep."

"Promise."

She quickly walked down the trail calling out for help. Her voice got further and further away. I forced myself to keep my eyes open. Reaching down I tightened the belt the best I could. I felt like I was going to throw up when I saw the bone sticking out.

I need to rest my eyes. Just for a few minutes. I closed my eyes and the pain started to slowly go away.

"Luke! Luke, wake up! You promised me!" Libby yelled out.

"Stop yelling, Lib. My head fucking hurts." Libby began kissing all over my face. I opened my eyes and looked at her.

"I can't find anyone. There is no one. It's dark now and everyone will be at their campsites.

Libby's lips were trembling. "You're cold, Lib."

Shaking her head. "I'm scared. I'm fine."

"I'm so thirsty," I whispered. Libby grabbed the backpack she had put on and took out a bottle of water. She placed it up to my lips and I took a small drink.

"So. Good."

I barely had any energy to talk. "Lib, you're gonna … have to … leave me. Go … find … help and leave me."

She stared at me as a tear rolled down her cheek. "Lib, if I don't get help soon—"

"No! Stop talking like that. Stop right now. I can't leave you alone. You have to stay awake, Luke! You're going to be fine. We're going to be fine."

Chapter Twenty-Nine

Libby

I SAT WITH my knees pulled up to my chest as I rocked back and forth. Luke was drifting in and out of consciousness. My throat was hoarse from calling out and I was so cold.

Looking up I began crying. "Please, please don't do this. I beg of you. Please."

"Libby, darling. It's so cold out here."

Turning, I looked to see Mr. and Mrs. Lambert standing there. Jumping up, I went over to them. "W—what are you two doing out here? It's dark and so cold?"

Mrs. Lambert placed her hand on my cheek. "Are you giving up, Libby?"

I jerked my head back. "No? I just don't know what to do. I can't leave him. He keeps trying to sleep and—" I began crying. "I can't leave him. Please ... can you ... will you please go get help? Please!"

Mrs. Lambert nodded her head. "Of course, darling."

Mr. Lambert rested his hand on my shoulder. "Libby, you have to give him hope. He's giving up."

"I—I don't know how to!"

Smiling he looked over at Luke and then back at me. "You do, darling. You do. Tell him your news."

Luke let out a moan I turned and looked at him. "I need y'all to go and find—" I spun back to talk to Mr. and Mrs. Lambert

211

and they were gone. "Hello? Mr. Lambert? Mrs. Lambert. Wait! Please get help!"

"Libby," Luke called out in a weak voice. I made my way back over to him. My knee was killing me. I dropped down next to him. He smiled as I put his head in my lap.

"I saw Mr. and Mrs. Lambert. They're going to get help, baby. Please hold on."

Luke closed his eyes and opened them. A single tear rolled down his face. "I wanted to get married, have a baby. I had so … many plans."

I thrashed my head back and forth. "No, don't you give up, Luke Johnson."

"I dreamed of us walking along with a little girl. We … we were swinging her as we walked."

Tears flowed from my face as Mr. Lambert's words came back to me. *"You have to give him hope. Tell him your news."*

"We're going to, Luke. We're going to have that little girl."

He slowly nodded his head. "Libby, no one is going to find us until tomorrow. I can't wait … that long. I'm so sorry, baby."

"No, no, no. Luke I need you to listen to me. I had my own surprise for you. I was waiting to tell you at the falls, but then you surprised me when you asked me to marry you."

Luke eyes opened and looked into my eyes. "Luke, you can't leave me. You can't because we're going to have a baby."

Luke smiled weakly. "God, I wanted that so bad with you, Libby."

Placing my hands on his face I looked into his eyes. "Luke, listen to me. Look into my eyes and hear what I'm saying. We're having a baby. I'm pregnant, Luke. I found out the day before we left for the camping trip. We're having a baby in about eight months. So you can't leave me alone. You can't do this to me. I need you! *We* need you. The baby and I, we both need you."

Luke's face lit up. "A baby? We're having a baby? How?"

I giggled as my teeth began to chatter. "Well, if you really need me to explain."

He smiled bigger. "No, I mean I thought you were on the

212

pill?"

I shrugged my shoulders. "I am. I never miss a pill and I take them every day at the same time. I guess your swimmers were bound and determined."

The color in Luke's face instantly looked better. He sat up a little more. "I can't believe we're having a baby. Your dad is going to break my other leg."

I laughed as I pressed my lips against Luke's. *He's back. Thank you, God. Thank you!*

I heard voices. Pulling my lips from Luke's I turned my head to listen. "Over here! I see them, Luke! Help's coming!"

Carefully moving Luke's head from my lap, I jumped up. I started yelling out, "Here! Please help us! Over here!"

Two men came running up. They were both dressed in state park uniforms. I couldn't really see what they looked like since it was so dark out. They stopped and looked at me, but I pointed to Luke. "Please, he broke his leg and hit his head. He's lost a lot of blood. We need to get him out right away."

The one guy was carrying a medical case and looked back at the other guy. "Tell them we need StarFlight, stat!"

MY HEAD WAS resting on Luke's bed. I had only left his side twice—when the nurses forced me to get my knee cleaned up and when they had brought him into surgery for his leg. My knee had been cut but not enough for stitches. It was for sure banged up pretty good, but thankfully nothing was broken.

The sound of Luke breathing calmed me. They had brought him back from the recovery room about an hour ago. His surgery on his leg went well, but the doctor said he would be weak from all the blood he lost.

A chill ran through my entire body. One of the nurses had let me borrow her sweatshirt. I felt like I couldn't get warm. Because I had been hurt as well, I rode in the helicopter with Luke. The hospital hadn't been able to get a hold of my parents or Luke's until about two hours ago. They were driving up from the coast and should be here soon.

Lifting my head, I looked at my engagement ring. Smiling, I leaned back in the chair. The door opened and a young lady walked in.

"Ms. Hayes?"

I nodded my head. She walked up to me and extended her hand. She sat down and faced me. "I'm Doctor Colin. We got some results back from one of your tests."

I looked at her badge. She was an OB doctor. Smiling I nodded my head. "I'm about four weeks pregnant."

Her face relaxed. "Okay, I wasn't sure if you knew. You hadn't mentioned being pregnant when they were checking you all out."

Looking down, I felt guilty for forgetting. I felt her hand on my knee. "You had to have just found out. Don't feel guilty. You had other things on your mind."

Chewing on my lip, I sniffed. "What kind of mother forgets she's pregnant?"

"The kind who just went through a very terrifying situation."

Nodding my head, I looked at Luke. "I guess so." Looking back to the doctor, I had a moment of panic. "I don't want anyone in our family knowing yet. I'm not that far along."

She nodded. "Of course not. There would be no reason for anyone to tell them." Her eyes were kind. I took a good look at her. She had blonde, short hair. It was cut just below her chin. Her light-brown eyes were beautiful and you could tell she had a kind heart.

Standing, she shook her head slightly. "Please get some rest, Libby. You're taking care of a little one now. Eat something and get some sleep."

Nodding my head, I replied, "I promise I will as soon as our parents get here. I don't want to leave him alone."

She smiled sweetly at me.

"Thank you, Doctor Colin. Have a good day."

214

"You're welcome. Please remember, eat and sleep. Soon."

Smiling weakly, I agreed.

Watching the doctor leave the room I let out a sigh as I shook my head. I felt the tears building in my eyes. Closing my eyes, I felt a tear roll down my face. Wiping it away I whispered, "Some mother I'm going to be."

Leaning forward, I placed my elbows on Luke's bed and buried my face in my hands. I was so tired. My body hurt and I was so scared.

I started to doze off again when I heard something. Lifting my head, I looked around and then looked at Luke. He was staring at me.

I jumped, practically knocking the chair over. "Luke! You're okay, you're in the hospital. Everything is going to be okay, baby."

Leaning down, I placed my lips to his as he moved his hand to the back of my neck and deepened the kiss. The warmth of his kiss warmed my body immediately. It was as if his kiss made me realize everything was going to be okay.

"I love you, Luke. I love you so much."

A smile slowly spread across Luke's face. "Please tell me I wasn't dreaming when you said you were pregnant."

I half laughed, half cried as I nodded my head and placed my hand on the side of his face. "You weren't dreaming."

His smile turned into a full-blown grin as his eyes filled with tears. "Libby, your daddy's gonna kill me."

Giggling, I said, "Me too! I think I'm more afraid of my mother than I am my father." I slowly looked back into Luke's green eyes. "I was so scared I was going to lose you, Luke. I can't live this life without you in it. I just can't. You're my entire world."

Luke reached up and wiped a tear off my face. "You didn't lose me, I'm fine, Lib. A little broken and bruised, but I'm going to be fine. It's gonna be you, me, and baby makes three."

I chuckled and shook my head. It wasn't going to be as easy as Luke was making it seem. He still had a little more than a year of college and I had two years. Looking down I took a deep breath.

"What about school?" I asked as Luke narrowed his eyes together.

"We'll finish this semester and take summer classes. We can find an apartment in College Station for us while I finish out my last year. If you want to keep going, we'll work something out. Maybe we can hire someone to help you, but you'll fall at least a semester behind." He smiled. "When are you due?"

"November sixth."

Luke's eyes searched my face. "Libby, I'll support you and this baby and if that means I stay in College Station and work at a damn gas station while you finish school, I will."

I let out a chuckle as I rolled my eyes. "We still have some time to think about it. I don't want to make too many plans, just in case."

"Don't say that. She's gonna be a beautiful and healthy baby girl."

Raising my eyebrows I tilted my head. "She, huh?"

Luke shrugged his shoulders. "Or he. I'm not going to be picky." Winking he tried to adjust himself in the bed.

"Oh shit! I was supposed to let them know when you woke up." Reaching up, I hit the call button.

A woman's voice came over the speaker that was built into the side of the bed. "May I help you?"

"Yes, um, Luke's awake."

"Okay, thank you for letting me know. I'll let his nurse know."

"Thank you," I said as I watched Luke's face. He seemed really happy about the baby. I was betting we were going to be the only two who were happy. I needed to brace myself for the lectures I was going to get from my parents.

"Libby, look at me," Luke whispered. Turning, I looked into his love filled eyes. "It's going to be okay. I promise you. It's all going to be okay. I love you and I already love this baby because it is a part of you and me. We're going to be okay."

Chewing on my lower lip, I felt like I was on an emotional

roller coaster. "I don't want my parents to be disappointed in me. I swear I didn't miss a pill, Luke. I swear."

Luke patted the side of his bed. "I need you in my arms, Lib."

I crawled up as Luke attempted to move. I knew he was in pain. I snuggled up the best I could as he draped his arm around me. "Libby, we decided together when we made the decision to trust just using the pill. What happened is a miracle and I don't really give a shit what my parents or your parents think. To me, our child saved my life."

I lifted my head and gave him a knowing look. He rolled his eyes. "Okay, I do care. I'm not going to feel bad though. Everything happens for a reason and I really honestly believe that you got pregnant and it saved my life. I was ready to give up, Lib. I was weak and tired. I wanted to make it all go away. Then when you told me you were pregnant, this feeling rushed through my body. I was ready to stand up and hobble the hell out of the place." Luke placed his hand on my stomach. "This baby is our saving grace."

Tears fell from my eyes as I let Luke's word sink in. It was true. In this moment, I believed that our baby was a miracle from God because he knew we were going to need her to pull through last night.

I lifted my head and let out a gasp. "The Lamberts."

Luke pulled back and looked at me. "What about them?"

"They were on the trail last night and I was ready to give up. I was cold and in pain and you were slowly slipping further away. Mr. Lambert was the one who reminded me about the baby. Not in a direct way, but, it was as if he knew I was pregnant." Shaking my head, I thought back to last night. "Come to think of it. They weren't able to find them and the park rangers said someone called and just told them to check the falls trail. Someone was hurt."

Luke made a face. "Huh. Maybe they called."

"From where? We know they didn't have cell phones." I went to say something else when the door to Luke's room opened. An

217

older gentleman walked in and smiled when he saw me in bed with Luke. I quickly scurried my way off of the bed. Smiling I said above a whisper, "Sorry."

Holding up his hands, he smiled. "No worries." Turning to Luke he reached out his hand as Luke shook it. "Well, Mr. Johnson you're looking better than you were last night when they brought you in. I'm Doctor Grambs. I performed the surgery on your leg earlier this morning. You had a pretty good break in your right leg."

Luke chuckled. "I'd say so."

The doctor glanced to me and smiled. Looking back at Luke he continued to talk. "You suffered an open fracture, or some call it a compound fracture, of your right tibia. We needed to go in and place a plate and screws to help with the bones healing. Typical healing time for this type of fracture is about four months, although it can take as long as six months or longer. I'll want you to do some physical therapy as soon as possible."

Luke nodded. "When will I be able to put weight on it?"

"Fairly quickly. I'll want you to use precautions of course and fracture pain will go away long before the bone is completely healed so I want you to take it easy. Just because it feels better, doesn't mean it's one hundred percent better."

Luke nodded his head. "Yes, sir. I understand."

Pointing to Luke's forehead he said, "The gash in your forehead was pretty deep. We ended up putting thirteen stitches in. You'll need to come back and get those taken out."

The doctor and Luke talked for a few more minutes before he told Luke to take it easy and get some rest.

I stood and walked the doctor to the door. After closing the door, I leaned against it and smiled. "I guess I'll have to play nurse to you when we get home."

Luke gave a pretend disgusted look as he rolled his eyes. "I guess I'll have to suck it up and take it like a man."

I began to make my way over to him, I needed to feel his lips on mine when the door opened again. Jeff and Ari walked in. Ari had tears rolling down her face as she rushed over to

Luke's side.

"Oh, my poor baby." She leaned over and kissed his fore-head next to his stitches. Luke's left eye was black and blue. Turning Ari looked at me. She gave me a quick once over and then walked up and pulled me into her arms. "Are you okay, sweetheart?" Pushing me back at arm's length she searched my face. I smiled and nodded.

"I'm fine. I promise. Just a sore knee and a broken phone." Peeking back to Luke my heart dropped. "Nothing like Luke though." I pushed back my tears as I looked into Ari's eyes. She placed her hand on the side of my face. "You look tired, honey. You need to get some rest. After your mom and dad see Luke, I want you to let them take you to the hotel."

I nodded my head. I didn't want to leave Luke, but I wanted to sleep and rest. I didn't want to add any stress on my body because of the baby. "I will. I promise. I didn't want to leave him until someone else got here."

Jeff was talking to Luke and asking him about his injuries. Luke filled them in on his leg and the bump on his head. I was so thankful he didn't have any other serious injuries.

Clearing my throat, all three of them looked at me. "Um, I'm gonna head on out to the waiting room and fill my parents in." Walking up to Luke, I gently kissed him on the lips. "I love you," I whispered.

He smiled and said, "Before you go—"

Panic set in. Was he going to say something about the baby? We agreed to wait.

"Isn't there something you want to show Mom and Dad?"

My eyes widened in horror. Luke quickly saw my concern. "What's on your finger," he said, clearing up my confusion.

Glancing down, I saw my pale-yellow engagement ring. Smiling I held my hand out. "Luke asked me to marry him next to the falls. Before the accident."

Ari's hands covered her mouth as she let out a squeal. She took my hand and held up the ring. Glancing over to Luke, she smiled. "See, I knew all those times I dragged you shopping with me and Grace, it would pay off. Oh Luke, darling this is beautiful."

I bit on my lip and beamed with happiness. Ari looked into my eyes and I could see how happy she truly was. "It's perfect for you, Libby."

Jeff pulled me into his arms. "I'm so happy for you both." Kissing me on the forehead he whispered, "Thank you for loving him like you do, Libby."

My heart dropped and I swallowed hard. Pulling back, I nodded my head as I smiled at Jeff.

Turning, I headed to the door and out to see my parents. As the door shut, I dragged in a deep breath and blew it out before I made my way to my parents. I prayed to God they didn't see through my charade.

Chapter Thirty

Luke

SITTING ON THE back porch, I looked out at the rain. Libby was now twelve weeks pregnant and we still hadn't told anyone. It was early May and school was about over. Libby and I talked about how we were going to tell our parents. My leg was healing well, but I was still taking it easy. The last thing I wanted to do was reinjure it.

I heard the screen door open and I smiled. I could sense Libby before I even knew it was her. Inhaling a deep breath, Libby's perfume filled my senses. Her arms wrapped around my neck as she leaned over and whispered in my ear. "I'm feeling a little frisky and everyone is home. Boo."

I chuckled as I took her hand and brought her around to sit on my lap. She sat down and wiggled as I raised my eyebrow. "Are you nervous?"

Letting out a sigh, she nodded her head. "I think Grace knows."

"Really? What makes you say that?"

Looking over my shoulder to see if anyone was coming, she turned back to me. "The morning sickness. I tried so hard to keep it on the down low but a few times it just hit me when I was with her. Then yesterday, she ran into me at the mall when I was picking up our shirts."

I chuckled, causing Libby to bounce on my lap and my dick

to jump. "The shirts. I can't wait to wear them."

Libby placed her hand over her mouth and giggled. "I'm not sure they are going to lessen the blow."

I ran my hand up and down her back. "Libby, they're going to be thrilled."

Libby lifted her thumb and began chewing on her nail. I pulled it from her mouth. "Stop it. They're going to be happy."

"Who's going to be happy and about what?"

Libby closed her eyes as I looked at Grace walking out the door and making her way over to us.

Think Johnson. Think.

"Will and Alex. We're going to surprise them with a weekend in Fredericksburg this summer."

Libby's eyes widened as she nodded her head in approval.

Grace pursed her lips together and nodded her head. "What a nice thing to do. How come y'all are doing that for them?"

Libby's smile faded as I felt the sweat bead along the top of my forehead. "Um, I don't know," I said as I shrugged. "Just thought it would be a nice thing to do. We plan on doing nice things all summer for our friends."

Libby got off my lap as she nodded her head. "Yeah, like I'm going to treat you to a manicure *and* a pedicure."

Grace gave Libby a pretend smile. "Awe, that is so sweet. My future sister-in-law is buttering me up."

"That's not true. It's just we haven't hardly spent any time together and I thought this would be nice. There's no hidden meaning behind it."

Grace grinned bigger. "Well I think that's awesome. Will you let me go shopping with you and buy the baby clothes?"

Oh shit.

Libby's head snapped over as she looked at me. I gave her what I hoped was a stay calm look.

Libby scrunched her nose and plastered on a fake confused look, as she let out a nervous chuckle. "Baby clothes? Why would you want to buy baby clothes?" Libby asked with a nervous smile.

Grace tilted her head and crossed her arms as she looked from Libby, to me, and back to Libby again.

"Do you think I'm stupid? Really? I know the two of you better than you know yourselves." She pointed to me. "You, you walk around with that goofy smile on your face all the damn time. You place your hand on Libby's stomach and whisper into her ear at least twice a day when you don't think anyone is watching."

Swallowing hard, I peeked over to Libby. Grace turned and pointed to Libby. "And you. Since we were fourteen you have asked me for pads or tampons because you never have any. You don't think I haven't noticed how you haven't asked for any in about three months. You don't think I haven't noticed you not wearing blush anymore because the color of your skin is just radiating."

Libby closed her eyes. "Shit. I forgot about the pads and tampons."

My mouth dropped open. "Lib!"

Throwing her hands up in the air Libby pointed to a smiling Grace. "She knows, Luke."

Grace started jumping up and down. "Oh my God!" Running over she placed her hands on Libby's stomach. I watched as tears began to build in my baby sister's eyes. "I'm going to be an aunt?" Turning to me she wiped a tear away. "I'm so glad you didn't wrap your stick!"

I tossed my head back and laughed. "Me too, Sweet Pea. Me too."

I PARKED THE truck and looked over at Libby. She was either wringing her hands together or biting her nails. "Lib. It's all right."

Placing her hands on her stomach, she began to cry. "They're going to hate me. I failed at being a good daughter. I got myself knocked up halfway through college." Her hands came up and buried her faced as her body jerked from sobs.

"Libby. Please look at me."

Dropping her hands, she turned her face and looked at me. The look she was giving me reminded me of how Grace used to look at my parents when they lectured her in high school.

"Are you happy?"

Sucking in her top lip and jetting out her lower lip she nodded her head.

"I'm happy too. This is our miracle baby. Don't ever forget that."

Nodding her head, she spoke above a whisper. "I won't. I promise."

I slapped my hands together and jumped out of the truck. I jogged around the front and over to Libby's side. Opening the door I looked down at her T-shirt. I smiled as I read it.

My daddy's swimmers are strong.

Glancing down, I looked at my T-shirt. Grabbing Libby's hand I led her to the front door. We had asked to talk to our parents and they informed us they were over at Gunner and Ellie's place getting ready for the barbecue later this afternoon. Libby and I were heading back to A&M so that I could take summer classes and our parents wanted to have a get-together with everyone. With how I had busted my ass in school and with taking classes this summer, I was going to be able to graduate this December.

I knocked and opened the door. I peeked down at Libby and smiled. We made our way through the living room and into the kitchen. Ellie, Heather and my mother were all standing at the island. Each with their hands in something they were making. My father, Josh, and Gunner were across the kitchen. Gunner was sitting at the table husking corn. Josh was leaning against a counter with my father standing next to him.

Smiling, I turned to face them. My father looked over as he was lifting his beer to his mouth. The rim stopped at his lips as I watched his eyes read my shirt. He dropped his beer some and shot me a dirty look.

224

Libby hugged and kissed Heather before turning and kissing Ellie and then my mother on the cheek. She came up beside me and whispered, "Here we go. Your dad sees your shirt."

Glancing down, I looked at my T-shirt again. *My swimmers are strong.*

I turned my head away and leaned to whisper in Libby's ear. "He thinks it's a joke."

Libby turned and looked at me. Her hot breathe hitting my face and causing my dick to come to attention. *Jesus. Even in a room filled with our parents, she turns me on.*

"What? Why would he think—oh!" Libby said as she giggled.

"Hey, baby girl." Libby and I both snapped our heads up as Josh came walking up to Libby. He slowed down and read her T-shirt out loud.

"My daddy has strong swimmers?" Josh looked up at Libby. "That's not cool at all. Lib, I don't think I like that T-shirt." Stopping in front of us, Josh stood there looking at Libby and down to the shirt. Turning, Josh pointed to my father. "Your damn T-shirt ways have rubbed off on my daughter."

Gunner laughed and shook his head. "Remember the beaver T-shirt?"

Josh turned and faced Gunner and they both laughed. I took a look at my father who was still staring at me. I leaned slightly over to Libby. "They all think it's a joke and your dad thinks your shirt is talking about him."

"Ew," Libby said in a whisper.

I looked into my father's eyes and gave him a smile. It didn't take long for him to figure out what our T-shirts meant. I held my breath. Glancing over I noticed Gunner stopped laughing when he looked at my dad. Turning back to look at Libby and me, a smile grew across Gunner's face. "Josh, you still like whiskey?" Gunner asked.

Josh laughed. "Hell, I haven't had whiskey in a long time."

Looking up at Josh, Gunner said, "You're fixin' to need some."

Libby grabbed my hand. I wanted to drop her hand 'cause

it was all sweaty from her being nervous, but I held onto it. Closing my eyes I took in a deep breath and glanced back over to my dad. He pushed off the counter and walked toward Libby and me. He stopped in front of Libby and searched her face. The slow smile caused me to let out the breath I was holding. "Just tell me one thing."

Libby sniffled next to me. I knew she was scared to death. "Anything."

"I'm not really going to be called Pappy, am I?"

Libby started laughing. "You can be called anything you want."

Josh walked up. His mouth was gaped open. Libby's smile faded and tears streamed down her eyes. "Daddy, please don't be disappointed in me. I couldn't take it if you were."

A tear escaped the corner of Josh's eye and he shook his head. "Isabella, I could never be disappointed in you. Do I wish it was years later? Yes, but I'm certainly not disappointed in you."

"Are you angry with me?" Libby asked as she squeezed my hand.

Reaching up with his hands, Josh wiped Libby's tears away with this thumbs. "Are you happy, baby?"

She nodded her head and whispered, "Very."

Josh pulled her into his arms and Libby began crying. "I love you, Daddy."

Grinning, my father reached out and pulled me to him. "Is this the reason for summer school? Graduating in December?" Pulling back, he looked into my eyes. "Yes, sir. The sooner I can start working, the sooner I can get a place for us."

"What in the world is going on with y'all?" my mother asked as she walked over. I turned around and saw Heather watching Josh and Libby. My mother was looking at Josh and Libby also before she looked at me. "Is everything okay? Why is Josh crying? He never cries."

My father walked up to my mother as Heather made her way over to Libby and Josh. "Do you know you are going to be the hottest grandma around?"

My mother chuckled and then looked at me as her eyes moved down and read my T-shirt. Her hands came up to her mouth and I watched as tears filled her eyes as she shook her head. "Mom, she's our little miracle."

"Okay everyone just hold the fort here. What is going on?" Heather asked as she looked around.

Libby walked up to me and I wrapped my arms around her as I rested my chin on the top of her head. "Mom, please don't be angry."

Heather turned and looked at Josh and that's when it hit. A sob escaped her mouth as she turned back and looked at Libby. "Libby? You're pregnant?"

Libby nodded her head and Heather quickly walked over and pulled Libby from my arms into her arms. "Why in the world would you think I'd be angry?"

"I didn't want you to be disappointed in me."

Heather placed her hands on the sides of Libby's face as my mother walked up to me and hugged me. "Oh Luke, honey." She pulled back and smiled. "A baby?"

I nodded and glanced back to Libby and Heather.

"Libby Hayes, there is no way I could ever be disappointed in you."

"This is what I want, Mom."

Heather nodded and looked at Josh and then me. Smiling she looked lovingly at Libby. "Let's all talk about everything later okay?"

Libby bit down on her lip and nodded. I knew Heather wanted Libby to have a college degree and so did I. I would do whatever it took to make that happen.

Gunner walked up and grinning like a fool. "I gotta tell ya, you handled that a hell of a lot better than I would have. Had that been your son," Gunner slapped Josh on the back, "I'd have killed the little bastard." Josh turned and looked at me.

"Believe me, that urge is there. I'm thinking a walk down to the barn may be in order."

I took a step back and everyone laughed as Ellie hugged Libby. "Does your brother know?"

Libby shook her head. "No, we wanted to tell y'all first."

My father slapped his hands. "Well hell, this just turned into a party!"

"Wait!" Heather called out. Looking at Libby she smiled. "How far along are you?"

My mother jumped up and down. "Oh yeah!"

Libby's face blushed. "Twelve weeks."

My mother looked like she was counting back. "Before the accident? Did you know you were pregnant then?"

Nodding her head, Libby smiled.

Heather's shoulders dropped. "Oh, Libby. I wish you would have told us, honey. You went through all of that alone."

Peeking over to me, Libby smiled. "We weren't alone, Mom. We had each other, and a very magical older couple."

Grinning I winked at Libby. Turning back to her mother, Libby asked, "Mom, can we talk later about Grandma and Grandpa Lambert?"

Pulling her head back in surprise Heather said, "Sure we can."

Alex came walking into the kitchen and looked around. "What's going on?"

We all looked at each other. My mother tilted her head and gestured for me to tell Alex. "Well, um, we were just telling our parents how November sixth is going to have to be a clear schedule for everyone."

Colt came walking into the kitchen. "Why the heck are y'all blocking the kitchen?" Colt stopped talking.

Colt looked around. "What's going on?" Shifting his head he looked down at my T-shirt, eyes widened in surprise. Spinning around he read Libby's T-shirt. "Holy shit."

"Hey, watch your mouth young man," Ellie said as she slapped Colt across the back of the head.

Grinning like a fool, just like his daddy had been earlier. "Awe man." Reaching his hand out to shake mine, I pulled Colt into a hug. "Congratulations, dude."

"Wait. What is going on?" Alex said as she threw up her hands.

"Libby and I are expecting a baby, Alex. November sixth."

Alex's mouth dropped open and tears quickly formed in her eyes. Alex walked over and pulled Libby into her arms. "I'm so happy for y'all!" Pushing Libby back to look at her, Alex smiled bigger. "We're totally going shopping for maternity clothes!"

Libby giggled and nodded her head.

"Does Will know yet?" Alex asked.

I walked up and took Libby into my arms. "Not yet. We wanted to tell our parents first."

Colt laughed. "Dude, please let me be there when you tell him. I want to see him kick your ass."

I glared at Colt. Josh started laughing as Colt laughed harder.

It wasn't long before everyone started making their way over for the barbecue. The rest of the day was spent talking, planning, talking some more, and then eating. Grams and Gramps invited Libby and me over for lunch the next day. Josh took me outside and threatened my life if I didn't make Libby and the baby happy every day for the rest of their lives. My father insisted he wasn't to be called Pappy. My mother made plans to go to Paris to buy clothes for the baby, and Heather watched Libby's every move. I wasn't sure how to read Heather. I couldn't tell if she was happy or not. She said she was happy for us and even talked about Josh building the baby's furniture.

If only her eyes didn't tell another story.

Chapter Thirty-One

Libby

MY MOTHER AND I walked arm in arm along the dirt trail. I was exhausted. Once everyone found out Luke and I were expecting a baby, everything got crazy. *What plans were being made? Would I keep going to school? What about my degree? Where were going to live?* It was endless. When my mother pulled me to the side and asked if I would take a walk with her, I was somewhat relieved.

We walked along in silence for a few minutes before I couldn't take it anymore. "You're upset aren't you, Mom?"

Turning to look at me with a stunned expression, she shook her head. "No, I'm not upset with you, Libby. I do have to ask you one thing though."

Inhaling a deep breath, I got ready for it. "Okay."

She stared straight ahead as we walked. "Did you use some form of birth control?"

I stopped walking. "Yes. Mom, I didn't purposely get pregnant. I was on birth control. I've been on birth control ever since you took me that one time."

Her eyebrows rose. I looked away embarrassed for some reason. "Luke wore a condom any time we were together, up until Christmas break. We were together one night and it just felt right and magical. I feel so embarrassed talking to you about this."

I turned away from her. She walked up and put her arm around me as we continued to walk. "Libby, you're a grown woman and I don't live with blinders on. Your father and I knew you and Luke were in a sexually active relationship. I was your age once too, you know." She wiggled her eyebrows up and down.

"Gross mom, I just threw up in my mouth some."

She laughed as she moved her arm and we walked together holding hands now. "Libby, I'm not going to judge you or say you did something wrong. You used protection and you're not upset about being pregnant. I'm glad you're being honest. It's just, I would have rather you waited a few more years."

Nodding my head, I stopped and turned to my mom. "The day I found I was pregnant was the day we were leaving for our camping trip. I was scared, Mom. I knew you and Dad were going to be upset with me. I didn't want to disappoint either of you. I didn't know how Luke was going to react either. When Luke graduates, we had already decided he was going to get a job close to A&M, maybe at a ranch or something. Being apart wasn't an option."

"Did you ever talk about kids?"

I chuckled. "No. I mean sometimes we would talk about our future and we both wanted kids. The plan was to wait a year or so after I graduated. I would stop taking the pill. If it happened, it happened. Then, I started to feel sick. Like I was getting the flu. My period was a few days late, so I bought a test. I was positive I wasn't pregnant. I mean, I was on the pill. I took them every single day at the same time of the day."

Clearing her throat my mother asked, "Libby, did you ever talk to your doctor about being sexually active?"

"I was planning on it when I went to her for my yearly. Why?"

"Were you still taking the same birth control pills? I mean your doctor hasn't changed the type of pills or anything has she?"

I shook my head. "No. It's been the same pills I've taken all along. Why?"

Stopping my mother looked at me with such a loving face.

231

"Baby, you were on the lowest dose of birth control pills. You were supposed to talk to her *before* you became sexually active."

Thinking back to that day in the doctor's office, I remembered the doctor telling me I would need a higher dose once I became sexual active. My mouth dropped in horror as I slammed my hands over my mouth. "I'm so stupid! I totally forgot about her saying that, Mom."

Shaking her head she winked. "Well, what's meant to be will be."

"Luke says the baby is a miracle. That she saved his life."

Lacing her arm with mine, we began to head back toward Gunner and Ellie's house. "How so?"

"Mom, it was bad on that trail. Luke had lost so much blood and he kept going in and out of consciousness." I shuddered as if I could still feel the cold wind blowing on me. "A cold front had moved through and the temperature dropped so fast. I was beginning to think Luke wouldn't make it through the night. Then Mr. and Mrs. Lambert showed up."

My mother stopped walking. "Who?"

"It was this older couple. We had met them before we went hiking. They walked by our campsite and it was really weird because they even warned Luke to watch where he stepped when we went on a hike. And Mrs. Lambert even told me to bring my phone. I thought it was kind of ironic that their last name was the same as your maiden name."

My mother was just staring at me. "Keep going, Libby."

I continued. "I don't even know what time it was, but it was dark. I heard someone talking and I looked up to see Mr. and Mrs. Lambert. I was shocked they were out late and in the cold. I was panicked and asked for them to go get help. I didn't want to leave, Luke. That's when the really strange thing happened."

"What?" my mother asked in a whisper.

Thinking back to that moment I got a chill. Inhaling a deep breath, I slowly blew it out. "Mr. Lambert told me I had to give Luke hope because he was giving up. I cried and told them I

232

didn't know how. Mr. Lambert smiled and told me I did know how, I needed to tell Luke my news. Luke had let out a moan and I turned toward him. When I turned around—they were gone."

My mother let out a gasp. The look on her face was like none I had seen before. I couldn't tell if she was shocked, scared, or just plain confused. The color in her face had drained as she continued to stare at me. "Go on, Libby. Keep talking," she whispered.

"Then the paramedics came. When I asked them if the Lambert's had told them where to find us, he said they had received a call saying someone was badly injured on the falls trail so they immediately came looking for us."

Standing there, I stared at my mother. She wasn't moving, talking, and I wondered if she was even breathing. "Mom?"

Wiping the tears from her eyes before they could fall she let out a small laugh. "Do remember when you were little, Libby, and I used to tell you stories about how your grandparents were watching out for all of us?"

Tingles moved through my body. "Mom! I knew there was something special about them. I told Luke Mrs. Lambert kind of looked like you."

Pulling me into her arms, she held me for the longest time before she pushed me back and moved her eyes up and down me. "I have to agree with, Luke. I'm pretty sure this little baby was your miracle, hand delivered by your grandparents."

Breaking down into tears, I stood there as sobs rolled through my body. "I don't know why I cry all the time, Mom!"

She giggled and said, "Welcome to motherhood."

"I HATE THE month of July," Grace said as we walked into the mall. I breathed out a sigh of relief when the cold air hit my face.

Placing my hand on my stomach, I smiled. "She kicked again!" I said as I stopped walking. Grace fell to her knees and began talking to my stomach. The first few times she did this in public I wanted to crawl under a rock. Now, I just laughed.

"Kick again for Auntie Grace. Come on, baby girl. Give mommy a giant kick so Auntie Grace can feel you. I'll sing to you. The itsy bitsy spider went up the waterspout."

I looked up and drew in a breath of air. *Noah.* He was smiling as he walked toward us. "Shit," I whispered.

Grace told Luke and me how she had seen Noah with another girl and they were talking about their wedding. It was the day Luke was picking out my engagement ring. I tapped Grace on the top of the head. "Grace," I said as I smiled at Noah. He stopped and smiled back at me warmly. Then he looked at Grace on her knees with her mouth up to my stomach.

"Out came the sun and dried up all the water and the itsy bitsy spider—"

Leaning down, I hit Grace harder. "Holy hell, bitch! I'm just trying to bond with my niece." Grace jumped and spun around, slamming right into Noah. Noah quickly reached out and took a hold of Grace.

The way his eyes lit up holding her, had me questioning if he was still getting married to someone.

"Noah," Grace said, barely above a whisper.

Noah's eyes roamed Grace's face as if he was trying to memorize this moment. "We have to keep running into each other more often Grace. I've missed seeing you."

Taking a step back, Noah dropped his hands from Grace's arms. "Um, what are you doing in Austin?"

He looked surprised by her response. "My parents live here. It's summer break. What are you doing in Austin?"

Grace turned and looked at me with pleading eyes. I knew her mind had gone to jelly.

"Baby clothes." I pointed to my stomach. "I'm due in November and well, the mall in College Station doesn't have ... the um ... the um ..." I snapped my head over to Grace. She was staring at Noah. Glancing back to Noah I laughed. "Well, hell. Pregnancy brain already. I can't remember what I was saying."

Noah laughed. Grace snapped out of it and chuckled, about

thirty-seconds too late. "Yeah, we're here buying some stuff for the baby."

"Congratulations, Libby," Noah said as he smiled that knock-me-over smile of his.

"You," Grace blurted out. Noah and I both turned and looked at her. She chuckled nervously. "I mean, what are you doing at the mall?"

"There you are, Boo Bear."

Noah's face instantly blushed.

A beautiful, tall dark-haired woman grabbed Noah's arm. She had on a tight, thin, white sweater that hugged her breasts and accented her thin waist. Her black skirt hugged her perfect hips and stopped just short of her knees. Her sky-high black leather boots rounded out the whole outfit. "I'm sorry, we're going to be late. I need to make my appointment to get registered for the wedding or they will bump us."

Glancing to Grace, she attempted a smile.

The girl pulled Noah away. "Sorry gotta run. I hope I see you around, Grace."

I bumped Grace's arm. She turned and walked away. I quickly followed. She was mumbling something as we made our way to the MAC store to buy more make-up. "What are you saying, Grace? I can't hear you."

I was rushing to keep up with her, when I reached out and grabbed her arm, pulling her to a stop. "Grace! Stop and talk to me. Are you okay?"

"Boo Bear? What the fuck kind of pet name is that? What, do they play footsies also while they're fucking in bed?"

"Grace!" I said as I looked all around us. "Keep your voice down for Pete's sake."

Grace threw up her hands. "I give up. I hereby announce to the world that I give up on men. I mean he's going off to register for his wedding and not two seconds earlier he had his hands on me like he wanted me. What kind of an asshole does that sort of thing?"

I shrugged my shoulders. "I don't know, but he's a cute asshole."

Rolling her eyes, Grace sighed. "And he's good in bed. Bastard." Turning on her heels, Grace marched into the MAC store and proceeded to buy over one-hundred dollars of make-up.

LUKE REACHED AND took my hand in his. I couldn't wait to get out of the truck. We were heading back to College Station for Luke's last semester of school. It had to be one of the hottest Augusts on record. The further along I got, the more miserable pregnancy was.

"What are you thinking about?" Luke asked.

I had been staring out the window when I turned and smiled at him. "I can't wait to get back to the house. I'm ready to be alone with you."

Will and Alex were in Mason this weekend talking about wedding plans with my parents. Grace and Lauren were planning on going out tonight so the house was all ours.

Luke lifted his eyebrow and ran his tongue along his bottom lip. My body hummed with the idea of him kissing me between my legs.

I jumped and started laughing as I placed my hand on my stomach. "That was a big kick."

Dropping my other hand, Luke placed his hand on my stomach. I moved it to where the baby was kicking. His hand jumped when the baby gave another good kick. Looking at me, Luke laughed. "Damn, it might be a boy. That was a good strong kick."

Biting my lip, I nodded. "I can't believe we have less than three more months to go."

"I know. I can't wait to see if it's a boy or a girl," Luke said with that panty-melting smile of his.

Nodding my head, I looked down at my stomach. "We're going to be a family soon." Luke took my hand in his and squeezed it. I thought back to our conversation last night with our parents.

LUKE AND I sat on the sofa in my parents' living room. Four sets of eyes watched our every move. I began chewing on my lip, but knew what I was about to do was the right thing. I took in a deep breath and blew it out.

"Mom, Dad, you've always told me to follow my heart. I made a decision about school." My mother sat a little straighter. I knew getting my college degree was a huge deal for my parents.

"Okay," my mother said as she smiled gently. I glanced around the room and looked at our parents. When Ari winked at me I instantly felt at ease.

"Luke and I have talked a lot about what we thought was the best thing to do for us. Luke wanted to stay in College Station after the baby was born so that I could finish school. I'd have to take a full load and I don't see doing that with a newborn baby. I don't want to live in an apartment and have Luke working and doing something he doesn't want to do. He wants to be here. Learning and taking on more things with the ranch."

Jeff smiled as he looked at Luke.

I took in another breath and went for it. "I talked to Ellie yesterday about learning more things on the business side of the ranch. She's been handling it with the help of Gunner's mother, Grace. With Grace and Jack now leaving and going out of town more often, and the cattle ranch growing bigger, Ellie needs help. Gunner and Ellie have agreed to pay me a salary to be Ellie's assistant, with the expectation that I'll be training to take on more things."

Glancing over to Ari, she gave me a huge grin. She had been so supportive of my decision. I had talked to her about it first to feel her out on how my mother would react. I didn't think my mother would be supportive, but Ari assured me she would.

Luke took my hand in his. "Once I graduate, we'll be moving back to, Mason. I'll be working full time on the ranch. Libby will be starting off part-time and increasing her hours. I talked to Aaron and Jenny yesterday, also. With them building a new house, their place will be empty come December. They've agreed to rent it out to Libby and me."

Aaron used to work for Alex and Will's father, Gunner on the ranch. He and his brother Dewy started a construction business that ended up being very successful.

I watched my parents' faces closely. My father would nod every so often and smile softly. It was my mother I couldn't read.

"I'm going to also be taking distance courses. I have every intention of finishing my degree. It will just take a bit longer than I had planned," I blurted out as I looked at my mother.

Luke and I looked at each and then back to our parents. My mother smiled as she took my father's hand and said, "I think the big question on the table here guys is—what is the baby gonna call us?"

LUKE AND I walked into a quiet house. "Grace? Lauren?" Luke called out.

Silence.

Luke quickly reached down and picked me up as I let out a small squeal. My heart began pounding faster as he carried me up to our room.

Luke shut the door and locked it as I giggled. He turned and headed to the bed. Gently placing me down, he pushed my blonde hair from my face and smiled at me. "Do you have any idea how my heart pounds in my chest knowing I'm about to make love to you?"

Tears filled my eyes. "Luke," I whispered as he lifted his shirt over his head. I watched as his hands moved down and began unbuttoning his shorts. My mouth parted and I let a small moan escape my lips as he pushed his shorts down, letting his hard erection spring out.

"I want to be tangled up with you all night, Lib. The feel of your warm soft body up against mine is the only place I ever want to be."

I melted into the bed. If I thought I was hot before, I was burning up now. The tugging in my lower stomach had nothing to do with the baby I carried.

Luke moved over my body and brushed his lips along my jaw line until I felt his breath on my sensitive skin. My hands pushed through his hair as I let out a moan. "Libby, I want you."

My breathing increased as Luke pulled back and began lifting me up to take my shirt off. Lifting my arms above my head, I inhaled his musky scent. It filled my body and warmed me to the core.

I watched as Luke's eyes fell to my chest. My breasts were bigger and spilled from my pale-yellow bra. When his fingers lightly traced along my cleavage, I bit on my cheek to keep from throwing myself at him. He began to place soft kisses on my chest as he reached behind me with expert hands and unclasped my bra. The moment my breasts fell free, I dropped my head back and let out a sigh.

"Lay back, Libby."

Doing as he asked, my head crashed back into the pillow. I watched as my chest heaved in excitement. It had only been three days since we were together, but because we were staying at my parent's house it was the longest three days of my life. I had wanted him so badly. At one point, I followed him into the men's restroom at a restaurant only to have Will guide me out. Will informed me he would have nightmares for the next month over what I said to Luke in my state of need.

Lifting my hips, Luke pulled my shorts and panties in one quick move. Oh God. I wanted nothing more than for his lips to kiss between my legs. I needed the throbbing ache to go away.

I arched my hips up and made a grunt noise, only to have Luke move and focus his attention back on my chest.

Luke kissed around my nipples as I began to plead with him. "Luke! I need to come. Please don't make me wait longer."

His eyes looked up into mine as he smiled that breathtaking

smile of his. The left side of his mouth rose just a bit higher and my heart was lost to him that much more.

"Stop smiling at me."

He pulled back and laughed. "Why?"

"It turns me on even more."

His eyes lit up and he smirked. "My smile turns you on, Lib?"

Nodding my head, my eyes searched his face and then his naked body. "Everything about you turns me on, Luke."

Luke grinned bigger and I was lost forever. "Ah, gah! Luke, do something before I get myself off!"

Chuckling, Luke went back to giving my nipples attention as his hand moved down my body. He rubbed my stomach some before he moved his hands further down. I spread my legs and whispered, "Yes," as he began to softly rub my clit. His kisses moved to my stomach and I closed my eyes to ward off the tears when he began talking to the baby. He pulled his hand from between my legs and began rubbing my stomach with both of his hands. Goose bumps instantly covered my entire body.

"Hey, baby Johnson. You've been so good for Mommy today."

"Oh God," I panted out. Something about him talking to our child like this was hot as hell. I swallowed hard as he kissed my stomach.

"Libby, you're the most beautiful woman I've ever seen. The sight of your swollen belly turns me on so much."

Lifting my head I saw him take his hard length in his hand. Luke moved his hand slowly up and down his shaft.

"Oh my," I whispered. It felt as if my orgasm was already building.

Licking my lips, I watched him touch himself as his eyes moved along my body. Bucking my hips, I cried out, "Luke!"

He was between my legs and sucking on my clit before I even knew he had moved. I cried out in pleasure as he pushed his fingers inside me and began sucking and licking my sex.

"Yes! Luke yes!" I screamed out as my orgasm rolled through

my body. The baby began moving and I was so overcome with all the different feelings, my body launched into another orgasm. "Luke! I can't ... take ... anymore!" I called out.

My brain was in a fog as I slowly came down from my orgasm. I could feel Luke's tip teasing my entrance as I tried to focus again. My hands ran up and down his body as he slowly pushed in.

"Fuck," he hissed as he pushed all the way in and slowly pulled back out. The way he made love to me about brought tears to my eyes. "Libby, I feel the baby moving against my stomach as I'm making love to you." His lips pressed to mine in a passionate kiss. I never wanted this moment to end.

Moving his hips and pushing in further, another orgasm rushed through my body. Luke moaned as his body shuddered and he poured himself into me. Never breaking his lips from mine, he kissed me until our bodies both came down from our euphoria.

Blue eyes captured green as we looked into each other's eyes. "That was amazing."

Luke covered my face with soft kisses as he said, "Life doesn't get better than this, Libby."

Chapter Thirty-Two

Luke

STANDING AT THE kitchen sink I took a sip of my coffee and waited. Alex came bouncing down the stairs, her hair pulled up in a ponytail as she laughed at something Lauren was saying.

"Hey, morning!" Lauren said with a smile.

Alex walked up and kissed me on the cheek. "Where's Libby?"

Grinning, I took another sip of coffee. "Taking care of something for me."

Alex poured a cup of coffee and looked at me. "This early in the morning, you sent your seven-month pregnant wife-to-be out to run an errand for your ass?" Alex asked me as she put her hand on her hip.

That's when I heard it. "Oh my God! What the fuck is wrong with my mouth?"

Alex dropped her coffee cup as Lauren and I both jumped out of the way. I was shocked the mug didn't break. I saw Alex running back upstairs.

Alex screamed out as Lauren looked at me with a terrified expression. "I'm afraid to go up there."

Then we heard Alex yell out. "Libby! Why are you filming this? Will! Oh my God, Will!"

Laughing, I set my coffee cup down and smiled at Lauren as I headed upstairs. Lauren was quickly on my heels. She began to giggle. "You used the red food coloring powder prank didn't you?"

I nodded my head and said, "Yep."

"Luke! That shit didn't come off of my skin for weeks!"

Throwing my head back, I laughed harder. I walked into Alex and Will's room to find my bride-to-be laughing so hard she had tears coming from her eyes as she sat on the bed holding her stomach.

"Can't. Breathe!" Libby said.

Alex flew out of the bathroom. "Why is he bleeding?"

I walked into the bathroom to see Will trying to rinse out his mouth. "It doesn't even taste like blood!" Will said as he stopped moving. He turned and glared at me and yelled out, "It's a fucking dye!"

Biting the inside of my cheek, I tried like hell not to laugh harder. Will stood up, red coloring all over his lips and down his chin. "You bastard. You asshole!" Will pushed me and I stumbled back as Alex let out a scream. Then it hit her. Dropping her mouth open, she looked between Will and me.

"You did not," Alex said as she narrowed her eyes at me. She spun on her heels and pointed to Libby who was still laughing. "Libby! You're fixin' to be a mom and you still let this jerk talk you into pranks! Why?"

Holding up her hand Libby tried to talk. "Can't. Stop. Laughing."

Will shook his head and turned to go back into the bathroom. Slamming the door behind him. I peeked over at Alex. She tried to act mad but when I busted out laughing she did too.

"Nice! You're supposed to love me, Alex!" Will called from the other side of the door. This had all four of us laughing so hard we had tears.

The bathroom door opened and Will walked out. His lips looked like he had put red lipstick on. I couldn't tell if Will's chin was red from the dye or from Will scrubbing his face.

"I fucking hate you, Luke Johnson. Payback is a bitch."

"RUN, COLT!" LIBBY yelled out next to me. Smiling, I watched Colt run it in for another touchdown. I wasn't sure why Bruce was hesitating to throw the ball to Colt, but he was. The A&M coach had called a time out and talked to both of them on the sidelines. I had a feeling it was because of Lauren. She had broken up with Bruce after spring break last year. Not really giving anyone a real reason other than he was too high maintenance. They had started dating again two weeks ago. It was right about the same time Colt came over to the house one night drunk out of his mind.

Libby kissed me on the cheek and then Alex did as I leaned over and high fived Will.

Libby's breath was on my neck and my pants felt two sizes too small. "Do you feel okay?" she asked in my ear. Shaking my head, I pouted.

"I'm exhausted," I said.

This semester was starting to take its toll on me with my heavy workload. Libby was due in two weeks and she tossed and turned all night, which kept me up.

Frowning she leaned over and yelled to Alex. "Hey, we're heading out. I'm feeling really tired."

Alex nodded. "Get some rest."

"I will. See y'all later." Turning to me, Libby smiled and winked. I could take her in my arms right now and kiss the living day lights out of her I was so happy. Smiling, I grabbed Libby's hand as we made our way out of the stadium and back to the house.

My head no sooner hit the pillow and I was out. I felt Libby pull the covers over me as she leaned down and kissed my lips. "I'm sleeping in Grace's room. I love you, baby."

Pulling the covers up to my chin, I mumbled that I loved her back and drifted off to sleep again.

BRUSHING MY HANDS down my face I swung my feet to the side of the bed and forced myself out of bed. Glancing at the clock, I saw it was almost noon. "Shit, I must have needed that sleep."

I slowly stood and started to make my way to the bathroom when the bedroom door flew open.

Will came running and skid to a stop right before he knocked me over. "Dude! You weren't answering your phone."

Laughing, I turned away from him. "Because I was sleeping."

"Luke, Libby's in labor. She's at the hospital."

I stopped walking and let Will's words sink in. Turning around, I whispered, "What?"

"Labor. Baby. No one could get a hold of you." Will reached over and threw me a pair of jeans that were over the chair. "Come on and get dressed. You need the bag and we need to hurry. She was starting to push."

I stood there, stunned. "She's not due for another two weeks. We were at the doctor's yesterday."

Will shrugged. "Well the baby decided to make a grand entrance. Where is the bag? Libby said she needed her focus doll or something like that."

I pushed my hands through my hair and quickly began putting on my jeans. My foot got caught and I began hopping. "Fuck. The bag. Where did Libby put the bag?"

Will spun around and looked at me. "You mean you don't know where the bag is?"

"Dude, I didn't even know she had a fucking bag!" I shouted as I finally lost my balance and fell to the floor.

Scrambling to get up, I saw Will bent over laughing his ass off. "Funny. Real funny dickhead, but you wait for the day Alex has a baby. I'm missing the birth of my child!"

I ran into the bathroom and rinsed my mouth out with mouthwash and pulled a T-shirt over my head. "I'm almost ready!"

I yelled out in pain as stubbed my toe on the scale that was for some odd reason sitting in the middle of the bathroom floor. "What the fuck? Son-of-a-bitch that hurt like a mother!"

I rushed out hopping on my other foot. Will was now sitting on my bed, still laughing. I glared at him. "I hope you have twins." He stopped laughing and stood up and pointed at me.

"Don't say that."

I smirked as I pulled my boots on. "What? Don't say twins?" I wiggled my fingers toward him. "Twins, twins, twins. I hereby wish for you to have twins. And I hope they're girls."

Will shook his head. "That's fucked up, Luke."

I started laughing and looked to my left to see Libby standing there. "Hey, sleepyhead. You finally decided to get up."

I stopped moving as I looked Libby up and down. She came walking into the room and up to me. She leaned down, kissed me sweetly on the lips then turned and walked over to Will. "Hey, big brother. What are y'all doing?"

Dropping my mouth open, Will held up his hands and laughed as he said, "Paybacks are a real bitch."

"You bastard!" I jumped and ran after Will as he took off running.

As I rounded the corner I heard Libby call out, "Don't run down the stairs!"

WILL SAT DOWN next to me on the sofa. We both let out a long sigh. "I'm over school. So. Over. School."

Will laughed. "Dude, you're almost done. I've got a year and half left." There was a knock on the front door before it opened and Colt walked in.

"Hey," he said in a tired voice.

I frowned. "Hey, you alright?"

Colt walked to the love seat and let out a long frustrated sigh. He looked like he hadn't slept in a week. "I don't fucking understand life. Someone explain this shit to me 'cause I'm about to give up."

Will sat up and put his elbows on his knees. "Colt, what's going on? You look like you've had a few rough days."

Letting out a hoarse laugh, Colt said, "What isn't going on? Coach is all over my ass for drinking. I got suspended for one game for punching Bruce."

Standing I said, "Whoa, what?"

Colt rolled his eyes. "He won't stop taunting me with Lauren."

"Does he know you have feelings for Lauren?" Will asked.

Colt chuckled. "Lauren of all people told him."

I sat back and let out a breath. "Wow. No shit?"

"Why would Lauren do that? It doesn't make any sense?" Will asked.

Colt shrugged his shoulders. "I don't know. Once Bruce found out he has done nothing but fuck with me."

"Dude, you need to find a girlfriend," I said as I stood and walked into the kitchen. Colt followed me. He sat at the bar stool and nodded his head.

"I know. It's hard, ya know? I can't push her from my head. I guess it's pretty clear she doesn't feel the same way about me and I need to move on." Will walked up and slapped Colt on the back.

"Dude, you have girls falling at your feet. Find someone you have an interest in and move on."

The front door opened. Grace, Libby, and Lauren walked in. They were all laughing. Lauren's expression faded a bit before she put another smile on her face. This time it didn't touch her eyes. They all made their way to us. "Hey little brother," Alex said as she kissed Colt on the cheek.

Colt smiled weakly. "Hey, sis. You doing okay?" Nodding her head, Alex made her way over to Will and kissed him. Libby walked up to me and I placed my hand on her stomach.

"Damn, your stomach is so hard." Libby blushed and nodded her head. She had to be the sexiest pregnant woman I'd ever seen. Her blonde hair was done in two braided pigtails.

247

The glow on her face was breathtaking. Leaning down I took her mouth in mine and kissed the hell out of her. I pulled back and she laughed. "I missed you, Lib."

Libby's eyes lit up. "I missed you too."

Grace made a face. "Gag me, you just saw each other this morning and I'm pretty sure you were doing some funky sex position because I heard noises that will be forever etched in my brain."

Everyone laughed as Libby blushed and looked away.

"Hey, Colt. How are you?" Lauren asked as she sat next to him. He looked at her and I knew he was confused as hell. One minute Lauren avoids him at all costs and the next she acts like nothing is wrong.

Colt flashed that panty-melting smile of his. "I'm doing great, Lauren. How are you?"

Lauren's smile faltered a bit. "Doing good."

Colt began texting someone as Grace and Alex talked about the darling outfit they found at the mall for the baby to wear home.

Libby looked around at everyone. "Are y'all sure you are okay with Luke and I staying here after the baby is born? Things are going to be different."

Grace's mouth dropped open. "I'm not going to be able to see my niece as it is, the longer y'all stay here the better."

Alex chuckled. "I don't think Colt is too worried about moving in right away, I heard you had a pretty fun date the other night."

Colt's head snapped up, and so did Lauren's. By the look on Lauren's face, she didn't get the memo that Colt was moving in after Libby and I went back to Mason.

Speaking at the same time, Colt and Lauren said, "What?" Colt's phone buzzed and he looked down at it before looking back to Alex and asking, "What fun date?"

"What do you mean Colt is moving in here?" Lauren asked as everyone looked at her. The smile that spread across Colt's face for a brief second was caught only by me. He looked back down and sent someone a text.

Alex looked at Lauren and then Colt. "Marie James told me you took her out and y'all had a great time. She seemed to be taken with you."

"Huh, interesting," Colt said as Lauren looked at him.

"Wait, you're moving in here?"

Nodding his head, Colt answered Lauren without looking at her. "Yeah, Lauren I am."

He stood and pushed the stool back. Taking in a deep breath he blew it out. "Speaking of Marie, I've got plans with her so I guess I'll see y'all around."

Colt started to head to the door when Lauren got up and turned toward him. She began to follow Colt and it appeared she wanted to say something. Finally she was going to talk to him. Lauren was about to say something when she stopped walking. Looking away from Colt, she turned and sat back down.

Stupid. So fucking stupid.

WILL AND I were standing in the backyard grilling steaks when Libby walked outside. Her face looked flush as she had her hand on her stomach. Tomorrow was her due date and I knew she was miserable. She was now sitting up in bed at night so she could sleep. Most of the time she went to Grace's room and slept in the other bed.

"Hey, beautiful," Smiling I looked into her eyes. Something was off. "Lib? What's wrong?" I asked setting down my drink and making my way to her. Will was right behind me.

I took Libby in. Her face was pale, the normal beautiful flush missing from her cheeks. "Libby, you don't look so good."

Libby frowned and shot Will a dirty look. "Thanks a lot, Will."

Shaking his head he, mumbled, "That's not what I meant."

Libby's hand came up to her mouth and she began to nibble on her nail. "Um, well I wanted to let you know that, um, well—"

I widened my eyes and moved my head as if I was trying to will her to spit it out.

She rolled her eyes. "I'm having contractions."

Dropping my mouth open, I said, "Come again?"

She smiled and nodded her head. "Contractions, I think baby Johnson is ready to make her appearance."

Will jumped and let out a yell as he pumped his fist! "My baby nephew is coming!" Running around Libby, Will ran into the house calling out for Alex. "Alex! Alex!"

I walked to Libby and placed my hands on her arms. "Don't be scared, Lib."

Her eyes filled with tears. "I'm trying not to be scared, but I am scared."

I pulled her into my arms and held her. "I just have to ask you one question."

"Yeah?"

Smiling I pulled back. "Do you have a bag I don't know about that you'll be needing at the hospital?"

Laughing Libby wiped a tear away. "The only bag is my overnight bag and that has everything, including two outfits. One for a boy and one for a girl."

Libby and I talked for hours the day before we were set to have the sonogram to find out the sex of the baby. When we finally decided it was a yes, the baby was positioned to where we couldn't see. We took that has a sign the baby wanted to surprise us.

Looking into Libby's beautiful blue eyes, I was frozen for a moment. This woman standing before me changed my life forever. The miracle we made changed both our lives. I couldn't wait to hold the baby in my arms.

Leaning down, I gently kissed Libby on the lips and then spoke against them. "Are you ready to go have a baby?"

She giggled and wrapped her arms around my neck. "With you by my side, I'm ready for anything."

Chapter Thirty-Three

Libby

LUKE SAT NEXT to me holding my hand as his fingers moved gently through my hair. I closed my eyes as another contraction started.

"Breath through it, baby," Luke whispered. I wanted to tell him to shut up, but I knew he was trying his best. I did as he said and breathed the stupid exercises that do not do anything for the pain. I wanted an epidural like it was no one's business.

There was a knock on the door and it slowly opened. My mother walked in carrying a Starbucks coffee for Luke.

So wrong. So wrong on so many levels.

Smiling, my mother set Luke's coffee down and made her way to the other side of the bed. "Hey, sweetheart."

I closed my eyes and shook my head. "How did you do this with two in there? No wonder you never had more kids!"

My mother chuckled. "Trust me, you forget how painful it is the moment you hold your baby in your arms.

Rolling my eyes, I grunted. "When are they giving me the epid—" Another contraction hit me as I squeezed Luke's hand and his face grimaced. The door opened again and this time it was the nurse and someone else.

"Alright, Libby. Let's give you that epidural."

Luke and I both smiled and whispered, "Thank God."

"ONE MORE PUSH, Libby. Come on. I see the baby's head," the doctor said as I fell back onto the pillow. I was fighting to catch my breath.

I thrashed my head back and forth. "I can't. I'm so tired. I can't push anymore."

The doctor looked up at me. "Libby, one more good push, I promise."

I was too tired to push anymore. Exhaustion was beginning to take over. Tears streamed down my face as I whispered, "I can't."

Luke placed his hands on my face and turned me to face him. "Look in my eyes, Libby. Baby, you can do this. You are the strongest woman I know. Libby, one more time and I promise you will be holding our baby. Our miracle, Lib." His green eyes were burning with passion. But not the same as when he made love to me. This was different.

"For me, Lib? Do one more for me?"

Biting on my lip, I stared into Luke's eyes. I loved this man more than anything. There wasn't anything I couldn't do with him by my side. I nodded my head. "I love you, Luke."

Kissing me quickly, he whispered, "I love you, too."

"Okay, Libby, push now and give it all you've got."

I leaned forward with Luke's help and pushed as hard as I could. I felt the pressure release as I fell back to the pillow. Lifting my head, I watched as the doctor asked Luke if he wanted to cut the cord.

Luke moved to cut it and the doctor said to us both, "You have a beautiful, healthy baby girl." I didn't think I could possibly cry any more, but tears streamed down my face. I let out a sob as I watched Luke crying. The nurse placed the blanket over my stomach and laid our baby girl across it. I reached down and traced her soft cheek with my finger.

"Hello there, princess. Mommy's been waiting for you."

Luke leaned over and kissed her head and then kissed me as he whispered against my lips, "You are amazing. Thank you."

The nurse took our baby girl and said she was going to clean her. Luke walked over to the table and watched as they cleaned up our daughter and wrapped her in a blanket. Luke held out his arms and I began crying again when they placed her in his arms.

"Libby, I'm going to slowly lift you up okay. Tell me if you feel sick or not." I nodded my head as the nurse began to lift the bed.

I couldn't take my eyes off the most beautiful sight I'd ever seen. The man I loved more than anything, holding our baby girl.

Once I was settled and comfortable, Luke walked over to me. He had been singing to the baby and my heart was about to burst in my chest. One of the nurses looked at me and winked.

Stopping next to my bed, Luke looked at me and smiled the most breathtaking smile I'd ever seen. "My God, she's stolen my heart and I don't think I'll ever be the same."

Wiping my tears away, I tried to calm my beating heart. I loved this man so much. When I thought he couldn't make me love him more—he said something to make me fall even more in love with him.

As Luke reached down and placed our daughter in my arms, he kissed me. Smiling I whispered, "She's so tiny."

Luke chuckled. "Seven pounds two ounces."

I held her in my arms as I looked into her big blue eyes. It was as if she was looking into my soul and knew exactly how I was feeling. I had fallen just as fast as Luke, and it appeared our daughter had as well. We continued to look into each other's eyes as Luke ran the back of his hand down my face.

"I love you, Libby."

Peeking up at him, I smiled. "I love you, Luke."

Luke and I spent the next hour alone bonding with our daughter and looking at every square inch of her body. From her toes, to the tip of her head that was covered in light-brown hair.

There was a soft knock on the door. "Come on in," Luke called out. The door opened and Luke's parents and my parents all walked into the room. Ari and my mother both started crying. I glanced at my father and saw him wiping away a tear.

"Are you crying, Josh?" Jeff asked.

Looking at Jeff, my father chuckled and said, "Are you crying?"

Glancing at Jeff I noticed he quickly wiped a tear from his eye. "No, something got in my eye."

"Who would like to hold her first? I asked. Ari and my mother walked up. "We had to draw straws to see and Heather won," Ari said with a huge smile.

Looking down, my mother whispered, "She looks exactly like you, Libby."

I lifted up the baby as my mother scooped her from my arms. The love that swept over my mother's face caused my stomach to drop and a smile to spread across my face. I knew she held that same look when she gazed upon me and Will for the first time.

She began swaying slightly as she looked down lovingly at the baby.

Glancing up, she smiled as a tear rolled down her cheek. "What did you decide on the name?"

Luke walked up next to me and took my hand as I nodded for him to tell them. "Mireya Hope Johnson is our precious little girl's name."

Ari covered her mouth in an attempt to keep her sobs back. My mother smiled and whispered, "Mireya, meaning miracle."

Luke kissed me gently on the lips and said, "She truly is a miracle. She also brought us hope when we needed it the most."

LUKE AND I sat down on the sofa, dropped our heads back, and let out a sigh as I said, "She's finally asleep."

Nodding his head, Luke said, "She's got a full belly, a clean diaper, and a comfy bed."

I giggled and let out another sigh. "So much has happened in the last three months. We had a baby, you graduated college, and we moved into our very first house." I turned my head to look at Luke. "No more sharing a house with four other people."

Luke turned and wiggled his eyebrows up and down. "You can scream tonight when I make you come over and over again."

My core clenched at the idea of Luke having his way with me. We had hardly been together. Luke refused to touch me while we stayed at my parents' house. I was ready to scream all night while Luke had his way with me. "Do you think Mireya will sleep through the night? She only woke up once last night," I said with hope in my voice.

Luke closed his eyes. "I sure hope so. How awesome would it be to sleep a solid six hours?"

I laughed. "Six? I'm thinking at least eight." Grabbing my hand, Luke pulled it up to his mouth and kissed the back of it.

"I'm giving us two hours of playtime, Lib."

"Oh," I chuckled. "I like the sound of that." I looked around at our little house. It was darling. We were renting Aaron and Jenny's house that they had lived in until their daughter left for college. They had built a smaller house on the other side of their property, closer to Aaron's daddy. The white beadboard on the walls added charm. Aaron had remodeled the house a few times over the years. The kitchen was huge and had everything we could ever dream of. The master bedroom downstairs had been added only a few years back. It included a huge master bedroom with a separate sitting area that had Mireya's bassinet. I wasn't ready to put her in her room yet, but Luke talked me into trying it out for tonight. We were using the guest room downstairs as her bedroom for now. No way was I having my three-month-old daughter alone upstairs.

I slowly pushed and stood. I took a few steps back and lifted my shirt over my head. Luke sat up and licked his lips. I loved how Luke admired my body like I was a goddess, especially after having the baby. I quickly learned to love my new curves.

"Do you like what you see?" I asked as I ran my finger along my cleavage and black lace bra.

Luke let out what sounded like a growl. He stood and began making his way to me.

I turned and headed to our bedroom, stripping out of my jeans as I walked along. When I made it into our room, I turned to see Luke slipping off his jeans and tossing them to the side.

"You drive me crazy with your body, Libby."

"Good. That was my plan all along."

I sat down on the bed and slowly scooted back as I leaned against the headboard. Luke crawled onto the bed and licked his lips before he pressed them to mine. Pushing my hands into his hair, I tugged and moaned. Luke pulled back and looked into my eyes. "When are you going to marry me?"

Smiling, I whispered, "As soon as you want."

"Valentine's Day."

Shaking my head, I laughed. "That's next weekend."

"I know."

I slowly ran my tongue along my bottom lip. "Where?"

Luke's eyes lit up. "Port Aransas, under the pier on the beach."

I felt the tears build as I thought back to that day. "Why there?"

Luke's eyes sparkled and filled with love as they searched my face. Capturing my eyes, it was as if we were looking into each other's souls.

"I was watching you walk away, but you stopped when I called out to you. When you looked back to me, I knew I could never give my heart to anyone else but you."

Wrapping my arms around his neck I whispered back, "Yes, I'll marry you next weekend."

Leaning down, Luke brushed his lips against mine as he kissed me gently. Pulling slightly away, his eyes met mine as he whispered, "Libby, I'll love you for the rest of my life and I'll forever cherish the moment your love saved me.

The End.

Turn the page for a sneak peek at Holding You.

Coming April 30, 2015.

Coming April 30, 2015

**Book 3 in the Love Wanted in Texas Series
HOLDING YOU**

Chapter One

Lauren

LEANING AGAINST THE rail, I watched Colt talk to one of Libby's cousins. The way she was flirting with him turned my stomach. I'd like to pull her by that tight bun on the top of her head and slam her against …

"Lauren? Are you okay?"

Pulling my eyes from Colt and the blonde, I turned to face Grace. "Yep. I'm fine. Why?"

Grace smiled a knowing smile. "Well, to start with, you look like you want to kick that blonde's ass from here to Timbuktu. Second, you're gripping that bottle so tight your knuckles are turning white."

Glancing at my hand, I loosened the grip on the bottle. Sighing, I looked back to Colt and the blonde. "He drives me crazy."

Grace chuckled. "Why? Because a hot girl is attracted to him? Poor Colt can't help it if he is a mini version of his daddy, Lauren. Girls are going to flock."

Rolling my eyes, I looked away. "He sure looks like he is interested in her."

Grace sucked in a deep breath and let it out. "You know what I see, Lauren?"

258

Turning to look at Grace, I asked, "What?"

Not taking her eyes from Colt, Grace smiled. "I see a guy who is being polite and talking to one of his friend's cousins. I see that every time she takes a step closer to him, he takes a step away from her. His smile isn't touching his eyes, and he looks bored out of his fucking mind. I think you need to go save him from what clearly is a conversation he doesn't want to be in."

My head jerked as I looked to Colt. It was then, for the first time, I noticed he was wearing a fake smile. When she threw her head back and laughed, she took a step closer and Colt turned his body away from her and took a small step away. Lifting his Coke bottle to his lips, his eyes caught mine. I couldn't help but smile. I wasn't smiling because he looked at me. I was smiling because I saw how miserable he was. He didn't want to be talking to the blonde and in that moment of realization I was ecstatic.

"See what I mean?" Grace said as she nudged me with her shoulder.

Colt smiled back, and this time his smile did reach his eyes. They lit up for the first time in weeks and I loved that it was because of me smiling at him. Ever since he moved into the house we were all sharing, all we did was argue about the stupidest things or avoid each other all together. I knew my frustration toward Colt was from him turning me down the night I asked him to make love to me. Then of course there was the fact that my father seemed to think I couldn't take over the family business without Colt's help. Part of me knew I was being unfair to Colt. His love and knowledge of horses would be an asset to our breeding business and my father could see that. And Colt explained his reasons for not making love to me that night, yet it still didn't lessen the blow when he turned me down. The embarrassment from that night still clung to my heart and was the main reason I avoided Colt. Well, that and the fact that anytime I was near him I wanted to jump his bones.

But tonight I'm not going to avoid Colt. Tonight I would be

a good friend and save him from the blonde who clearly wanted more than just a causal conversation.

"Excuse me, Grace. I can't pass up this moment. I'll be able to rub it in Colt's face later how I rescued him from this situation."

Grace laughed as I began walking toward Colt. His grin turned to a full-blown smile, as his eyes never left mine. Seeing the blonde out of the corner of my eye, I glanced to her. She was staring at me with daggers as I made my way over to them. Her eyes moved up and down my body. I knew I looked good. The chiffon, platinum colored bridesmaid dress that Libby had picked out for us to wear fit me like a glove. Even Meg said my breasts looked killer in the dress. Colt hadn't been able to keep his eyes off of me when I walked down the aisle.

Walking up to Colt and the blonde, I smiled bigger. "Hey, Colt."

"Hey, Lauren."

Turning, I smiled at the bitch. *I mean, the blonde.* "Hi. I'm Lauren. You are?"

Flashing me a fake smile she said, "Tina."

I nodded my head. "Nice to meet you, Tina." Tilting my head slightly, I looked back at Colt. "You promised we would dance."

Colt's mouth dropped open. He, of course, hadn't promised this. He hadn't even talked to me since last night when we got into another argument over something stupid. I didn't even remember what the fight was about to be honest.

Coming to his senses quickly, Colt placed his hand on my arm. I prayed like hell he hadn't felt my whole body shudder under his touch. "Right. I wouldn't want to go back on a promise."

We started to walk off when the blonde reached for Colt's arm. "Wait! Is Lauren your girlfriend, or are you … free later?" Moving her eyes up and down his body while biting her lower lip, Tina gave Colt a naughty as hell smile.

What. A. Bitch.

Colt pulled is head back and gave her a shocked look. Good. I'm glad to see he was as shocked by her advancement as I was.

"Yes. Yes she is, Tina. See you around."

Colt's hand slid down my arm as he took my hand in his. My heart jumped and my stomach felt like I had just gone through about ten loops on a roller coaster. Leading me out to the dance floor, I turned and gave Tina a dirty look. "Oh my God! How rude. I mean … holy sheets! She practically asked you to screw her later. In front of me!"

Colt's laugh was a low rumble as he spun me around and pulled me into his arms. I couldn't take my eyes off of Tina as we danced.

"Thank you."

Looking into his eyes, my breathing increased. It was then I realized where I was. In Colt's arms. Up against his body. Really, really up against his body. How many times had I dreamed of Colt holding me in his arms again?

Too many times. Asshole. Ugh. I hate that he makes my body feel like this.

"Thank you for what?" I asked, lifting an eyebrow.

"Saving me from what was probably the worse conversation of my life."

Stifling my giggle, I couldn't help but glance to Colt's lips. He noticed because the bastard licked them.

Oh God. Calm yourself, Lauren. Quickly looking away, I tried to focus on something else. Anything else.

"You look beautiful, Lauren."

Shit.

"Thanks. You look pretty handsome yourself," I said as I continued to scan the dance floor.

"How would you know? You've barely looked my way all night."

My head snapped to him. "Are you kidding? I've been star-ing at you for the last …"

Shit. Shit. Shit. Way to play it cool, Lauren. Hello world. The Lauren who throws herself at Colt has finally shown up and she's looking to get her heart stomped on again by him.

Closing my eyes, I dropped my head to Colt's chest to hide

my embarrassment. I wanted to crawl under a rock.

"Hey, Lauren. Please look at me."

Colt's voice was a whisper. A hot sounding whisper. One I imagined would sound pretty damn amazing in my ear as he made love to me.

Ugh! Stop this, Lauren.

I pulled my head back but didn't look up. Placing his finger on my chin, Colt lifted my eyes to him. "Lauren ..."

His eyes fell to my lips as I instinctively licked them. Finally finding my voice, I whispered back, "Colt."

Colt leaned closer to me and I felt his hot breath against my lips. I moved my hands to his arms and gripped them. Feeling his muscles flex under my grip, I let out a small moan. His eyes moved to mine. My head wanted to argue with my heart, but I was tired of denying my feelings for Colt. I wanted him. All of him.

"Tell me what you want me to do, Lauren," Colt said as our eyes found each other again.

My heart was pounding so loudly, I barely heard his words.

Swallowing hard, I said, "Kiss me."

Darrin – You know the drill and how this works. I love you!

Lauren – I am rushing to type out my thank-you's since you are in desperate need to get your nails done for your winter dance tomorrow night. Yes. Yes I am the greatest mother in the world ... you just told me that ... I'm putting it in print.

Kristin Mayer – Thank you for being such an amazing friend. Thank you for reading my stuff, brainstorming with me, making me laugh, being there when I just need to vent, and most importantly ... you just being you.

Nikola Siervert – Thank you for always being there for me when I need you to be the last eyes! You're the best!

Ari Niknejadi – Thanks for always being there for me. Your daily Voxers to me crack me up and make me laugh. I'm super proud of you and all that you have done this last year. I can't wait to see what you come up with next year.

Katelyn Finnegan – The pictures that you shot for this book cover were beyond breathtaking. Thank you so much for understanding my vision and going with it.

The Chaser's – Y'all know who you are! I'd be lost without you. You make me smile every single day. Thank you so much for your support!

Kelly's Most Wanted – I could never thank y'all enough for your support! Thank you for spreading the word about all my books. I truly appreciate it more than you will ever know!

KELLY ELLIOTT

To all my friends/readers – A HUGE thank you. Without y'all, none of this would even be possible. I hope you enjoy reading Luke and Libby's story as much as I loved writing it.

Mantz Brothers – One Kiss At a Time
Luke and Libby in truck headed home over Thanksgiving.

Taylor Swift – Fearless
Luke and Libby dancing in the rain in the HEB parking lot.

Amy Grant – Cry a River
Luke kisses Libby then tells her they could never be together.

Blake Shelton – Do You Remember
*Luke and Libby's song they danced to the night he first kissed her.
Played in the truck on the way back to Mason.*

Dan + Shay – Nothin' Like You
*Luke and Colt watching Lauren dance with her friends
at the party in Mason.*

Diana Krall – Let's Fall In Love
Luke and Karen dancing at the Italian restaurant.

Frank Sinatra – It Had To Be You
Luke and Libby dancing at the Italian restaurant.

Dierks Bentley – How Am I Doin'
Luke dancing with Claire at the barn dance.

Cascada – What Hurts The Most
Luke and Libby dancing at the nightclub.

Sara Evans – A Real Fine Place To Start
Luke telling Libby he loved her on the beach.

Leona Lewis – I Will Be
Luke and Libby make love for the first time.

Jason Walker – I Feel Like That
Luke and Libby at the pool house together.

SoMo – Ride
Luke waking Libby up and playing with her.

Annie Lennox – I Put A Spell On You
*Grace dancing with football player/Luke and Libby
dancing during the party.*

Blake Shelton – My Eyes
Luke dancing with Libby in the parking lot of HEB.

Cole Swindell – I Just Want You
*Luke and Libby making love on the roof outside
Libby's bedroom.*

Dan + Shay – Nothin' Like You
Luke and Lauren dancing in the kitchen.

Chase Rice – Gonna Wanna Tonight
Luke and Libby camping.

Lady Antebellum – I Did With You
*Luke asking Libby to marry him. Libby
telling Luke she is pregnant.*

Lady Antebellum – One Great Mystery
Libby giving birth to Mireya.

Hunter Hayes – Still Fallin'
Luke and Libby living in their first house.